best gay stories 2014

edited by Steve Berman

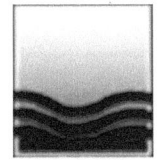

LETHE PRESS
MAPLE SHADE, NEW JERSEY

BEST GAY STORIES 2014

Published in 2014 by LETHE PRESS, INC.
118 Heritage Avenue • Maple Shade, NJ 08052-3018 USA
www.lethepressbooks.com • lethepress@aol.com

ISBN: 978-1-59021-502-9 / 1-59021-502-8 (library binding)
ISBN: 978-1-59021-505-0 / 1-59021-505-2 (paperback)
ISBN: 978-1-59021-510-4 / 1-59021-510-9 (e-book)

The works in this volume are fiction or semi-fiction. Names, characters,
places, and incidents are products of the authors' imaginations or are
used fictitiously.

COVER DESIGN: Alex Jeffers.
INTERIOR DESIGN: Matt Cresswell

COVER PHOTO: "Maranui Surf Life Saving Club 'cock fighting' at Lyall
Bay, Wellington." Glass negative by Sydney Charles Smith, Melba
Studios, 1914.

introduction
steve berman

OH, THE QUIRKS OF QUEER HISTORY. In 1823, the royal homosexual, Karl Friedrich Alexander, third King of Wurttemberg was born, the Rev. William Webb Ellis invented the sport of Rugby as a safer means for grasping other sweaty men while grunting, and French physician Marcel Duchamp (not the Dadaist) was the first to detail in print the phenomenon of "growing pains" suffered by children. In 2013, Wurttemberg is more known for its annual Bear Festival in the Black Forest than its blue bloods, the organization governing gay rugby clubs has the acronym IGRAB, and, well, homosexual fiction still revels in the douleurs de croissance, as evident in the aches and arguments and anguish that can be found in the many fine stories published last year which I have picked as the cream of the crop. The men you will meet in these pages are pained by the realizations that they are no longer young boys who can leap off rocks into a swimming pool or can happen upon a tryst without consequence. Some are at the precipice of adulthood, some are already across the great divide of years and looking over their shoulders at whom and what they have passed by.

Wistful. Sometimes somber. Sometimes nostalgic. But before you fear that the dreaded fate suffered by homosexual men in olden days and olden stories has returned—when he pays for his social transgressions by being martyred—be assured that the growing pains written by the authors in this anthology are more caring, more considerate even as they yield catharsis, convalescence, and the wisdom that maturity brings. In the last hours of 1823, a young boy in Kingsport, Massachusetts, left his father's house, the mayor's residence, to seek a life at sea, with other men, because it offered him the escape from prejudices of the time. And while we, as gay men, today face many of the same societal woes, we can take comfort that young sailor rescued from Paris the preciosities of Philippe I, Duke of Orleans, before Catholics burned down the vaults of the bibliotheque housing scandalous works penned by royalty. Our stories can survive the history of oppression and offer comfort. Please take comfort this year in our recent words.

Steve Berman
Spring 2014

contents

the stories

there's a small hotel
andrew holloran

HE HATED HAVING TO STAY IN HOTELS—OR RATHER THE FACT THAT HE HAD ONCE
lived in New York City made him feel demoted to an inferior status when
he came back on visits. Returning to Manhattan was like seeing someone
who'd once been your lover but was now with someone else; like going
back to a house you used to own but can no longer enter, so you park your
car across the street and look at it from a distance. For a long while he
did something like that. The first thing he would do when he came up out
of the subway was walk over to a building on St. Mark's Place—as if his
apartment should still be waiting for him, with the same lock, fitting the
same key he had kept as a memento. But he'd lost the apartment when the
building was sold and the new landlord discovered he was not living there
full time. Now someone else was, and after a few trips back he stopped
walking past the entrance to peer up at his old windows—which led to the
issue of hotels, which led to the issue of money.

People complain that New York is expensive, but the truth is you can
live there very cheaply. It helps if your apartment is rent-controlled, of
course, or rent-stabilized, as his was. Those years of low rent, however, had
given him an artificial sense of what a room, even a temporary one, should
cost. So it was hard to adjust to the idea of paying for one night in a hotel
what he had once paid for a month in his apartment. Once, when forced
to stay in a hotel that cost two hundred fifty dollars, he had lain awake all
night, having divided the room rate by the hours he planned to sleep, as
if there were a meter ticking in the headboard. He could not even enjoy
the luxury that one got for that amount: the fluted shell-shaped soap, the
thick towels, the herb-scented moisturizers and mini-bar, the deep carpet

1

and enormous bed made up probably by a woman from some Central American country who certainly could not afford to stay there either. An expensive hotel room produced nothing in him but guilt; he didn't see the point of the luxury, since there was something wasted about a hotel room to begin with. A hotel was a place you could sleep; and sleep was an unconscious state. You couldn't appreciate the potpourri as you snored. You were sleeping. He wanted a hotel whose price seemed to him to make some sort of fiscal and moral sense.

Everyone he knew, however, chose hotel rooms in precisely the opposite way. A museum curator, an old friend who came to New York frequently on business, always insisted on staying in the current "hot" hotel, like Morgan's or W or the Paramount when they first opened. Once, he and the curator had gone to Paris together. While his friend had stayed at the Grand Bretagne, he had found a nondescript place on the rue Maubeauge, which shocked his Parisian friends when he told them where he was. "Rue Maubeauge?" they said with stricken faces. But he liked his drab plain room where there was no servile attempt to please. "Genet," he reminded them, "just chose the hotel nearest the train station."

What he did not say was that he found an allure in the nondescript, slightly sad establishment. There was something lonely and forlorn about checking into a hotel that could be a positive pleasure. In fact, he divided hotel rooms into two categories: rooms in which you wanted to make love, and rooms where you could imagine killing yourself. Most rooms, of course, were neither one nor the other but something in between, or a blend of both; especially when you were dealing with cheap hotels. In reality all he wanted was a room that was quiet, which had some natural light, perhaps a view, and a feeling that one could comfortably read the paper in bed before falling asleep: in other words, something like his bedroom at home.

What baffled him about New York was that he had been unable to find, in the years he'd been visiting since losing the apartment, just that sort of place—the modest, small hotel one could always find in Paris, say, or Madrid. He knew it must be there but he couldn't find it. One friend told him it didn't exist, for the same reason public toilets were scarce: Manhattan wasn't welcoming. Manhattan wasn't cozy or domestic. It demanded you sink or swim, and which you did depended on money. Of course the city was filled with hotels, but even when he lived there, and visitors had come to stay, he'd known of no place he could recommend, no hotel that met his own requirements. The Gramercy Park, which had the right look and location, was not cheap; the Hotel Chelsea charged for its mystique; and though he always looked on his walks uptown for little hotels on lower Madison Avenue, where there should have been just the sort of place he was looking for, he could find nothing.

Now he needed one himself—the place one could come back to over and over again, the place a traveler needs in every city he visits, a home away from home. One year he thought he had found it in the Leo House—a hotel on Twenty-third Street run by an order of Catholic nuns that offered rooms with shower down the hall, and did not even charge tax because it was a religious organization, and was popular with Europeans, sensible people who did not want to pay more than one had to, and had a splendid breakfast that was all you could eat that included muffins baked by the sisters. This could have been like Shangri La, except for one problem: He was never able to sleep, even when he took down the crucifix that hung above the bed and put it in the closet. Some residue of Catholic guilt, some drabness in the always vacant sitting room, with its library of religious literature, its brown curtains and high window looking out onto the busy street, its echoes of the sad interiors Henry James gave to certain of his heroines, the ones who had no money, inspired not nostalgia for his Catholic childhood but a vague depression; and though he tried to make it funny, telling friends it was like a movie set from Going My Way, it wasn't really. An odor of hard-won gentility, of denial and sacrifice, pervaded the place, though that was not the deal breaker; the final proof that it would not do was the simple fact that whatever the cause he could not get a good night's sleep there, and so, after several dark nights of the soul, tinctured by the crucifix in the closet, he had faced reality and given it up.

So he was grateful when one day an editor he knew recommended a place publishing people liked to stay called the Pickwick Arms, in the east fifties, just opposite the Sutton Place Synagogue.

It was fun at first to stay in midtown. The rooms, with a bathroom down the hall, were only seventy-five dollars, though they were the size of a cabin on a sailboat; there was barely enough room between the bed and the wall for a small table, lamp and chair, much less a person to stand. It was not a room in which one cared to make love or commit suicide. The window looked out on a brick wall. When he awoke in the morning he could hear the watery echo of taxi horns in the street below—that immemorial sound he associated with the midtown hotels of childhood, when his parents took him to New York. But it didn't quite work. The neighborhood was fairly swank, and he wondered as he crossed the lobby whether the man at the desk held him in contempt for being willing, at his age, to share a bathroom down the hall. Poverty was forgiven young people in New York (artists are supposed to starve), but people in middle age were expected to be prosperous; otherwise they're failures. So the next time he came to town he found another hotel off Madison Square.

Madison Square he had always loved: the Flatiron Building still looked just as it did in the photograph by Steichen—that vanished, snowy, mystical New York. The Hotel Arlington was just a few blocks northwest of that glorious icon and had exactly the atmosphere he liked: It had seen better days. Everyone working the desk appeared to be Chinese. The block was drab and dingy; the lobby small, the floor linoleum, the counter stacked with brochures for Circle Line cruises that looked as if they had not been touched for decades, and there was still a pay phone on the wall. He felt no guilt checking in. Off the lobby was what had to be the world's smallest gift shop, with, when he peeked in, a beautiful young man behind the counter, looking as bored, in the fluorescent light, as an animal in a cage at the zoo. Surely no one ever bought anything. Surely the young man was living on dreams of Broadway. Rather than trust the tiny elevator he walked to his room on the third floor. When he opened the door he realized he'd found that priceless thing: a painting by Edward Hopper—a room that was as dreary and faded as its blue chenille bedspread, a room that was drenched in loneliness, and made his stomach immediately tighten—because in it he could imagine having sex.

At sixteen, on his way home from school for Thanksgiving and Christmas, he had always stayed at the Hotel Taft. The moment the heavy door of that room—a beige, metallic door that bulged out, like a bay window—closed behind him with a solid comforting click, he'd started to masturbate—an act then considered a sin, but which, there in the middle of Manhattan, all by himself, seemed not likely to draw anyone's attention except God's. The black-and-white tiled bathroom, the heavy porcelain wash basin, the tub with its stopper on a silver chain, the kiosk in the lobby lined with candy bars and newspapers, the quaver of taxi horns in the street below, and masturbation: that's what New York had meant to him at sixteen.

Forty years later not much had changed—though forty years later the city had acquired other meanings. One of them was the reason he was checking into the Hotel Arlington that August afternoon—when, after dropping his duffel bag in 312, he walked up one more flight and knocked on 416. When the door to 416 opened, he stepped back in horror—the cloud billowing out was so thick. Miles had been smoking. The smoking, over the years, had made a beautiful face even more lined than it would have been normally; but there, among the effects of alcoholism and skin cancers and drugs and cigarettes were still the outlines of the man he had once loved, which made the Hotel Arlington more than a hotel that day—it made it a rendezvous.

Miles was in New York for a less romantic reason: He was there to have his colostomy reversed. He had been given such a run-around by the surgeons at St. Vincent's who had performed the operation that removed a small portion of his intestine inflamed by diverticulitis, it had been cancelled and postponed so many times, that he had become so depressed he had finally walked into the psychiatric unit one day and told the clerk he was on his way to the Hudson River to kill himself. Then they had given him an appointment. They had also kept him under psychiatric care for four months, which, since he needed a place to live anyway, was fine with him. His room had a view of lower Manhattan that was spectacular, particularly at night. The stay had altered Miles, however; the antidepressants had thickened and slowed his voice so that he sounded drunk; though Miles was still the person he was happiest to see.

In fact, once the door had closed behind him, he no longer felt like a tourist, or a stranger wandering the streets of a city in which he'd once lived. Miles was someone he'd lived with in his apartment on St. Mark's Place—someone who'd known him then. It hadn't worked out: Miles had moved on to another boyfriend, another neighborhood, the Upper East Side. He was now living on welfare. But they both still loved Manhattan, and when they went to a coffee shop on the other side of Madison Square, the moment the Greek waiter brought him his eggs and toast, he felt as if he was living here again.

Miles, however, was so weak from his months in St. Vincent's that after eating they walked arm in arm up Madison Avenue toward Brooks Brothers, something he would never have done in the seventies, when they were lovers, but that now, in late middle age, he did for support. In Brooks Brothers he bought Miles two shirts and a sweater Miles said he needed, and then they took a cab down to the Village to have dinner. It was understood he would pay for everything. Miles hadn't a cent.

He had fallen on such hard times, in fact, that he seemed irretrievable—the ne'er-do-well in every family, the one whom life had crushed, the one whose fate, thank God, had not been yours. He wasn't sure why this was, but Miles didn't seem to have the will power to get himself out of the hole, or the toughness, or gumption, or whatever it took; he seemed blunted and faded and numb, and there was nothing to do but give him money when he asked, even though he'd told Miles more than once that he should leave New York, that he couldn't afford it, advice Miles had refused—because he couldn't imagine being anywhere else, because, he said, he'd rather starve here than leave Manhattan.

For this he gave Miles credit—this devotion to a city they both loved—though no one they'd known when they both lived here was still around; or, rather, the few who were, Miles said, after running into them on the street, looked like vampires. Yet the Village was packed when they got out of the cab at a restaurant on Greenwich Street. "I always liked the city on weekends when everyone was at the beach," he told Miles as they waited to be seated. "You could do whatever you wanted on summer weekends—nothing, if that's what you wanted. There was something almost rural about it. The pressure was off." This time they took a table outside Sapore, a restaurant Miles said he had been able to see from the window of his room at St. Vincent's.

"You know, you have to admit one thing," he told Miles. "The hospital solved your housing problem. It gave you a place to live. I can't find a decent hotel."

"I know one," Miles said. "This guy I met in St. Vincent's told me about it."

"Why was he in St. Vincent's?"

"He tried to kill himself," Miles said. "He thought the CIA was watching him. He was a nice guy. He spent all day reading Henry James. And he told me about a hotel on the Hudson River called the Riverview where you can get a room for thirty dollars a night. So after I was discharged I went down to check it out. You can live there for two hundred and seven dollars a week," Miles said, "though the rooms are very small."

"How small?" he said.

"Very small," said Miles.

"Well, the rooms at the Pickwick Arms are small," he said. "I don't mind a small room."

"The rooms at the Riverview are really small."

"But that's such a bargain," he said, "and on the river! That could be the place I need."

"I don't think so."

"But the only other cheap place is the Leo House," he said. "And I can never sleep there. I'd love to see the Riverview. Let's walk down after dinner."

Miles shook his head in wonderment.

"What are you saving your money for?" he said. "Why don't you stay at a good hotel, like the Carlyle?"

"Are you crazy?"

"No. You are," said Miles. "You won't spend the money that you've got."

The waiter put their plates in front of them. They sat for a while in silence, Miles devouring his linguine, while he absorbed the rebuke. Then he said: "The man who was reading Henry James in St. Vincent's—which James was he reading?"

Miles thought for a moment.

"*What Maisie Knew*," he said.

"Ah. *What Maisie Knew* could make you paranoid."

"Why, what's it about?" said Miles.

"It's about a little girl in a divorce case whom everyone lies to." He put his fork down, sat back, and looked around. "What do you think Henry James would have made of this?" he said. It was a warm night, and the sidewalk was thronged. "Do you notice how many gay men are holding hands?" he said. "But they don't need to do that anymore—you don't have to hold hands to show you're gay. It seems to me a little cute."

"They probably do it because they can't in the town they came from," said Miles.

"But," he said, "I've seen four couples doing it now. That makes it a trend." He took a sip of water, realizing he sounded like an old fogey, and said, "It's so wonderful to be back in New York. There's no place like this—no place."

The couple at the table behind Miles was a perfect illustration: a young man with a tiny rat's tail of hair hanging down the back of his neck—a little curlicue of hair, a strange, asymmetrical addendum to his otherwise neat haircut, an arbitrary detail worn purely for the sake of style. The more he stared at it the more the curlicue of hair seemed to him symbolic of New York. It was like a cord you could pull—pull the cord, he imagined, and the man's legs would part. He'd not had sex in a long time. When, after paying the check, the young man stood up, turned toward them, and slipped his knapsack on, his T-shirt rose halfway up his stomach—a fragment of Greek sculpture at the Met, an image that remained even when he and Miles abandoned their table an hour later and started walking westward through the sensuous summer streets. "The Village has changed, you know," said Miles in his slow, medicated voice. "These townhouses are now even more expensive than ones on the Upper East Side."

It's the real estate conversation, he thought, the one people have in every city but New York because there's nothing else to talk about; their relationship had come down to the real estate conversation. Walking down Jane Street toward the river it was easy to see why, however: the high ceilings, molding and chandeliers—the enviable rooms of people who did not need a hotel, who actually lived in settings James had used. But that was not his fantasy. "I never really liked the West Village," he said to Miles, "I don't know why—at least I never wanted to live there, did you? It seemed so bourgeois. I came over here for the bars. But I was always glad to go back to St. Mark's Place when they closed." But now he did not have that option, so, still walking toward the Hudson, he suggested they look at the Riverview.

"Do we have to?" said Miles. "I may actually have to move there and I'm not looking forward to it."

"But we have nothing else to do," he said, "even though it is Saturday night. We have nothing else to do," he repeated, in astonishment.

The sad truth was just that, so they went to the hotel.

The Riverview turned out to be a large, red brick, nineteenth-century building that had once been a sailors' home. It was right at the end of Jane Street, which the city had closed off so that it no longer intersected with the West Side Highway; in its place was what looked like a curved driveway edged with flower beds, like something in Miami Beach. Upon entering they went up an echoing flight of worn marble stairs. At the top, inside the lobby, in a cloud of fluorescent light gleaming on linoleum, there was an enormous cage with a man inside it. An old man with white hair was bent over the counter talking to him—the sort of old man, he thought, who shouldn't have to end up in a hotel like this.

The old man was trying to find out how much a room for two nights would cost.

"Eighty-three dollars," said the man in the cage.

The old man bent forward at the waist, as if hit in the stomach, and stepped back. "Go ahead," he muttered to the two of them, and took a step away from the counter.

He smiled, and nodded at the old man, and stepped up to the cage. "Is it possible to see a room?" he said in a voice that sounded to him overeducated and la-de-da.

The man in the cage spoke into a walkie-talkie and told someone there were people who wanted to look at a room.

The old man returned to the counter and took some money out of his pocket. "How much?" he said again.

"Eighty-three dollars," said the man in the cage. The old man rocked back once more, as if hit in the stomach a second time.

"That's more than you said it was," he whispered to Miles. "It must be the tax. They really screw you with the tax. Nothing costs what it's advertised to be, hotel rooms or airline tickets, because they always leave out the tax."

"Maybe it's thirty a night only when you stay a week," Miles muttered.

A Negro with grey hair and glasses came up from the street and pressed the elevator button. The man in the cage told him it was out of order. A young man with a Puerto Rican flag on his t-shirt came down the stairs and asked the man in the cage in Spanish what he wanted and the man in the cage said, "Show them 410."

The Puerto Rican, who turned to them with a dolorous expression, was about five-foot-eight and had big dark eyes, a mustache, and a long broken nose. He was dressed in black, with keys and a walkie-talkie hanging from his belt, and as they walked slowly upstairs there was plenty of time to admire the proportions of his body, the wide shoulders, and V-shaped back. The man was probably tired of going up and down these stairs, he thought. In fact their progress was so slow that impatience overcame him between the second and third floors and he went around the Puerto Rican and went up the stairs two at a time to the next landing. But there he stumbled, and the sound of his stumble, the slap of his shoe, echoed down the stairwell. "Are you all right?" Miles called up, laughing.

"Yes!" he said, his reply reverberating. Now that he was old he did not find a stumble funny; such things were in fact foreboding. He walked up the rest of the way with care and waited, when he got to the fourth floor, for the others.

The Puerto Rican seemed even glummer when he reached the final landing—tired of working, no doubt, in a place that got more and more depressing as he followed the custodian down the hall. The doors of the rooms were painted grey. Thin fluorescent tubes lined the ceiling; it looked like the interior of an air craft carrier—or a bathhouse. That's it, he thought suddenly. This is like following the attendant in a bathhouse—like the Everard, in fact, those old Puerto Rican guys at the desk who wanted you to know that though they were working there, they were straight and did not approve of what you were going there for.

He had never been able to decide if their contempt was a pill he had to swallow, or one of the ingredients that made the Everard so exciting, along with the rumor that the Police Benevolent Association owned the place. That question was moot now—yet the resemblance between this hotel and the Everard was so strong that, walking down the hall, he began to feel a strange nostalgia. The gleam of the fluorescent light on the linoleum, the sullen Puerto Rican, his beauty, his back, the total silence, were having an effect. The Everard had burned down years ago but the similarity was uncanny.

The Puerto Rican stopped two doors from the end of the hall, opened one of the rooms, and stepped back to let them look inside.

"You see?" said Miles.

"You weren't kidding," he said. "This is an incredibly small room. This is smaller than the Pickwick Arms. This is like a submarine! This is like those Japanese hotels where they slide you in an out in a drawer. This is like a morgue!"

"I told you so," said Miles.

There was nothing in the room but a television set suspended over a bed, like a security camera. If the television were to come off its perch, it would fall right on the person watching it, he thought, like the bookcase that killed the rabbi in Paris when he reached for a volume on its topmost shelf.

He stepped back. The attendant led them to the end of the hall and pointed to a doorway. He poked his head into a large bathroom consisting of gray walls, showers and toilet stalls. A shower head was dripping and there was a breeze coming through an open window. It reminded him of the changing rooms in the roofless pavilion at Jones Beach, the big open-air changing rooms that were like a souk in Morocco, patterned with light and shadow. But it was the drip of the shower he loved, above all else; that took him back to the Everard, to the silence at four in the morning, when most people were having sex or sleeping and no one was walking up and down the halls and the shower room was empty. He had loved the shower room when it was empty, for the same reason he loved walking the city late on Sunday night when there was no one on the sidewalk. There was something restful about both. That was the thread he had lost when he'd left New York—the Everard, the Club Baths, at four in the morning, lying in his room near the showers with his door slightly ajar—wondering who could possibly still be up, especially on a week night, the only time he went to the baths. He knew now that this had probably been the happiest time of his life. Safe and sequestered in the middle of life, equidistant from birth and death, hidden from responsibility and expectation, wide awake in what felt to him then like the center of the universe. The dripping of the shower was the drip of Time passing, Time suspended and caught.

He turned and looked at Miles. Miles had never liked the baths; he'd found them degrading and unromantic. The Puerto Rican led them back down the hall as the Negro with glasses was knocking on someone's door, which opened as they passed to reveal a man lying on his bed in his Jockeys—a big fat man on the narrow bunk in the tiny room, putting down the paperback he was reading and turning, like a beached sea lion, as he greeted his visitor. It's just like the baths, he thought—people used to bring books to the baths, too, and used to knock on friends' doors, when they took a break from cruising, to talk and laugh.

Halfway down the stairs, he started talking to the Puerto Rican in Spanish, and by the time they reached the lobby he was glad to see the Puerto Rican smiling. But when the man in the cage asked them if they wanted to rent the room, he explained they had just wanted to see it, for future purposes, thanked him, and went out into the street.

"You mustn't even think of living there," he said to Miles. "It would plunge you into a depression you'd never get out of, it would undo all the work you did at St. Vincent's."

"I may have no choice," said Miles. "It's all I can afford."

"Better to leave New York," he said, "better to live in Sayville, or New Jersey, or anyplace you can find a cheap room."

"No," Miles said. "I want to stay in Manhattan."

"At what price?" he said. "The Riverview is so depressing! It would be the worst possible thing you could do. It would drag you down. You have to take care of yourself, mentally. You can't just stay in a room watching television all day smoking cigarettes. That's what you can't do. You have to go out, get back on your feet—start a new life."

"How?"

"Any way you can!" he said. He thought a moment. "That's a line from Henry James. The doctor tells Milly Theale, who's dying, that she must be happy, and she asks how, and he says, 'Any way you can.' Well, it's the same thing for you. You're not dying, but you're in danger. You have to find your way back. You can't go to the Riverview. You'd turn into an old man in his underwear watching TV all day."

"But I am an old man," said Miles. "At least, I look like one. Unless I wear my baseball cap and dye my beard. Then I get cruised."

"You see!" he said. "You could still find another lover—and that's what's always been important to you—having a lover. Without one you fall apart."

They walked back the rest of the way in silence to Madison Square, through the throngs of young people who seemed like fish swimming in a different sea, one in which only they could breathe, and they parted on the landing at the Hotel Arlington. The next morning they had breakfast in the same coffee shop on Madison Avenue. After that they said goodbye.

"Remember," he said to Miles, "even if you have to live in Brighton Beach or some place really far out—you can always come in on the subway. But you mustn't stay in the Riverview just so you're in Manhattan. Manhattan isn't worth that. You have to get a job, and have a place that is reasonably cheerful when you come home. You have to take care of yourself. You can't stay home all day watching TV."

"But that's all I want to do," said Miles.

"Well, that's what we all want to do, on some level, but you have to fight that instinct," he said. "Anyway, I'll call you tomorrow!" They embraced, and he started walking to Pennsylvania Station to get the train. But with each passing block he realized he did not want to leave the city quite yet; he wanted to stay another night. Yet he didn't want to return to the Hotel Arlington; and he didn't want to see Miles again. Miles was preoccupied with his own problems, and his problems were depressing; New York was not just Miles, there was more to it than that.

So he went to the Metropolitan Museum. When he got there he headed immediately to a room with a small Roman cameo whose presence there had always amazed him: a carving in ivory, no larger than a brooch, of a man with powerful legs and a very long penis that was clearly stuck in the buttocks of another man. Then he went to see the Greek fragments—those small torsos, devoid of arms or legs, whose grace and beauty always astonished him. Then he wandered around till the museum closed. It's not worth the money I would save, he thought, on the subway downtown. The room is too small. And it's not the Everard. Or Jones Beach. I don't watch TV, so there will be nothing to do. And even if I take a shower, the chance that the Puerto Rican will come in is slim to non-existent. The Puerto Rican will be working. The Puerto Rican is straight. I cannot even be sure the Puerto Rican will be on duty, or if he is, that there would be any reason to run into him. Nor can I lie on my bunk, with the door open, and wait—the way we used to at the baths, when the waiting was more sexual than sex. No, he thought, as he stood on the steps of the Riverview, this will be like going to prison. He turned and walked back down to the street. An hour later he was on the train leaving Penn Station, going through the tunnel that always seemed to him like a birth canal, after which they emerged on that marsh beyond which the towers of the city rose so improbably. Around him everyone was already reading or looking at their phones and he felt himself sinking into exhaustion and exile. It was always sad, leaving Manhattan. He looked back through the dirty train window at the city, and then rested his head against the seat and closed his eyes. There was nothing to look forward to. He could not help Miles. He was lucky to have escaped himself.

the rest of us
guy mark foster

IT WAS VERY WARM IN THE ROOM BECAUSE OF THE BROKEN AIR CONDITIONING, and because the breeze coming through the opened window had not cooled, though it was nearly eleven thirty p.m. Hanging on the walls were various black and white photographs of selected parts of the human body—arms, backs, distended necks—in which the models' faces were in shadow or otherwise hidden from view. These images were all of men: dark-complexioned men with well-developed musculature and gleaming, hairless torsos. Atop the chest-of-drawers sat two playbills from a recent production at the Public Theater, and next to them a pair of silver-rimmed, antique eyeglasses, the type worn curled about the ears; in addition, an autographed copy of Rupert Kinnard's comic serial *B.B. and the Diva* sat propped open on the steamer trunk, beneath the window. A few feet away, two men lay next to one another, in bed—one fair, the other a shade or two darker, and in terms of physique not remotely like the models in the photographs—each having a difficult time trying to fall asleep.

One of the men, Martin, pushed back the rose-patterned linen bed sheet, and sat up.

"I don't think you should blame me," he said. Martin had a slender build and hazel eyes, with flecks of dark coloring about the irises. As he spoke, his delicate hands beat the air like wings.

"I'm not blaming you," answered Paul, his lover. The second man did not turn around to say this, but instead kept his back facing the room.

Martin countered. "Yes, you are. Don't say you aren't doing something when it's as plain as the nose on your face that you are doing it. You're blaming me. I don't like to be blamed for what I didn't do. No one would."

"Nobody's blaming you, Marty," Paul answered, looking now over his shoulder at the other man. "All I said was that maybe it didn't show good judgment. If that's blame, then what more can I say? You won't let me say anything else. If I do, if I try, then I'm being a sonofabitch. Well, I'm not a sonofabitch. And I won't accept being called one."

"You're twisting my words," Martin said.

"Oh, I am?"

"Yes."

Paul turned completely around, so that he and Martin were facing one another.

"Fine, then. I'm twisting them. And I'm sorry. Now can we get some sleep? It'll be morning soon."

"It's eleven thirty at night," Martin said, pouting all of a sudden. "It won't be morning for hours yet."

The other man, Paul, sat up in bed and yawned. He was built more stoutly than his lover, and had a shaved head. At Syracuse, Paul had played fullback on the football team; but he hadn't lifted weights in years, and now his body had softened and spread.

"Okay," he said, patting his fleshy stomach. "You win. I do apologize if I blamed you. It's just that I didn't want you hurt. I care for you. Is that so horrible?"

Martin stepped out of bed and went into the bathroom for a quick pee. He considered taking a pill for his back pain, but because the medication often caused him to awake groggy he decided against it. When he returned, Paul had sat up and was flipping the pages of a fitness magazine.

"I know why you read those," Martin said, climbing into bed. He wanted to assert himself, to make up ground for his earlier tantrum. "It's for the photos of near-naked men, and not for the poorly written articles on health and fitness. Those beefy white boys turn you on. Admit it."

Paul grimaced and threw the magazine across the room at Martin, who quickly ducked to avoid being struck by it. The two men smiled at one another. Everything was going to be okay between them. After all, they had survived worse fights.

"Those guys could have hurt us," Paul said, his voice louder than he had meant it to be. "You know? I don't want anything bad to happen to you. Tell me, what's so wrong with that?"

"What about yourself?"

"I don't want anything bad to happen to me either. Satisfied?"

Martin offered a rebuttal. "But it isn't as if I haven't done it before—laid my head on your shoulder. I've done it lots of times."

"I don't remember you doing that," said Paul, shrugging.

"Well, I have. And what about taking your arm? Or placing my hand in your lap or on your thigh? I've done that, too. What makes things so different this time?"

Paul's voice was so loud it surprised even him. "Because we were on the subway, that's why, Marty. On a subway we wouldn't have been able to get help, or to escape were something to happen."

"But I was tired," his lover offered. "I laid my head on your shoulder because of that, not because I wasn't worried about us being attacked. I was worried. But I don't always think about that. Sometimes I just want to be tired, or I want to take your hand. I don't want to have to think about other people. Other people don't matter. They do, but they don't. Or they shouldn't. I'm all confused."

A small, adjustable lamp sat on a table next to the bed, spreading a faint glow of illumination against the white wall. Martin, who, like Paul, was nude, scratched himself between his lightly perspiring thighs, and then sniffed his fingers.

"It's fucking hot," he said.

"Yes," echoed Paul. "Did you call the repair people again?"

"They told me the guy would be by tonight."

Paul glanced at the clock next to the lamp on the table. It was now almost midnight.

"Maybe he'll still make it."

Martin turned to him and smiled.

"Sure," he said. "And I'm Diva Touché," referring to one of the more flamboyant characters in Rupert Kinnard's comic serial.

They both laughed, and punched one another about the arms and chest a little roughly.

After a while the two men fell silent. Paul casually picked up the fitness magazine and opened it to a photograph of a dark-haired man dressed in snug-fitting workout shorts, and no shirt, gripping a set of dumbbells in each hand—the classic heterosexual strongman pose. The man was drenched in sweat, and every muscle in his body was tensed and on display, including the slightly elongated bulge of his penis.

And not a hair was out of place. From this, alone, Paul felt the stirrings of an erection. He hated himself for being so easily manipulated. Martin was right of course. The magazine was clearly marketed primarily towards gay men. However, its slick production was aimed also at straights. And as the dominant consumers, the egos of these men needed to be protected from the horrible implication that they *might* be queer—hence, the ambiguous presentation. This, thought Paul, at the cost of the dignity of all gay men.

"Do you think," he blurted out, "we would have been able to defend ourselves had they come over to us, those guys?" The sound of his own voice surprised him. Because the subway car they had taken earlier that night had few available seats, several of the riders had to stand, including a trio of youths who stood together, near the door, speaking in elevated voices among themselves. Most of the passengers were either black or Latino, and ranged in age from the very young, five or six, for instance, to middle age. As it was late, however, no one seemed to notice anyone else. For that reason, Martin hadn't given it a moment's thought that maybe he should remain alert until the train reached their stop. It was only after he'd already done what he did that it struck him that he was taking a risk. But it was too late, then. So he decided to just "go with it." Someday, he thought, people would hardly pay attention to such things—just as most white people no longer raised an eyebrow, for instance, at seeing blacks seated at the front of the bus. The future had to begin somewhere. Why not with the two of them.

Disgusted with himself for his programmed attractions, Paul quickly lowered the magazine to his lap, to conceal his arousal.

"I don't know if we could have or not," Martin answered, flexing his wrists. "But I would have been happy to die trying."

He could feel Paul looking at him as if he had said something no one in their right mind would ever have said. "You don't mean that. Tell me you don't mean that."

"I can't tell you what isn't so, can I? So, I won't."

"Jesus fucking Christ!"

Martin said, "Now you're angry at me. What did I say?"

Disgusted, the other man turned his back. He pulled up the bedclothes and once again pretended to fall asleep.

"It's simply my truth," Martin said after a while. As he spoke, he disturbed the air now and again with a flurry of fingers. "You should be happy I speak the way I do. Other people say other things, and for them it's their truth. But for me it isn't. It's simply my truth, Paul, that if anyone were to come up to me and tell me that I couldn't do what I do, be what I am, that I had to be, instead, like them, and do what they did—and if they were to strike me for it—then I would have to strike them back. And if one of us had to die in that exchange, then I would be happy to be that person, though I wouldn't prefer it. I'd prefer to be the one to live. Honestly, I would. Sometimes a person isn't able to choose his death, it just comes—like a phone call in the middle of the night. Or a concrete slab falling down on you from the sky—so suddenly you couldn't do anything, make any decisions or choices. If I could choose my death I'd choose to die for being myself—for being myself in the face of those who would say I couldn't, that I was an offense to their eyes. It's a thing to be proud of, Paul—not backing down from a choice like that. Not many people get the chance. Not that I'd want it, or I wouldn't be afraid; I would. But I wouldn't back down. I couldn't live with myself. I'd *want* to die, then."

While Martin was speaking, Paul rose slowly from bed. He went to stand before the rather ornate, expensive chest of drawers they'd invested in a few of years ago, after one of them had been promoted.

As he was listening, Paul picked up his silver-rimmed eyeglasses and secured them behind his ears. Pulling back the curtains from the window, he peered down at a couple, a man and a woman, strolling arm-in-arm on the street. The man, tall, with an easygoing, diffident manner, walked with his side pressed close to the woman's—apparently he was whispering some small lover's nothing into her ear—and she, in turn, stretched her smaller, lithe frame upwards to meet him, as if at some midway, neutral point. What he had to say to her was, of course, no one else's concern.

Nonetheless, for an instant, Paul tried reading the man's lips; however, it was too dark and he couldn't make out any words. For starters, he wanted to know if the things this couple said to one another were in any way different from the types of things he and Martin, during their own small intimate moments, said to one another. Simply, he wanted to learn if such differences might truly be a reason for others to cause bodily harm to him and the man he loved.

He followed the couple with his eyes until they had crossed Montague

Street and had disappeared into one of the brownstones that lined the neighborhood. Their privacy, he thought, was sealed and completely uninvaded. That other people could inhabit the world so freely and he and Martin could not angered him.

Paul turned from the window. "I don't like it that you say the things you do," he said, gesturing at Martin with his fist. "The things you say sometimes—crazy, just crazy. I could kill you myself. With my bare hands. No one would know. I'd say you got sick and one day you simply didn't wake up. Everyone would believe me. Who'd doubt me in this day and age? No one, that's who. Oh, they'd feel sorry, for a while. Of course, they would. For a few days. A couple of weeks. They'd genuinely mourn. But, then, they'd let it go. They'd have to. My god. What else is there?"

In bed, Martin leaned far forward, to stretch his stiffening back. He was tired—not exactly like before, on the subway ride home earlier that evening after the play they'd seen, a new one by Susan Lori Parks, but tired nonetheless—and it was already one a.m. and he had to get up at seven, shower, dress, and be at City College by nine o'clock. He wanted Paul to slip into bed next to him. It was cooler in their bedroom, not as cool as it would have been had the repairman come by to fix the broken air-conditioning unit, but cooler than an hour before; that was saying something. Now, at least maybe they would be able to rest.

"I'm not saying what I said to hurt you," Martin offered, in conciliation. "It's just very important for me to live in the world in a certain way. And to accept whatever consequences that come to me because of that choice. Not 'accept' exactly—that isn't the word; but you know what I mean. I want to be proud of myself. You can see that, can't you?"

"I see it," Paul said.

"You do?"

"Hell, yes. I just don't know if I could make the same choice, and stick by it. Or that I even necessarily believe in it. I don't know, Marty. It's as though if I don't believe in it I'm something less in your eyes."

"But you're not."

"Well, then, in my own. I don't think I like that."

Paul walked into the bathroom and looked at himself in the mirror, at the darkened circles around his eyes, and the freckles about his nose, which as a boy had made others call him "cute," or "white boy," but which as an adult only marked him as old—at only thirty-six—in the way that liver spots did for the elderly. Besides, he was also overweight and needed badly to diet. He thought of the question Martin had asked him, and which he had dodged: Why was he upset now, and not before? Perhaps it was only because he was getting older, and was noticing it. More and more, he felt the necessity to guard what little time he had left, not to expose it to any potential harm. To tread upon the earth lightly.

He splashed cold water on his face, and rinsed out his mouth. When he walked back into the bedroom, he realized Martin was waiting for him to finish what he had been saying.

Paul shrugged his shoulders. "I don't know, Marty," he said, standing before the chest of drawers. "I feel as if I'm being judged somehow. That if I'm not willing to offer up my life, then I'm a coward. I value my life. My life's important to me. And I'd do anything to keep it. Maybe that makes me a coward. For one thing, for not wanting those guys on that train tonight to see us in a certain light, a light they might have difficulty seeing in, so to speak, and so would therefore feel the need to strike out at us—to darken things again, so that they could see themselves. It's all about self-interest, you know. That's all anything is: 'What I can get,' 'What's good for me,' and so forth. Forget the rest of us."

Martin nodded. "I know."

"Do you, really? I wouldn't want anything to happen to us. To what we have made together. It's something that's important to me, as my life is important. Is it so goddamn wrong to want to protect that, Marty, at whatever the cost—even at the cost of my dignity?"

Paul slid the drawer open and took out a small box of antacids. While he spoke, he punctured one of the foil packets and popped a tablet inside his mouth.

He said, chewing: "Don't take this the wrong way, Martin, but people like yourself—people who've always refused to let others define you, who are individualists—think it's easy to stand up to those who have something over you. Who can decide whether you live or die, or at the very least who can make you damn miserable because, for starters, how you think and how you live, as far as they're concerned, is such a god-awful 'offense,' as you call it. I admire your indignation. Because it's my own. How could it not be? But what about those of us who aren't as brave, who haven't the courage you have to say 'Fuck 'em'? Who are afraid of losing the tiny bit of ground we've managed to gain in life? Why should we risk losing *that* for the sake of what other people are so righteously quick to call 'pride'? What's that word mean anyway? I confess, I never knew. Can a person be 'prideful' if he again and again offers the other cheek? Or ducks behind, say, a well-paying job, to avoid a life-threatening situation? I guess, what I'm asking—if I'm asking anything—is do we always have to *fight*? Can't we just refuse to? Just turn our backs and ignore the bastards—whoever 'they' are? Tell me, is that not an option anymore? And since when? I don't know, Marty, if you or anyone else has the right to condemn those content with what we have—not content with what we *want*, that's a different matter altogether: all of us *want* a heck of lot more than what any of us'll ever have—but content with what is *ours* already, what we've *earned*, by dint of our hard work, if just a bare minimum of ass-kissing?"

Getting out of bed, Martin stooped to pick up from the floor the fitness magazine Paul had earlier thrown at him. Martin tossed the magazine onto the chest of drawers and tried to place his arms around his agitated lover.

"Come to bed, baby," he said in a low voice. "It's late. Okay?"

But Paul jerked away. "Well, the hell with my dignity!"

He slapped his palm heavily against his thigh. "Will my 'dignity' keep me warm at night? Will it listen to me when I've had a lousy day, having had to hold my tongue with those white liberals at work? Or stroke my ego when I look in the mirror and see yet another age line, or can pinch more than a half a foot off my waist? What if I *do* get sick? You know—with You-know-what? Where's my dignity going to help out when I can't hold my bowels, or forget to pull out my dick to take a piss, and so it streams in a warm bath down my fat, ugly ass thigh?"

"I don't have the answers, Paul. I don't know who does. Anyway, you're not fat or ugly. You could lose a few pounds. But that's all."

Martin turned off the night-table lamp and slipped beneath the sheets. He waited for the other man, who continued to stand on the far side of the room, his arms folded stubbornly over his chest, to come to him.

"I'm too cool now," complained Paul, as he rubbed his arms.

Yawning, Martin patted the empty space on the mattress next to him.

"Come here," he said. "Like you said, it'll be morning soon, and we won't have slept. And then good heavens we'll look horrible. Something we *can't* have. We're fags, after all."

This last remark brought a slight smile to Paul's face, and his shoulders visibly loosened. Martin was relieved. After all, Paul wasn't like him, in that he had never grown up with other people pre-judging him because of the way he carried his school books, among other things. Or made disrespectful comments about girls one minute and then gone weak in the knees for one of them a minute later, like they did. Though he had often felt estranged from those around him on the inside, Paul had long ago learned to shape himself according to other people's specifications in order to belong. To fit in. And along the way he had earned rewards for doing so. But Martin, because of things that he had long believed were simply beyond his control (like, for instance, the way he used his hands when he spoke, fluttering in the air like bird's wings), had never been able to do that. Years ago he had tried several times to do so before he had finally just given up in frustration. It had been no use. He looked at the images of the nude men on the wall, looming over the two of them, and suddenly these old feelings of envy threatened to return. But it was late, he decided. Therefore, it was time to let go of troubling thoughts for which he had no resolution, and would likely never have any.

Martin shifted slightly when his lover slipped into bed next to him. He placed his head on Paul's shoulder after Paul had made himself comfortable. Next, he positioned one of his legs, bent at the knee, to nest in between Paul's legs, near the groin. One of Martin's arms lay pressed closely against his own side—the side onto which his slender frame was turned; the other, as usual, he flung across Paul's fleshy stomach.

Speaking in a hushed voice, Martin said: "I don't believe anyone can have what we have."

Paul sighed. "You don't?"

"No. They wouldn't deserve to have it as much."

"But then how is it that we deserve it?" Paul took his opposite arm and let it rest gently across Martin's ass.

"Because we took it and made it ours. No one gave us anything. It's like in that story, remember? Or was it a poem? That black gays are outlaws. 'Men in search of our own constitution.' That's us."

Paul flinched at the image.

"I know you don't like to think that way," said Martin.

Paul shook his head. "It's not that. It's just.... Well, it's just that I don't like to be romantic about my life."

"You think it's romantic?"

"I always did. But there's some truth to it, too. I don't have to like it."

The two men lay silent for a while, and listened to one another breathe. Finally, Paul reached over and switched off the lamp.

He said to his lover: "Put your head on my shoulder whenever you want. It's okay."

Martin's eyes had been closed. He opened them at hearing this, but he didn't smile. "We'll talk about it in the morning," he said. "Good night."

Paul kissed him on the top of his head. "G'night, yourself."

the trick
ed kurtz

I woke up next to Steve on the morning he died; didn't wake him up to say goodbye, just left the coffee on and locked the door on my way out. Steve is an insomniac, tosses and turns all night when he doesn't just get up to read or watch television. Was, I mean. He's sleeping pretty damn soundly now. First time for everything.

I met him in a bar in the so-called warehouse district, where most of the queer joints are these days, bought half a dozen drinks from him before the manager made him call me a cab and kick me to the curb. Next time I came in I was effusive with the apologies. He just smiled, and it was genuine as hell. I stuck with black coffee that time. He refused my tips.

Steve was working on a social-work degree at the time, and he got it right around the same time I got shit-canned—"reduction in force," they called it—and started to dream out loud about actually making a living with my writing. Good old supportive, big-hearted Steve. He went for it a hundred percent. We moved in together that June.

I turned forty-two in September; Steve was thirty-seven five weeks later. We stopped hitting the clubs and bars, and settled into the picture of a comfortable old couple, sitting across the room from one another while one read and the other watched reruns of crummy old sitcoms that weren't that funny when they aired the first time. The kind of couple the kids always said they wanted to be like, when they were "that age." Cute, but at least I didn't have to listen to that crap anymore.

That last morning, I shut the door gently. Just a tiny *click* was all. Ostensibly, I was heading to the deli on the corner for some breakfast and a bit of key-punching on the old laptop. In reality, I was going to see a man about a horse.

I never gave a rat's ass about the races. Seemed intolerably boring to me, watching a dozen stinking horses run circles around a track in the desperate hope a two-dollar bet might net twenty, two hundred, a couple thou. I dug money well enough, same as anyone else I guess, but even the cricket fights you saw in the alleys over in Chinatown were more interesting to me that the races. At least there was actually something at stake there—one of those little bastards had to die. But horses running? So what? If I wanted to watch horses run I'd watch old John Wayne movies.

Of course, that was before I met him—the trick.

Used to be a guy could cruise the Forty-Two, no muss, no fuss. Dead of winter or the peak of summer, just take a seat in the Rialto and watch half of a badly dubbed chopsocky flick from a scratched-all-to-hell print and wait for somebody to sit down in the next sticky seat. It sure as hell wasn't a honeymoon suite (and worse still when it was in the Grand Luncheonette men's room), but no one batted an eye and in those days it was pretty much a sure thing. Then came Giuliani, and along with him Mickey Mouse, and by then we were all a lot older, anyhow. So by the time Steve and I were sleeping two feet apart in that walk-up in what used to be Alphabet City, I'd become a bona-fide bathhouse man.

Some nights I lurked off in a corner, kept to myself. Watched. Other times I made special new friends, a few repeat customers but not usually. A week and half after my birthday, on an unseasonably warm November night, I met him. The trick.

There wasn't a word between us that first time, not even *hello*. Wham, bam, thank you sir, and a quarter of an hour later I was staggering onto the MTA with an unmistakable funk wafting about me, bleachy and vaguely embarrassing, that reminded me to shower before so much as pecking Steve on the cheek. Then again, I never pecked his or anybody else's cheek. I wasn't June goddamn Cleaver, for Christ's sake.

Week after next I saw him again. He flashed a Mona Lisa smile before slinking off with an almond-eyed twink sporting a ludicrous fauxhawk. Anyone else, any other time, I would've shrugged it off, reminded myself I had no business being there anyhow, so who gave a damn what a trick did, or with whom? Me, apparently.

I was jealous as hell, and over a reedy, green-eyed punk with a rose tattooed on his back and one eyelid that hung lower than the other. The sex was all right, better than Mr. Asleep-by-Ten-o'clock at home, but casualness was the name of the game here, if not outright flippancy. No one got owned in a bathhouse, which was more or less the point, which was why I should've shifted focus to somebody else or gotten the hell out of there. Instead, I waited.

What I got in fifteen minutes took my trick and his twink the better part of an hour. I was catching sidelong glances from solitary tourists too shy to put words to it, all of which I ignored. My eyes were glued to the steam billowing out of the adjacent room, a misty cloak they came out of, one at a time. My trick came second, more slowly than the fauxhawked guy, and pouted playfully when he saw me with a terry-cloth towel around my waist and my hands in my lap. What a rube.

"Poor, pretty boy," he cooed, belying the fact that I was old enough to be his father. Bastard.

I was reminded of high school, back in the seventies, asking that uptown cow to the prom and her replying by way of asking what my father did for a living. I told her I didn't have a father. She laughed. I knitted my brow at the memory, my eyes narrowed and trained hard on the trick's pale, sweat-slick face.

What the hell was wrong with me?

"Come on, then," he said musically, cocking his head to one side and making for the lockers to get dressed. He was talking to me like I was his dog. It pissed me off. But I trotted along after him, anyway.

We went at it hot and heavy from the second he dragged me through the door. His place was tiny, maybe five hundred square feet of rent-controlled squalor, with dirty clothes draped over every available surface and cigarette butts smashed into the threadbare rugs. He had a few posters tacked up on the walls—underwear models, hold the underwear, and a couple of Broadway bills (*Cats*, for shit's sake)—but they weren't enough to disguise the dinginess of the crumbling plaster, the mystery stains where the paint hadn't chipped off yet.

None of this caught my eye at first, of course; my attention was not to be divided. A thumb dug into the elastic waistband of my drawers while I clumsily hooked his shirt up over his chin, where it promptly got snagged. Shoes kicked off, my left much more fluidly than my right, but the socks stayed right where they were, because they weren't in the way and we were in a goddamn hurry. There was an awkward little two-step from the door to the ratty love seat against the wall, where we collapsed onto a spread-out newspaper and made it crinkle like a son of a bitch.

I think it must have been about half past twelve. Steve would have been in bed for hours.

The building only had one bathroom per floor, so we had to wait for a disgruntled Korean lady to finish up before we could scrub the sex off one another's skin and move on to awkward goodbyes and bullshit I'll see-you-laters. What was the point when we both knew it wasn't true? Just part of the game, I guess. All games had rules to keep them from falling to pieces.

And my trick broke the first one straightaway by asking me back in for a nightcap. I broke the second by consenting. He had bargain Scotch. Peaty, from a big plastic jug.

I remembered a guy who'd picked me up in the Arcade on the Deuce when I was seventeen, eighteen years old, grumbling about skid-row cocksuckers. I hypothesized now this might have been what he meant.

The trick dumped three fingers of the syrupy mess down his throat and groaned with his next breath. He rasped, "Gets the job done."

"Yeah?" I asked, mostly to keep from being silent. "What job is that?"

"Makin' you forget, or not care. Whichever."

I nodded like I was in full agreement with his assessment, though I didn't really have a clue what he was talking about. Mostly I just stared at the cluster of small, pink scars that surrounded his left nipple. I'd noticed them when I was biting the hell out of it the first time we met. They looked like cigarette burns. I didn't ask about them.

The newspaper crinkled under my ass and I tried to sit still. He poured another three fingers of shitty scotch into his glass.

"Listen," he said, letting the liquor slosh around the sides of the glass a bit before sucking some of it down. His voice was high and a little whiny. "You got any money?"

"Come on, man," I complained, slamming my glass down so hard I was surprised it didn't shatter. "Don't hustle me."

"Shit, no—that's not me. See these?" He teased the scars on his nipple with his fingertip, leering at me while he did it. "That's what hustlin' gets you. Roughneck married dudes, want to punish you because *they're* fags. The hell with that—I'm on the level."

I must have grimaced, because he grinned guiltily, like a kid caught with his hand in his pants. His droopy eyelid seemed to droop even more. I lifted my rear, finally swept the damn newspaper away, and sank into the scratchy corduroy cushions to hear what my trick had to say.

To my complete astonishment, it was pretty goddamned interesting.

Steve left me a note on the kitchen counter explaining how he'd be staying late with a patient, prissing that I'd already know that if I'd get a mobile phone. I hardly ever answered the regular one—why the hell would I want one with me all the time? I crumpled the note into a tight ball and tossed it in the trash.

A patient to Steve meant some eldritch crone a few years past her expiration date, all chalky and wet-sounding and pissed off at the indignity of having to hire somebody to help her shower and shit. He was paid well enough, though, to float a useless would-be writer on his salary, so there was definitely something to be said for wiping ancient asses. Still: better him than me.

Heart of gold, that guy.

I poured myself a drink in the kitchen—top shelf compared to the airplane fuel I drank at my trick's place—but it still went down punching. I wheezed for a few seconds before killing it off, washed it down with tap water, poured another. My mind was reeling with possibilities, with anticipation and fear. The gin only made it worse, intensifying the scenarios playing out in my head as my vision blurred and knees buckled. Somehow I made it to the couch and ended up half-on and half-off it, my face squashed up against a silk throw pillow, one of Steve's embellishments. The floor pulsed up at me and then away, back and forth. My mouth wouldn't stop watering and all I could think about was how much cash a person had to have to afford an around-the-clock, on-call caregiver at their beck and call. A lot, I reasoned. Enough to pull this off, at any rate.

Ten-to-one payout, a sure thing. Doping, the trick explained—he had insider knowledge, no doubt about it, Colonel's Fortune was going to win that race. They even had gatekeepers paid off to delay the other horses; just a second or two, but enough. Best part was, nobody *knew* that he knew. As far as anyone apart from us would be concerned, luck would be a lady that night.

A hunnert grand'll be a mil, five hunnert thou two ways—can you get it?

"I'll get it," I mumbled into the throw pillow, probably less than a minute before I blacked out.

The race was three days away when I finally got my chance. I'd been hanging on to Steve like a love-struck teenager for over a week by then, sharing every goddamn meal with him and tagging along on the most inane errands. I followed him to the DMV, a check-in at the office, a sit-down with the snotty son-in-law of a potential patient (he made me wait in the car). Over lunch at a HoJo's, he said I was being sweet, his eyes full of questions he didn't dare ask. Gift horse, and like that.

Between finishing stomach-churning Monte Cristos and receiving the long overdue check, he got curious about me eyeballing the racing form.

"Since when are you interested in horse races?" he wanted to know.

"Research," I lied. "It's for a novel."

That launched me into a big, sticky web of bullshit about the great big novel I was about to start writing, and about the literary agent I knew through a friend of a friend who wanted to see some pages as soon as possible. Naturally, Steve wanted to hear all about it. I spun off some crap about not wanting to jinx it. The conversation got awkward then, punctuated by long, droopy silences. My chance came when his beeper chirped and Steve smiled apologetically, excused himself to make a call. He touched my hand, a gentle brush that barely rustled the hair on my knuckles, and vanished. I dumped the rest of my coffee down my throat and waited. When Steve came back to the booth, he was all sheepish and leaking sighs.

"Patient," he said, a double meaning I wasn't sure he intended. "Want to ride along, see how the other half lives?"

He was goddamned right I did.

We never talked about Steve's patients, but from what I'd gathered or imagined, my expectation was that we'd head for the Hamptons. Instead, he zipped us over to New Jersey and across the terrifying Bayonne Bridge, during which I squeezed my eyes shut and focused on the way my guts spasmed inside. I hate bridges.

Staten Island was a surprise. The house ended up in Tottenville, which sat on the southernmost tip of the Island and felt like the outermost edge of the world. It was the most provincial spot you could find within the city proper and it always had been. The narrow, rambling Arthur Kill channel bordered Tottenville to the west with Jersey's gloomy oil refineries looming on the other side. There were marshlands all around overrun by cattails and tall cord grass that hid burned-out cars concealing God knew what horrible mysteries. It smelled stale and rotten out there in the marshes and I had no plans to investigate.

The house was a sprawling, crumbling Colonial on Main, hidden from the street by a copse of overgrown poplars. Old money, then. Steve parked on the drive, beside a structure that looked like it might have been a guest house before the roof caved in. I felt like we were about to visit Miss Haversham. If the disintegrating old joint wasn't haunted yet, I figured it would be as soon as Steve's charge croaked. I almost said so, but Steve was ushering me out of the car and over the weedy walk before I could formulate a complete thought.

"I hope this doesn't take too long," he said while stabbing the lock with his spare key, "but there's a ton to read in the library if it does."

The library. I gave an airy snort as we went inside.

The house smelled like wet dog and warm hot dogs. I wrinkled my nose and hung back a bit while Steve switched on a few faux-Tiffany lamps fitted with low wattage bulbs. The effect was that of an old-timey parlor, the kind where tuxedoed hosts with thin mustaches presented their wives to their friends' wives and played at not being totally miserable. I felt like William Powell or Edmund Lowe could have fit in this room, back before the wallpaper started to peel and the residents gave up on dusting.

Steve pushed open a paneled door and gestured at the room on the other side—the library, natch. I nodded, went in. He said, "I'll let you know if this goes overlong."

The room was humid, dank. I turned on a lamp and surveyed the floor-to-ceiling shelves lined with musty old volumes. Not a paperback in sight. The heavy curtains obscuring the window were gray with dust and moth-eaten. I peeked around for a liquor cabinet—the library seemed as good a place as any for one—and found a safe, instead.

It was tucked away between Gibbon's *History of the Decline and Fall of the Roman Empire* and three and half feet of old Sears, Roebuck catalogues, just a little black iron box with a dial on the front, the kind masked banditos blew up with dynamite in black and white westerns. Cute. All I needed was the combination.

By the time Steve poked his head through the door, I was seated uncomfortably in the room's only chair, a book open in my lap. I didn't even know which book I'd pulled from the shelf.

"He'd like to meet you," Steve said.

"Who would?"

"Mr. Baldwin."

"That who lives here?"

"Yes."

"What's he like?"

"Old. A bit of a queen. Come see for yourself."

Mr. Baldwin, as it turned out, was a bit of a queen like Mayor Bloomberg had a few bucks in his account. He was sitting up against a carefully arranged mountain range of pillows, the blankets turned down crisply at his middle, a sagging silk cap on his spotted pate to match his silk pajamas. He looked about a hundred years old, but his eyes were bright and cagey. When they lit on me, they never let go. His crinkly lips pursed and curled, a sarcastic smile.

"The wifey, I presume?" he rasped, his voice like onionskin.

I feigned a grin and fantasized about punching the old queen square in the throat. He kept his eyes locked on me, a staring contest I lost when I averted my gaze to the bronze wastepaper basket on the floor. It was filled with crumpled tissues, and I recognized the full scope of a care-giver's responsibilities for the first time. I can't say I was astonished.

"My castle is falling apart," Baldwin hissed with a flourish of one blue-veined hand. I noticed an impressive collection of orange pill bottles on the night stand, more than a dozen in all. *For whatever ails you,* I thought, my mind turning to the steroids the trick said Colonel's Fortune would be pumped full of come race day.

"Mr. Baldwin is a really fascinating person," Steve chimed in. "He's done a lot."

"I did them all," the old man quipped. "Everyone you've heard of, at any rate."

Steve laughed uncomfortably as Baldwin chortled and licked his papery lips. I was starting to wish I'd found that liquor cabinet.

"Do you know," the patient went on, "why I called Steve here today, Wifey? I pissed myself. I pissed the bed and I can't get up to do anything about it. Steve had to come straight away, you understand, to clean me up, change the sheets. I fart every time he picks me up, and it is humiliating for me."

He smiled all the while with that deadeye glare, and wondered how much I'd have to get paid to jerk off a dying old queen who pissed himself and farted all over the place. A hundred thousand dollars ought to do it.

"You young, fresh-faced little queers, always prattling on about *pride.* Wait until you get so old you can't..." He trailed off, and Steve clutched his bony hand. His eyes were watery anyway, so I couldn't tell if he was about to cry or if he always looked like that. "Pride goeth before the fall, Wifey."

The trick turned over onto his side and jutted his ass at me, the way cats sometimes do. I was spent—out of breath, feeling giddy, feeling old. He shook a cigarette out of a pack, a fancy one with brown paper and a gold band around the filter, which he lit and handed to me. I leaned up against the wall in lieu of a headboard and relished the smoke that arrested my lungs. After the trick got one going for himself, he straightened up and drew a bead on me.

"I know him, you know. Reggie Baldwin. Wrote a book in the Seventies, everybody read it. I'll bet he's got half a million in that little safe of his."

"We won't know until we get into it," I grumped. Neither of us had a clue how to crack the damn thing open, and to my mind that meant bringing in a third party. Someone else to split the take with, someone else to know what I'd done. And, judging by the people who populated my admittedly limited social circle, someone I didn't even know. Not good.

"We'll find out when we get it back here," he said, his voice lilting like a song while he ran an index finger down the length of my face.

Here.

Smart boy.

I took in a movie with Steve in the afternoon, day of the robbery. It was one of those theaters that play old movies all the time, and Steve was thrilled at the chance to see whatever it was on the big screen. I'd never heard of it. I don't watch a lot of movies anymore.

Women with modern-art hairdos and ruffly, Elizabethan blouses pontificated in the coolness of the auditorium and my better half soaked it up like a hot bath. For my part, I worked out the details of my visit to Tottenville in just a few hours. Baldwin's rotten old house was so decrepit I figured I could punch a hole in it and climb right through, though I knew I wouldn't have to—I'd found a side door in a rank hallway, behind a rusted-out washing machine, which I unlocked. I expected to find it still unlocked when I returned. From there, it was simply a matter of pulling the safe down and carrying it out to the car waiting in the drive. If the old queen heard us crashing around down there, so what? He couldn't get out of bed, anyway.

Us. The trick and I, of course. But only because I couldn't carry a heavy iron safe by myself. I needed help, and he was the only one to do it. Him and his droopy eyelid and scarred chest and certain knowledge of the big payout come Saturday. Hell, I even planned on returning good old Reggie Baldwin's investment to him. It was the least a newly rich man could do, and the old bag could report the burglary until he was blue in the face, good luck getting the NYPD to give a shit when everything was accounted for.

That put Queen Reggie out of our danger zone, and I took care of Steve about halfway through the movie. Red devils in his root beer, courtesy of a street dealer I knew from my misspent days on the Forty-Two. Night-night, Stevie. I had to half-carry him home.

With Steve down for the count, I took the MTA to the trick's hovel, where he had an Impala waiting. He'd borrowed it from a cousin, or so he said. Duct tape was holding the upholstery together inside and it smelled badly like cat piss. The car rattled like a cage the whole way to Staten Island, and I rattled along with it. Neither the Impala nor I had fallen apart when we reached Tottenville, which I decided was something just short of a miracle. I just hoped it would make it back with the extra weight of Baldwin's safe in it.

The trick shut the car door much too loudly and said, "I can't believe I'm about to rob Reggie Baldwin's house."

I furrowed my brow and hushed him. He dismissed me with a girlish hand wave.

The side door remained unlocked, just like I left it. The musty, old-people smell of the house assaulted me instantly. I swallowed and focused on Colonel's Fortune, my ship that was finally coming in. I wondered if I'd stay with Steve or not, once I had all that cash in hand. The weird truth of it was I hadn't given it any thought. My eyes had been so unassailably fixed on the prize that I hadn't given the slightest consideration to what my life was going to look like with five hundred grand in the bank. Probably I'd set up in better digs. Maybe be somebody else's sugar daddy for a change.

"This place is a shit hole," the trick observed, again in a stage whisper that could probably be heard Jersey side.

"Beats working for a living," I said.

"I expected...I don't know, something else."

"The old man's so bad off he shits himself. The house is the least of his worries. Come on, over here."

I guided him toward the library door, careful to avoid stubbing my toes on any of the furniture crowded around the room. I was ready to lift the safe and get the hell out of there. I was not ready for the door to be locked.

"Now what?" he asked me, all of his playfulness sloughed off like a layer of dead skin.

I could hear the blood in my ears then. Dragging a long breath into my lungs, I gritted my teeth and listened to the house. There wasn't anyone in the place but Baldwin, me, and the trick. It didn't really matter how I got into that room, so long as I did it, and tonight. After all, I had a sure thing to bet on.

So I kicked the damn thing in. Not that hard, or as hard as most people probably think. It was an interior door, more or less hollow on the inside, and the little brass knob caved under the third kick. The racket resonated in my head, and with a hand on the trick's shoulder I cautioned him, listening for the inevitable yawp of the pants-crapping old queen upstairs. It didn't come. About three quarters of a second later, I knew why.

He was sprawled out on the dirty rug, his legs twisted up like ropes of raw dough. I thought he must have dragged himself down the stairs and into the library, though couldn't fathom why he wouldn't have blown his brains out in the comfort of his own bedroom. Maybe he kept the gun in there.

Baldwin's head was a nightmare, his face gray and slack like the skin was sliding off, a messy crimson exit wound at the crown of his skull. It looked like knockwurst when it's cooked too long, at too high a temperature—it just *pops* apart at the ends. Presentation is everything to some cooks. Reggie Baldwin had presented himself in the most dramatic way possible, as if he knew I'd be back, looking for his secret dragon's hoard, and wanted to give me a nasty little shock. If so, it was a grand success. I was shocked as hell.

Beside me, the trick chortled.

"Jesus jumped on Mary, what a way to go."

"Getting old ain't for sissies," I said. Bette Davis said it first, but I didn't see the need for a citation. The only thing pressing on my mind at that particular moment was getting the hell out of Staten Island as fast of that piece of shit Impala could take us.

"He's not getting any *deader*," he announced. "Let's get what we came for."

"There's a body at our feet," I reminded him. "We need to go. Now."

"It's *right there*," he said, pointing a steady finger at the little black safe.

"All we have to do is step over poor Reggie here, take it down, and we're gone."

"I was going to return it. Pay him back."

"He doesn't need it now. Come on, give me a hand."

The boy had a point. Not a nice one, but it made sense. At the time, at least.

I stepped over the corpse, as I was told, and slid a few inches in the blood pooled on the hardwood. The trick said something like "Whoa, Nelly!"

and I wanted to punch him, choke him, leave him to rot with "poor Reggie here." Instead I a grabbed a shelf, dumped half a dozen books on the floor, and steadied myself. *Colonel's Fortune*, my brain repeated rhythmically, chanting like I was trying to summon a devil. Whatever we found in that safe was a day and a half away from being decoupled. I helped the trick pulled the safe away from the wall, all the while wondering idly if people dreamed when they were bombed out on Seconal and if so, of what.

The safe was about a hundred times heavier than I thought it would be, and I expected it to weigh half a ton. My trick's neck transformed into a bundle of bulging cords, his face turned a weird shade of purple.

"Down?" I whispered. I don't know why I whispered. There was no one around to hear who wasn't already dead.

He gave a sharp, desperate nod and we both squatted, letting go a few inches from the floor. The safe cracked the hardwood, kicked up a cloud of dust. The trick huffed and laughed, wiping the sweat from his brow. I waited for him to compose himself.

"The hell's this thing made of?" he said, a quivering grin on his lips.

I sighed, peered at the doorway, eager to get a move on. Then I felt his hand at my groin and warm, nicotine-infused breath at my throat. Crazy—that was the only word for it. I figured somebody had to have heard the shot, called the police. Wasn't that what people did when they heard a gun fire? Dial 911, even if maybe it was just a car backfiring? I tried to think back to all the dozens upon dozens of times I'd heard those crackling pops, some of them disturbingly close. Life in the Big City. The trick's fingers working my zipper down and worming into my fly did nothing to expedite the memories. One thing was for sure: I'd never called the cops over a noise that didn't involve me. Not even once.

A soft grunt roiled out of my throat and I lay back on the rug, careful to avoid all the blood.

While the trick drilled through the face of the lock, I sprawled out on his loveseat and clutched a light beer I'd fished out of the fridge. The drill was an enormous, industrial thing, not the sort of equipment you found just sitting on a shelf at the hardware emporium. I wondered if he'd gotten this from his cousin, too. I didn't ask.

"This thing's as old as Reggie was," he commented, his forehead dappled with sweat. Not so much as a twitch of his mouth putting Baldwin in the past tense; it didn't bother him at all. "Newer ones usually have a cobalt plate, makes it so you can't hardly get through to the cam housing." He wiped his face with his sleeve and blew out a long puff of air. I had no idea what he was talking about, nor when he'd suddenly become so knowledgeable about safecracking. I was starting to feel like I was being played, but I couldn't figure out the game. The last dregs of my beer went down warm and sour. I tried to recall if I'd seen another one or if this was the last of it.

"What kind of dope do they put in those horses, anyway?" I asked, just to have something to say.

"Hell, I don't know. Some kind of steroids, same as athletes, I guess. Speeds 'em up, and from what I hear Colonel's Fortune is already *fast*." The drill jutted in a quick couple of inches, jarring him. A smile spread across his face. "Gimme that punch rod."

I grabbed a long steel rod from the floor by its hammerhead end and passed it over to him. Absently, I tipped the empty bottle to my lips and sucked air. Disappointing.

"You hang out at the track a lot?" I pestered. Questions I should have asked before, at the start. I got up to ferret out another drink.

"Not really. Almost there."

There was a fruity looking wine cooler stashed behind a Styrofoam takeout box. I reached for it when I heard something clatter noisily.

"Better get back in here, lover," the trick called out to me, his voice like honey. "Time to find out what's in Al Capone's vault."

He might as well have cursed us with that little joke. He yanked the door open and the only thing inside the safe was the lock he'd knocked into it. Whatever game he was playing, it was over now.

I downed the wine cooler in one go.

I was three sheets to the wind by the time I got home, somewhere between midnight and one in the morning. I'd stopped off at a liquor store en route, drank half a bottle of schnapps on the train. Nobody noticed or cared.

I never gave a rat's ass about the races, and I still didn't. I had no intention to check the racing form, see if Colonel's goddamn Fortune won or not. It didn't matter, not when we came up so disappointingly empty. Goddamn trick. Goddamn Reggie Baldwin. I slid naked under the sheets beside Steve and damned him, too.

The last thing my trick said to me was, "Well, how much have you got?"

He still wanted to play, to make lemonade out of the rotten lemons we'd worked so hard for. I just laughed in his sweaty face and left the door standing open on my way out.

Lying flat on my back in the dark of our bedroom, I wasn't laughing anymore. I wasn't exactly crying, either. Mostly I just felt empty, like this was the last defeat I could stand for a while. In the morning I'd get up and sip my coffee and try to remember not to leave the apartment if I didn't have to, not to *attempt* anything. My ship had come in all right, but it kept on sailing into the night and I'm not a very good swimmer. Now I was standing alone on the dock with my thumb up my nose, confused as to how it all went south so damn quickly.

I resolved to patronize a different bathhouse from then on. I dropped into a restless sleep around two.

I woke up next to Steve less than five hours later, gently placed my hand at the small of his back. It felt cool to the touch. My guts pinched up straight away and I got up on my knees to look him in the face. I didn't need to be an As-Seen-on-TV forensic scientist to realize I'd killed him. The red devils I'd slipped him weren't exactly pharmacologist-approved, and apparently I *did* need a certain amount of scientific knowhow with regard to how much a guy Steve's size needed to sleep soundly through the night. My plan involved guesstimation. Death by. Accidental, but wholly, irrevocably my fault. I rolled him over and thumbed an eyelid open, the eye underneath glassy and dry, the pupil huge and black. Like an animal's. Roadkill.

Sorry, babe. I just didn't want you to know what I was doing behind your back.

Mea culpa.

What followed: tears, impotent rage, guilt, loneliness, panic. Panic was the main thing. I was looking at a manslaughter rap. Worse still, if I reported this thing, how long before I got tied to Baldwin's house, the kicked-in door, the missing safe and the corpse on the carpet? I certainly didn't expect the trick to protect me. If anything, he'd throw me under the bus to save his own ass. I was in trouble.

For lack of anything better to do, I put on a pot of coffee in the kitchen and let my mind wander over my non-options. I wasn't going to call the police. I wasn't going to call anyone. All I could do was slurp down some mud and think about what I could carry in a single suitcase and what I'd have to leave behind. With any luck—not something of which I had a surplus of late—Steve would have a little cash lying around, enough to get me to Port Authority and the hell out of town.

I tossed the bedroom, my eyes constantly jetting back to the body on the bed. At least it wasn't as gruesome as Baldwin's, something I told myself over and over to make it seem less nightmarish. He looked like he was only sleeping. I half-convinced myself he was.

There were twenty-eight dollars in Steve's wallet. I pocketed the cash and left the credit cards. No sense in leaving a trail. How far would less than thirty bucks take me? Back to Staten Island? The question was rendered moot when I checked the closet.

Though it wasn't the hundred grand I'd hoped for, the twenty-six thousand in hundreds and fifties I discovered buried under Steve's shoe rack was more than enough to elicit a shrill yelp from me. The fact that they smelled musty and vaguely like warm hot dogs made me giggle. After I counted through the bills for the second time, I squeezed my partner's cold, dead hand and said, "You sly bitch. You weren't ever going to tell me, were you?"

Of course he wasn't, the little thief. It wasn't as though I had access to his bank statements. He'd probably been ripping patients off for years. Naturally, I turned the rest of the apartment upside-down, looking for more secret stashes of pilfered cash, jewels—who knew what my poor, dead Stevie had gotten away with? Probably old Reggie was the first to take it so hard, but I doubt that would have slowed my man down.

I didn't find anything, not even change in the couch cushions. (Steve cleaned under the cushions regularly, the only person I ever met who did, and once bawled at me for the better part of an hour over an errant Skittle he'd discovered down there.) Still, twenty-six Gs wasn't anything to sneeze at, especially when I multiplied it by ten and didn't have to split the take with anybody.

I kissed the cadaver on the center of the forehead and headed out to see a man about a horse.

from "the graveyard of bitter oranges"
josef winkler
translated from the german by adrian west

In front of a tropical fruit stand in the Piazza dei Cinquecento, lit up by low-hanging bare bulbs, I stood and observed the red flesh pierced by black seeds of the melons, the yellow pineapples split in two, the ovular, yellow-green bunches of grapes, and the segmented coconut flesh laid out in large basins. I heard Arabian music, camels knelt down before a Corpus Christi altar covered over with flowers, blessed mendicants meandered through the streets among the dead cobras, playing panpipes. Starvelings from African countries squatted on the grass patches of the Piazza dei Cinquecento, ate and urinated on the spot, and, when night had fallen and the dew distilled, wrapped themselves in their rags and slept, until the sounds of the carabinieri and roving dogs awakened them. Nervous in their high heels, which clacked against the asphalt, two transvestites walked back and forth. Behind a cafe, where the street urchins and transvestites drink their cappuccinos and Camparis, I saw three Tunisian boys step into a dark side street, in the company of a forty-year-old Tunisian man. I followed them and sat down when they did, a few steps behind, on a stone bench. One of the Tunisian boys walked to a nearby public fountain and washed off a bunch of yellow-green grapes. I went up to the fountain as well, to wash my hands, which were sticky, as I had eaten a half a pineapple, and looked more closely into his face. The boy stared at me a moment, taken aback, while I knelt next to him and held my hands under the stream of water. He stood up and went back to his friends with the washed-off grapes, which he had placed in a brown paper bag. Plucking a round grape from the bunch, the older African asked me in a mix of Arabic, French, and Italian since when I had lived in Rome, how long I wished to stay, and what I did for a living. As I answered, he sat down to my right, wary of the pizza that had been vomited on the stone bench. The boy to my left wriggled closer, and the one who had held the grapes under the streaming water squatted down by my legs and gazed into my face. Vexed and apprehensive, I glanced left and right as their net closed in on me. Worried for my leather satchel, which contained my observation book, with its depictions of the desiccated corpses of the bishops and cardinals from the priests' corridor in the Capuchin catacombs in Palermo, I pulled it up onto my lap and laid my hand across it. I saw in the Africans' eyes that I had insulted them by this gesture. I had taken them for thieves before they had even been able to contrive to rob me of anything. The boys had freshly washed hair, their faces, staring back at me, were well-rested, their clothing was new as well, and I concluded from all this that they had only arrived in Rome a few hours before. The Tunisians stood up, left the dark street, and walked in the direction of the Piazza dei Cinquecento. Standing up from the stone bench as well, I pulled a banknote from my pant pocket. The brightly lit cafe, ringed with windows, cast a broad glow over the Piazza dei Cinquecento. With a shimmering gaze, the youngest of the boys whispered to one of his friends that I had a banknote in my hand. While the others walked on a few steps ahead, the boy who had been spoken to stood still, looked back toward me, and turned in a half-circle, waiting for me to address him. *Vuoi soldi?* I asked the African. *Far' l'amore?* the boy whispered. He asked me whether I knew of a suitable place and made arrangements with his friends, saying, in two hours at the latest, he would be back in the Piazza dei Cinquecento. I thought we could hide behind some shrubbery, but those heavily frequented areas smell of urine and feces and are eternally damp, dogs are always passing by and sniffing around, and patrolling policemen shine the headlights of their blue and white cars into their every nook and cranny. As we walked by the brightly lit stall of a music cassette vendor, the sixteen-year-old Tunisian recounted to me that he had arrived in Rome just hours before, with a few friends and his brother, from Tunis. They had come as stowaways on a ship from Tunis to Cagliari and from there to Civitavecchia and on to Rome by bus. We walked up the Via Finanze and arrived at a bus stop. The people there, standing at the border of an excavation site and waiting on the bus, eyed us with distrust. As we walked by our oglers, I rested my hand on Omar's shoulder and tousled his purple-black, curly hair. Continuing along, we came upon a wide-open iron gate and crossed the threshold. A few cars stood at the lit back entrance of a church leading into the offices and sacristy. But the arcades were completely dark. I laid my black leather satchel down on a stone bench, a few feet from Omar, because for a moment I was afraid he might make off with it. After I stripped off my pullover and laid my glasses over my bag, I walked toward Omar, who stood waiting in the corner and had already pulled down his zipper. With my lips I grazed his chin, his shampoo-scented hair, I slipped his pants down and spread the elastic of his tight white underpants, freeing his sex and his buttocks. After I had shed the clothes from my lower body, we pressed our stiffened pricks together. Amarcord! When I was sixteen years old, I used to go into the hayloft with the pictures of bare naked sixteen-year-old boys that I had clipped from the *Bunte Illustrierte*, push down my pants, and burrow with the black-skinned boys into a hay pile just under the swallows' nests. In the arcade I knelt down, stroked the thighs of the Tunisian boy with my lips, licked his black balls, sniffed at his pubic hair, and took his circumcised penis into my mouth. While I sucked his cock, he groaned softly and made copulating movements with his hips and ran his hands through my hair. I let it slip back out of my mouth and burrowed my nose in the boyish aroma of his black pubic hair. He dampened his prick with spit and gestured for me to turn around. But I felt an intense pain in my lower abdomen and curled up, so that his prick slid from my backside; I turned around, knelt back down before him, pushed his shirt up over his nipples and pressed my face into his belly and into his crotch. I breathed in the scent of his pubic hair, the scent of his balls and his glans, bored my tongue deep into his bellybutton, clasping his buttocks in my palms. I sniffed at his thighs and moistened his kneecaps with my spit and, when he turned around, I pressed my tongue deep between his buttocks, until I perceived the taste of excrement on my tongue. I nestled my nose and tongue into the black hair of his armpits, sucked with my lips on his nipples and buried my face again in his loins. Hearing a noise, we let go of one another and listened attentively for a moment. Then I knelt down again before Omar and pressed my chin into his nude belly; but hardly thirty seconds later, I heard the shutting of an iron gate, and a man stood behind us yelling, *Andiamo! Subito! Andiamo!* We dressed ourselves in haste. I felt after my eyeglasses and pullover. It was not until we stepped across the threshold of the iron gate that the monk saw he had chased off two faggots. The nerves in his face were twitching and he spouted curses in Roman dialect. We raced away quickly, with quivering legs, out onto the street, and laughed on our walk back to the Via Finanze and once again past the bus stop. In search of another spot, we walked further on, and came to the open yard of an enormous building, but the bushes were not high or thick enough; when we entered, we found a grimy stone pathway leading up toward the house. Under a dark archway, I again laid my eyeglasses and my leather satchel aside. Omar had already bared his genitals, he came up to me and pulled down the zipper of my pants. Repeatedly kissing his right hand, which smelled of cigarettes, I implored him softly, *Kill me! Kill me!* I knelt down again and took his hot cock in my mouth, sniffed at his thighs, burrowed with my nose and tongue in his pubic hair and moistened his balls with my spit. Emerging from the back-alley, my eyelids glued half-shut from his semen, I walked out onto the perfumed Via Veneto, passing by two wickedly expensive whores, one of whom accosted me and spit at her feet when I explained to her that women held no sexual interest for me; I bumped into a transsexual, who had dumped out a half-bottle of perfume over his body, and cut through the Villa Borghese to the Via Antonio Gramsci, down the Via San Valentino and finally out along the Via Barnaba Tortolini. When I entered the foyer of the apartment building, and heard the voices conversing, I knew the signora was being visited by one of the elderly ladies from the Swiss embassy. I gave her visitor my hand, but I was so afraid, in that moment, that she would strip away the groin-scent of the African from my fingers, that I drew my hand back at once, after only fleetingly brushing against her. I sat down at the table, resting my chin in my hands, to surreptitiously inhale the scent of Omar's hips. Later, when the visitor was gone, I sat on the divan and wept. I covered the left -hand side of my face with my hand, so that Signora Leontine Fanshawe, sitting next to me and reading in the leather armchair, could not see my tears. When I went to the bathroom and afterward used the sink, I avoided washing my right hand, so that I would not wipe away the boy's scent. Before I went to sleep, I cleaned my face only with my left hand and was careful that I did not accidently dribble toothpaste on my right. I went to sleep with the scent of Omar's loins on my hand. In the morning, when I awoke, the scent was gone.

the cervantino baby
trebor healey

"No MUCHACHAS EN MI CASA, BETO." She wagged her finger. "No muchachas en tu cuarto."

"Muchach-as?" I enunciated, with emphasis on the a. "No problema, Senora. Yo prometo."

She poked her finger in my sternum then to emphasize the point. "No muchachas, Beto, no."

What was I, a child? No—more like she had that elderly woman wisdom of knowing a cad when she saw one, even if she was wrong about what vowel to tack on the end of her word for trouble.

Señora Mendoza was my house mother in Guanajuato—*mi mamá*. I was attending classes at the Instituto Falcon to brush up on my atrophied Spanish before heading deeper into Mexico, and whatever adventures awaited me there. I'd signed on for a week at the school and then planned to take buses down to Querétaro, Mexico City, Puebla, Xalapa—for however long I could stretch my money. I'd been assigned to the Mendoza family when I checked in at the school, and paid them one hundred dollars for an almost completely private room. They lived in a tall house on the slopes behind the Universidad de Guanajuato's towering Spanish Colonial cathedral-like main building, and almost all their rooms were on the upper story, with just a washroom, and one bedroom—mine—on the ground floor.

Like the tourist propaganda that had enticed me there—and why the place was so rife with language schools—Guanajuato was truly more of an old European hill town than anything in Europe. Settled by the Spanish in 1559 as a silver and gold mining center, it was full of beautiful old structures and charm to burn, with a rich history from the War of Independence—and since not much had happened since, it was beautifully preserved, almost frozen in time. Which meant I had the pleasure of walking out every morning on to the ten-foot-wide cobblestone Calzada de Guadalupe that snaked its way up and down the hill, all the houses rising in their varied colors along both sides, giving me a feeling of delightful dizziness.

I'd stroll down the hill and across the steps of the big University Building, and then down past the big Basilica with its soaring belfries, and on to Calle Obregón, which took me into the plaza where businesses were opening up their doors, the gazebo in the middle of the square peacefully silent and solitary, watching it all, not inhabited yet by romantic lovers or the requisite mariachi players.

I'd usually see a cute boy or two, either opening up some store, hosing down the sidewalk, hurrying along somewhere on some errand, or more likely, rushing to class. They usually smiled wide and made eye contact in the way of Mexican men, which I quickly learned was just how they greeted you and not an invitation to queer sex as it would be in the States. Still, it warmed my heart and roused my longings.

Pero, "no muchachas en la casa Mendoza," I laughed out loud as I walked.

I'd keep that promise, and hold her to the feminine vowel when the shit hit the fan a week later. I'd also leave Isabel to clean up the mess. That wasn't fair, but it was partly her fault. It was she who invited Isaias inside, after all, setting a dangerous precedent. To her credit, she did defend me when everything went south—or so she claimed—but Mamá was in denial about a lot of things and would have none of it. And there's no more unreasonable woman than a moralistic Catholic who believes her daughter is a virgin when she's not.

Isabel had a story of her own, which she related to me one afternoon when I'd run into her in the plaza. I'd liked her immediately upon meeting her my second day in the Mendoza house and was thrilled to bump into her in town. She had a big infectious smile and sincere, kindly eyes. She was a schoolteacher and an athlete, a tad too feminist for her mother's tastes, but she played the devoted daughter to a T. Señora Mendoza, mi mamá, was someone who was willing to be bullshitted, and my mistake was that I'd end up telling her the truth. But that was later.

First there was Isabel and her sad tale. She'd been "ruined," she said over lunch at the Restaurant Valadez, a popular sidewalk cafe on the plaza, by a Swede who'd studied at Instituto Falcon. *Ruined.* She was only twenty-one. I wanted to say *"You'll get over it. We're all ruined at twenty-one if we fall in love and get dumped."* But you can't say that to a twenty-one year old, so I just listened. Isabel was intelligent—but goodness, she was dramatic too.

"I opened myself to him, like Jesus on the cross—" and she threw her arms out. "When he turned his back on me, I couldn't protect myself." Her arms were still out, beginning to shake now from the effort. I understood—or thought I did. He'd crucified her and she couldn't pull free of the nails.

One tear rolled nobly down her cheek, which she didn't bother to brush away as she turned back to her salad. *What could I say?*

"I'm sorry, Isabel," and I held out my open hand on the table. She didn't take it; she just smiled sighfully.

"Do you have a girlfriend?" she feebly asked.

"No, no, I don't." As I'd just moved into her very Catholic home and was in a foreign land, I didn't feel like telling her why just yet. She'd find out in time. Oh, would she. But I did feel a little bad in that she had just revealed a secret of sorts, and I'd held my cards firmly to my chest. But as I'd find out later, there was more to her story too.

She had friends at the Institute, which is how she'd gotten her mother the gig renting rooms to students. It was good extra income for minimal effort. Mamá fed me breakfast and dinner, and while I ate, she talked at length about the corruption of Mexican politics, the madness of the world, and her sister who'd moved to Chicago and become a Protestant. I couldn't follow all of it with my rudimentary grasp of Spanish, but I got the gist. "¿Eres catolico, Beto?"

"Sí, Mamá."

She smiled, until I told her that now I was a Buddhist. She scolded me, told me it was wrong to dispense with the faith of one's birth; that I couldn't in fact; that I was fooling myself and committing a grave sin; that I should go to mass with her.

"I'm late for my evening class," was all I could muster as she sat back, eyeing me suspiciously and reiterating, as was her wont, finger wagging with admonition, "No muchachas en mi casa, Beto. No muchachas."

I smiled big. "¡Absolutamente no!"

I began to wonder just why it kept coming back around to that subject.

Were the girls of Guanajuato so loose? Not from what I'd seen. It was Mexico after all, and the church kept most girls in major check, just like I'd seen in Catholic Italy or Portugal. But Guanajuato was an educated town—richer and more liberalized than much of Mexico—and that posed a threat to traditional folks like *mi mamá*. And then there was the Cervantino, which I wasn't even aware was beginning at the end of that week. And what came with the Cervantino were the dreaded Cervantino babies.

The Cervantino was a celebration of Cervantes and his work—primarily *Don Quixote*, of course. The town swelled with students from all over Mexico as the theaters staged myriad plays—some so obliquely interpretive as to seem completely unrelated—recounting the misadventures of the old Don, his sidekick Sancho Panza, and the requisite slews of chivalric and caddish knights, comely barmaids and damsels in high windows. Restaurants shifted their menus to medieval Spanish fare and tapas, the trousers of the wait staff ballooning with gaudy stripes and knee-high stockings. There were parades, complete with huge puppetted performers on stilts mimicking windmills, the old Don, the sun and the moon; galloping horses; flamenco dancing; and music in the plaza: mandolin solos interjected among the mariachi madness, and boys dressed as harlequins in too-long sleeves and big elfin shoes adorned with bells, flopping about like jesters.

I took a fancy to one of them, in fact. But that all came later. It was Wednesday, day three of my visit, with the Cervantino still three days away and Isabel now giving me tragic looks as if to remind me of her divulged secret, while Mamá had taken to eyeing me suspiciously one moment and then lovingly and ingratiatingly the next. She constantly offered food, comfort and refreshment, entertaining me with family photos and tales of her girlhood in Jalisco, but she always ended every story with something admonitory about mass and muchachas.

I didn't meet my padre until the third night. He'd been out of town on business—something to do with shoes, ironically, as he rarely wore his, being mildly crippled and looking like he was experiencing a lot of back pain, the source of which I was unable to figure out or broach, mostly due to his kindness, his dignity in handling his condition, and the sighs of his wife and daughter. He was their Tiny Tim, only not so tiny, certainly not a child, and obviously not named Tim. He was, as he proudly and boastfully stated, "Ernesto Quintero de León Mendoza y Vasquez."

I shook his hand heartily, introducing myself as "Beto Mendoza," and thanking him for adopting me, even if for but a week, as a member of his family. He beamed while Mamá nearly choked with emotion, patting my back as I stood before her husband. She guided me back to my chair, imploring, "¿Más café, Beto?"

"No, gracias."

"No, no, mamá, vamos a ir a una fiesta," Isabel chimed in half-whining.

Mamá was crestfallen, no doubt imagining an evening of family bliss, not the usual middle-aged night alone with Ernesto and the TV. Isabel was all they had left , their four sons grown and moved off to cities with more opportunity: León, Morelia, Monterrey, Mexico City. And now, even their newly minted son, in his maiden act, was heading out—and taking their last remaining child with him.

Mamá wanted to know whose party it was, and when Isabel related that it was Isaias' and Ezequiel's, she momentarily beamed before the disappointed frown returned to her face. Isabel rolled her eyes and guided me to the door, explaining to me as we walked Guanajuato's lamplit stone streets that Isaias and Ezequiel were twin brothers who had gone through school with her and had always been favorites of her mother's. Accomplished and dutiful, Isaias was a graduate student in the Archaeology Department where Isabel worked in administration, and Ezequiel was a fairly well-known and successful folklorico dancer. The party, she told me, was a reunion of sorts, inspired by Ezequiel's return home from touring through Central and South America with the Guadalajara Folklórico group. All their old friends would be there. I looked at Isabel quickly then, suspicious that she was taking me to meet some of her closest and oldest friends, worrying that she was setting herself up for yet another Swedish fall.

I stopped her on the street then, gently grabbing her elbow, and as graciously as I could, broached the subject. "Isabel, can I trust you with a secret?"

Her eyes lit up.

"Well, I hope you will keep this between us and not make it known to your mother. I'm gay...uh...as in I like men?"

She reached out and hugged me immediately, expressing her happiness at the fact, and that it meant we could now *really truly* be friends. I was surprised, considering my earlier suspicions, reminding myself once again that coming out to most people was a cause for celebration and not as loaded down with the dreaded rejection and abandonment I so often feared.

Apparently, I'd made Isabel's day. She skipped along now, grabbing my hand, finally free to love me. She kept looking at me, then bursting out laughing, perhaps because she was already formulating a plan for that evening, the players of which I had not yet met, nor had I any clue about how charming they'd be.

We climbed the stairs and heard the music before we reached the door of the little house of the Moreno family and the beginning of what can only, for me, be called a rendezvous with a Grecian sort of fate.

There'd been no omens, of course, nor prophetic oracles back in the States predicting chaos in Mexico, but I recognized Ezequiel immediately, almost as if I knew him. He looked the spitting image of a young Che Guevara. And when his friends insisted he perform the Vera Cruz dance for us all—that's the one sans shirt (which he quickly dispensed with)—I blushed in awe, not just at the spectacle of his naked torso, but at his amazing acrobatic talent and finesse. Beside myself as he put the finishing touches on his performance—all eyes upon him—my eyes scanned the room desperately for Isabel who, when I found her, was laughing hysterically—I think at my expense—and sitting next to Che's (I mean Ezequiel's) identical twin brother, Isaias, who was smiling at me seductively. I smiled back, stupefied at my good fortune, as Isabel motioned me over. My mind was racing as fast as my heart, and, full of that sexual greed typical of men such as myself, I was already wondering whether both boys were queer before I'd even met Isaias who'd just indicated in no uncertain terms that he was. *Wasn't there a lot of evidence that twins tended to have the same sexual orientations?* I thought to myself as I parted the bodies and made my way to Isabel.

Isaias put his hand out to shake mine in an epic gesture of physical contact that clearly communicated it was the beginning of something profoundly animal to come.

"Hola," he smiled brightly as electricity pulsed through the palms of our hands. *The Guevara twins. Good God.*

"Hola," I stuttered back, my hand grown clammy. What I wanted to say was *Let's go!*—not knowing where to of course. Instead, I behaved myself and practiced my Spanish flirtatiously as Isabel midwifed our romance into full bloom, sharing with Isaias the few stories I'd shared with her, and prodding me to ask Isaias about his most recent trips to Mexico City, or about his sojourn last summer in Puerto Vallarta. He shyly looked down at his lap, and then—when Isabel ran off to the bathroom—demurely claimed that he was bisexual, and that Isabel's fantasies about his adventures were just that—the product of her own imagination and wishful thinking. I shrugged nonchalantly, letting him know that, whatever the case, I was enjoying myself and had made no judgment about him based on Isabel's exuberant hearsay. But I sensed immediately his fear and trepidation.

Cervezas were proffered and dancing ensued, with Ezequiel—clearly the star—now and again taking over the dance floor à la *Saturday Night Fever* and treating us all to a stunning performance of his acrobatic prowess. My god, I was crushed out on him—and being that he was in some odd public sense exhibiting his body and what it could do in grand fashion—consumed with lust, almost to the exclusion of the man sitting right next to me who looked almost exactly like him. But, of course—and unlike Isaias—Ezequiel seemed completely unavailable—he'd only briefly said hello to me when I'd first come in, and not in the fashion of his brother, either. Ezequiel wore the knit brow of the straight boy, and practiced the laconic clipped Spanish and the macho aloofness characteristic of the heterosexual male.

The hours passed, during which I spoke with an architect, an anthropologist and a medical student—Guanajuato was clearly one of Mexico's old world upper-class havens—and saw not just one but all my teachers, among whom was José, a gruff, bearded, Marxist-looking character who was a bit of a taskmaster about the finer points of the Spanish accent—rolled r's and tildes, as well as the "*flow*" as he called it, which meant his futile attempts to get American students not to overemphasize consonants and syllables, which, while common to English, made one's Spanish clunky and mechanical. He sat in a corner brooding, clinging to his gorgeous Spanish girlfriend, watching the revelers with arrogant disdain. Maria and Magda were more fun, dancing up a storm, chatting with all the students who were there, including myself and four or five others, making an obvious effort to impress the gringos Mexican-style. And I was impressed.

When the party was down to five—Ezequiel and Isaias, an expatriate named Jill who was clearly enthralled with Ezequiel, Isabel and myself—we decided to head down to El Beso for a nightcap. As we boisterously made our way down the hill, Ezequiel all the while jumping and slapping at store signs and light posts, his energy seemingly boundless, Isaias grabbed my elbow lightly and we slowed down, creating a distance of six or seven feet between ourselves and the others.

"You can't be gay here," he said in heavily-accented English. "Is dangerous. No touch me en la calle. Soy bisexual."

I almost laughed at that last line, but I also knew to heed and respect his warning. I'd been a dumb American in my enthusiasm for him and his brother—even perhaps in my confession to Isabel—and it was instructive to be reminded that we were in a small, conservative town in Mexico, and just as you could get mugged for looking like an American, you could also get beaten or killed for acting queer. I looked at Isaias and nodded with understanding, seeing in his eyes the danger I could be putting him in. He had to live here after all.

We ended up at El Beso near the plaza soon enough, and it was full of middle-aged Mexicans. "*Chilangos*," Isabel whispered under her breath, voicing the derogatory name for Mexico City bourgeoisie who acted—when outside their cosmopolitan city—with all the grace of Germans in Greece. Drinks arrived, and I quietly watched Jill make a fool of herself with Ezequiel, who barely responded, sipping his beer and staring into the middle distance, while Isabel and Isaias chattered about university politics.

"What are you doing here in Guanajuato, Jill?" I finally ventured.

"I'm a writer. I'm writing a novel. I live in San Miguel actually. Lots of expats there." She said it like it was a good thing, and I suppose it was if you were actually living in Mexico and not just passing through. For my part, if I didn't see an American for my three weeks in Mexico, I'd be delighted. I had the mirror, and that was enough.

"So I've heard," I answered, not adding that that was why I hadn't gone there.

Ezequiel stood up and, alpha male that he was, the rest of us did so as well. We jauntily spilled down the stairs and onto the street under El Beso's delightfully Spanish sign—funky, gloopy, Miró-like—another indicator of Guanajuato's identification with the continent. Ezequiel did a sort of bow to us all, leaving Jill hanging, and headed home back the way we'd come. Isabel and I were going in the opposite direction, so Isaias offered to walk us home. As Jill's hotel was on the way, and since she looked somewhat disoriented from Ezequiel's brush-off , she came with us for two blocks until we bid her goodnight at the Posada Palenque and climbed up the twisty-hilled streets past the University, bathed in its eerie green light, to 125 Calzada de Guadalupe.

Isabel gave Isaias a big kiss on the cheek and turned to put the key in the door, allowing Isaias to look over at me and communicate with his eyes that he wanted to *do it* now.

"Adios, Isaias," Isabel smiled, leading me in the door. But Isaias put his foot on the doorsill when Isabel turned to close it and smiled mischievously at her. She opened the door wider, looked up the stairs, listened for a second, and then put her finger to her mouth and pulled Isaias in, pushing him behind me into my bedroom. Then up the stairs she clumped.

Un muchach-o en mi cuarto.

Things happened quickly. We laughed, we shushed each other as we stripped and wrestled together; we experienced the awe of our attraction for one another; the joy of how we made each other feel; the humor of how the bed creaked. Then came the quickening and Isaias bucking and growling under his breath, "Qué rico," as we lost ourselves to each other.

Without missing a beat, he rushed to gather himself up, gave me a quick kiss and his phone number, and tiptoed out.

I awoke to the calls of mi mamá: "¡Desayuno, Beto! ¡Cafe!"

This place was too good. My own private room, a mother who wakes me up and feeds me, a stroll through one of the most charming towns in the world to an hour or two of class, then to top it off I get to end the day with a beautiful naked man on top of me who knows what he's doing and can barely keep his passion in check.

"Buenos días, mamá," I greeted her with a kiss on the cheek. The exuberance of the laid.

She smiled in motherly bliss.

"¿Tienes la cruda, Beto?" she teased.

"No cruda, mamá. I'm a good boy."

"Un católico," she said with satisfaction.

"Hoy, soy un católico," I relented.

"... y no muchachas en mi casa."
"No muchachas!" And I laughed heartily.

Isaias dropped in that night around dinnertime and Mamá asked him to stay for supper, which he did. Mamá praised him to me, which I began to think was his point in dropping by. Isabel acted coy, saying little, and then rushing off to some engagement halfway through dinner while Papá just sat and listened with that beatific smile he always wore on his face, interrupted now and again with a little chuckle at the absurdity of his wife's flattery. I just nodded a lot, and interjected innocently with a lot of "¿como se dices?"; "más despacios,"; "repita, por favors."

"Both of you are like sons to me," she concluded as she cleared our plates and Isaias related that we were off to climb up to El Pípila, a hilltop statue of the torch-bearing Indian miner who had set fire to the Spanish fortress and launched the War of Independence.

We both gave Mamá a hug. We'd made her happy—at least in the kitchen. Because before we left , Isaias hustled me into my room for a quick jackoff —even as Mamá was shouting down to us about whether we wanted cocas or pan for the long hike.

"No, gracias, Señora Mendoza," Isaias called back up to her while he furiously worked the passion from his loins.

Isaias smiled and kissed me deeply when we'd completed our little task, seeming less and less bisexual all the time.

I was a bit smitten actually, as he was a delightful fellow, handsome, sweet, full of a friendly kind of mischief, chasing little kids, scaring off pigeons and handing me found objects—little flowers, centavos, discarded food wrappers which he'd make me read aloud to test my Spanish. But I couldn't quite shake that image of Ezequiel dancing like a Ukrainian. Truth was, I wanted them both.

We hiked up the series of steps to El Pípila in less than an hour, rewarded at the top by a grand view of the whole town—its churches and university, the little plaza and labyrinthine streets and tunnels, the colorful little boxy houses in purple and blue and orange, and the mountains all around and beyond—as the sky went yellow, pink and purple with the sunset.

Isaias dragged me into the bushes for another go, and then we went back down into town where he showed me the fort where El Pípila had thrown the fiery torch and been killed, as well as the little iron cages hanging atop the walls where the four heads of the rebellion's ringleaders had been put out for display on spikes after they'd been beheaded when the insurrection failed. We ended with coffee and pan dulce down by the plaza, Isaias staring longingly into my eyes.

Isaias had to work the next day, so I sought out one of the cliché tourist destinations from my *Lonely Planet* guide: El Museo de las Momias. And that's where the trouble really began. The trouble being Ezequiel, because he was there, sort of walking aimlessly about, as if he were waiting for something. I was surprised, frankly. He'd grown up in Guanajuato, and the mummies were the kind of thing you wouldn't frequent if you actually lived there. Basically, it was just glass case after glass case of the mummified remains of Guanajuato's residents of past centuries, who had unwittingly ended up mummified by accident due to the dry air and minerals in the soil where they'd been buried. There was a pregnant mummy, a baby mummy, a fat mummy, etc.

"I just like it here," was all he said, in his deep voice, by way of explanation.

He gave me the grand tour and seemed to know quite a bit about each of the dead displayed: "That's Alfonso—he was married to Elena over there." And he pointed with a jerk of his head.

Afterwards we took a crowded bus back up to town together and, upon arriving at the big open-air Mercado Hidalgo, he suggested we have a beer at one of the cafes in the adjoining plaza. We had a few, and chatted about folklorico and different kinds of music. As it turned out, he was a huge fan of Nirvana and grunge in general, and I had lots of such CD's in my room that I used for my portable CD player.

As for what happened next, maybe it wasn't so much Isabel's fault then as Kurt Cobain's. There'd been no indication that he wanted anything but a copy of *In Utero*, but I'd be disingenuous to say more didn't cross my libidinous mind as we headed back to Calzada de Guadalupe to peruse my CDs—though when I'd engaged the fantasy, I'd laughed to myself at the prospect.

But it happened all the same, and as it unfolded I knew I was not only stepping in a huge pile of karmic shit, but it dawned on me as well that Ezequiel was quite likely using the museum as his cruising ground for gringos—for guys who could never expose him. I was also thinking about how much I really liked Isaias, and how I would not want to do anything to jeopardize our little romance or hurt him. But Ezequiel's body was the kind that made you say, "Well, just this once," or "Who the fuck cares?" But my god, he was *his* twin brother—and Isaias and he really did look a lot alike, right down to the nitty, gritty details, if you get my drift , though Ezequiel was definitely more aggressive, selfish—even cruel. Things happened *with* Isaias; Ezequiel happened *to you.*

Mamá came home just as we were polishing each other off. I heard the door open, shushed Ezequiel, whose tough-guy face suddenly filled with the fear of God, and the two of us waited, suspended—in an odd position too—to hear her clump up the stairs. She didn't, and I knew then that my worst fears were just then manifesting. We heard her bags rustle, but no other sound. She was listening at the door.

"Beto?"

I said nothing. Ezequiel, panicked, looked at the window.

"¿Estas solo?"

"Sí...uh no...mi amigo está aquí." Ezequiel shook his head furiously. Mistake.

Why hadn't I just said I was with a friend in the beginning? Why the initial yes to her query of whether I was alone? Why the quick reversal to no?

She began screaming then, a lot of which I couldn't follow, but "dios" was involved as were "muchachas," "hombres," "mentirosos" and "promesas." Ezequiel took his cue and was out the window by the time she'd located the key to find me making the bed, the window wide open and wind blowing through the little frilly lace curtains. She turned on her heels, her face full of a quiet fury, and went back out the door and into the street, but Ezequiel was long gone.

When she returned, she barked, "Where's Isabel?!" And it was in the voice of a person who would kill to find out.

"No sé," I shook my head, hoping she believed me. It didn't occur to me until right then that this room might have been occupied by one notorious Swede, if not a whole slew of horny gringos that Isabel had fancied. I hoped to God then that Mamá *didn't think*...I mean, I was a cad, but I would never be that caddish. Yet, hadn't I been? How was it different really? Whether with Mamá's daughter, Isabel, or with Isaias' twin brother, Ezequiel, I'd transgressed in a family way.

My stomach sank and I thought the best thing for me to do right then would be to pack up and get out of town. But then I thought of Isabel, and I wanted to clarify things for her sake, as well as to reassure Mamá that nothing horrid had happened. And I wanted to at least say goodbye and thanks for the memories to Isaias. These people had been good to me.

"There were no muchachas en mi cuarto, Mamá. Un muchacho, Señora, un muchach-o!"

Her face went white. "¡Dios mio!" And she shouted for me to get out.

From bad to worse. I packed up while she stood there. "Gracias, Mamá, gracias," I meekly offered maneuvering by her with my bag.

"No soy tu mamá, Beto," and she crossed herself.

As I struggled out the door, Isabel appeared. Was that good or bad? Thank god she didn't look disheveled.

What's happening? her face seemed to say.

"Hola, Isabel."

By then Mamá was screaming to Isabel in very rapid Spanish behind me, and I simply walked away, down into town, where there were no rooms available because the Cervantino had begun.

Hordes of Mexican college kids were pouring into town, hiking up from the bus station, squeezed into the ubiquitous green VW cabs, or packed six-deep in little Fiats. Others were busy preparing for the festivities, running up banners, painting each other's faces. At a loss what to do, or where to go, I just sat down on the Basilica steps and watched, hoping something would come to me.

It didn't take long for Isabel to appear. Tears streamed down her face.

Ruined again.

I shook my head.

"Where's Isaias?" she gently asked.

Of course she thought I was with Isaias. "Did you tell your Mom it was Isaias?" I replied, feeling like a horrid criminal covering his tracks.

"Of course not, but I told her you were gay and that she shouldn't have kicked you out for that. She's got to get with the modern world." And she shook her head righteously, but softened before saying, "Oh, but it's my fault for letting Isaias in the other night. I'm so sorry."

"Did you tell her that?" I thought of Watergate.

"Of course not, I don't want her to know it was Isaias."

I thought how crazy this was all getting. Isabel didn't want her Mom to think it was Isaias; I didn't want Isabel to think it wasn't; and Isaias was out there somewhere, with just time separating him from the awful truth. And there I was, left to protect Ezequiel who would get away with it all.

Just then two huge puppets appeared of Don Quixote and Sancho Panza. The parade had begun.

Isabel began weeping in earnest. I comforted her the best I could, but she was coming apart. "What a world," she moaned. "People are so cruel, and intolerant." Her ire rose now. "Do you know about the Cervantino babies?"

I looked at her and shook my head, indicating I had no clue.

She explained how the college kids came to Guanajuato from far and wide; how they drank and sang and paraded about; performed in plays and skits; danced to music; played guitars; filled the posadas to bursting—and fucked like rabbits. Nine months later, the students all long gone, the town watched an alarming epidemic of young girls waddle about, all hugely pregnant and due pretty much all on the same day.

"Cervantino babies," she reiterated. "A lady from Texas came down here and opened an abortion clinic. They drove her out of town. She came back the next year. They drove her out of town again."

Mexico.

I just listened, too worried about what was coming down with Isaias to get into a political discussion about abortion in a catholic country.

But she had that ruined look on her face again.

"What is it Isabel?"

"I had a Cervantino baby once." And she sniffled her tears.

I put my arm around her shoulder.

"Lars took me to the Texan lady. He paid for it, and he left right afterward."

More to the story.

"Isabel," I whispered, and held her close as she wept on my shoulder.

I half-expected to see Isaias right then, but fortunately, it was just a gaggle of harlequins.

"Isabel, I wasn't with Isaias," I confessed suddenly.

She looked at me, perplexed.

I shook my head.

"Who then?"

"Just don't tell him about any of this. Please."

She stopped crying then. "You met someone else?"

I looked at her, waiting for her to turn on me.

"I really need to just go. Will you walk me to the bus station?"

"But what about Isaias?" And then she did get mad. "You can't just leave!"

"I was gonna leave anyway eventually."

She looked at me then with fury. Her mother's daughter.

"Isabel," I pleaded.

She took my hand, and she walked me back to the University, and right into Isaias' office, where a dozen or so graduate students scurried about or slumped over papers in need of grading. He played it straight to protect himself, but he understood what Isabel was saying: A misunderstanding about an American girl who was studying with Beto in his room, and how her mother had freaked out, thinking something was going on.

I looked at the ground. No one owed me this.

Isabel turned to me. "You can stay at the Moreños'. Pay them the same thing you paid my mother."

Isaias smiled.

So I spent the next week in the Moreños' house, sleeping on a pad on the floor next to a bunk bed where slept Isaias and his twin brother, Ezequiel, who pretended nothing had ever happened, though he surreptitiously handed me the two Nirvana CDs I'd given him when Isaias was in the shower, warning me, "Don't ever tell him."

Isaias came with me to Mexico City for a few days and we had a good time tromping through Chapultepec and hanging out in cafes in Colonia Roma and Coyoacan. We both decided we'd like to live in Frida Kahlo's house and particularly liked a painting there by Diego Rivera of a man on the seashore, under a huge bluff that made him look totally insignificant. Painted right after Frida had died, it was called, "Fridita, mi maravillosa". We toasted each other that way from then on—a year later in Zihuatanejo; two years after that in Chetumal, and once a whole five years after in Merida, when we'd long stopped seeing each other romantically (by then, Isaias had a lover and lived in Yucatán's capital city, where he was a professor of Archaeology at the University). Isaias had just told me about how Ezequiel had ruined his marriage when his wife caught him with a man, and that he was now drinking like a fish.

"Is he still dancing?"

"No, he gave it up."

I thought then of that first night's brilliant performance of the Vera Cruz folklórico; the shriveled faces at the Museo de las Momias; I thought of the sad end of Kurt Cobain; harlequins; I thought of Isabel. And I thought of telling Isaias everything now that the cat was out of the bag on Ezequiel. I didn't have to protect *him* anymore. But then, I'd never kept the secret to protect him. I'd done it for Isaias, and Isabel—for mi mamá. And I realized right then that Ezequiel was my Cervantino baby.

A tear pooled in my eye just as the waiter came by with two more beers, which we lifted up, and in the only way I knew how to tell him, I looked at Isaias, and raising my voice, shouted, "Para Ezequiel, el maravilloso!"

fend for yourself
james powers-black

I WAVE CURTIS OVER BEFORE I REALIZE JIMMY HAS WALKED INTO THE BAR BEHIND him. I can tell by the look on Curtis's face something's wrong.

"What's going on?" I ask.

Jimmy cuts in right between us and stands there, surveying the bar. Curtis hesitates, but he quickly tells. "We almost got the shit kicked out of us because Miss Thing here picks me up an hour late and parks us way the fuck over on 51st, nowhere near a streetlight, and skips down the sidewalk like we're going to a goddamn picnic!"

Jimmy should've known to show up earlier. It's not smart to walk around after dark in this part of Kansas City. That's the kind of mistake small-town guys make the first time they drive to the city to go bar hopping. Jimmy's got no excuse. When isn't the bar packed on a Saturday night? If you don't get here early enough, you have to park pretty far away, and in that case, you'd better put your head down and walk fast.

A few other guys turn toward us, half-listening to the story. Most of us have been followed on our way into the bar. Occasionally, someone gets beat up. No one comes here looking for that kind of drama, and besides us no one really cares.

Jimmy looks innocently at Curtis, his eyes barely up to Curtis's shoulder. Curtis is bigger than any of us. It's hard to believe anyone would take him on.

"One of them was blond," Curtis explains. "Aging twink, kind of cute. Probably skipped swim practice to get in a game of Smear the Queer." He keeps talking to me without looking at Jimmy. His voice booms. I can hear him over the music and everyone else in the bar. I think he played football in high school. I grew up as corn-fed as he did, but his family must have had better corn. I almost can't imagine him having sex with a man.

Jimmy moves onto the barstool next to mine, but Curtis still won't look at him. "And the other one," Curtis squints. "I don't remember him too well. All those breeder closet cases look alike." Curtis winks at me.

"What are you talking about?" Jimmy asks. I keep watching to see if he ever blinks.

"And she," Curtis says, shoving his chin in Jimmy's direction, "didn't even know what was going on. Oh-bliv-ee-ussss." Curtis looks right at me, lightly shaking his head.

Jimmy stares at me for three long seconds, like he hasn't seen me a thousand times before. His eyes are sparkling green. He seems cocksure of everything. My face feels hot, and I cover my crooked front teeth. Jimmy smirks and turns toward Curtis.

"You mean those two guys we saw on our way in?"

Curtis finally gives Jimmy his attention and glares at him, indignant as hell. They're like siblings or a divorced couple. Nobody's quite sure. Whatever his reasons, Curtis has been looking after Jimmy for years.

Curtis points a thick finger at me.

"Do you want another drink?"

"Sure."

"What about me?" Jimmy asks.

"It's time to fend for yourself, little princess," Curtis says, waving Jimmy off. "Go play? Let me know if you pick up a trick. I'll call myself a cab." Curtis sits next to me.

Jimmy rolls his eyes, then slips through the doorway that leads to the dance floor on the other side of the bar.

"Do you think those guys were really going to hurt you?" I ask.

"They definitely weren't just hanging out. Seemed they were looking to make trouble. Jimmy pranced right by them, and I kept walking." He takes a healthy swig of beer. His Adam's apple pumps with each gulp.

I work a corner of the label off my beer bottle. "They probably took one look and decided they'd better not fuck with you."

"I'm not too sure about that. They just got caught off guard by Jimmy's one-fag Pride parade. But they turned around and followed us for a while. I just kept saying 'uh-huh' to Jimmy's stupid story and made sure he kept walking. If we'd stopped, they would've jumped us."

He'd made such a big joke of it when they arrived. I'm surprised to see he's pretty shaken by the incident.

"But you could've taken them both," I say. "Easy."

"Maybe, maybe not. Wouldn't have made a difference if they'd had a knife."

"Jimmy didn't get what was going down?"

Curtis shakes his head. "He just chattered away the whole time. And he's got such a big-girl voice." He starts to grin. "At one point, he was telling me what a great buy he'd gotten on his new comforter."

I can't help but laugh at that.

He leans his head on his hand and smiles. "That's one of the things I love about him. He's unfiltered. But sometimes it's all I can do to keep the little princess from getting her ass kicked."

"Damn," is all I can say. I wish I understood why he cares so much. Jimmy treats him like shit most of the time.

"And I swear I saw him looking those guys over when we first passed them." He smiles broadly, but tries to hold down the corners of his mouth. "I mean, he did it real quick, but he wasn't too subtle about it, either. Subtlety isn't really his thing."

I laugh but it comes out more like a snort. Curtis doesn't seem to mind.

"Yeah," I say, "he's always looking."

"He's going to get himself hurt if he's not careful," Curtis says. "He doesn't think half the time. Worries the hell out of me."

"How long have you known him?" I wonder if Curtis and Jimmy were ever together, even just once. Something about that idea just doesn't seem right to me.

"A long time. Since he moved here after college. Maybe ten years?" He speaks softly, but I can hear him clearly. "Jimmy used to have a real sweet side, although I haven't seen it in quite a while."

Curtis finishes his beer and sighs. I've nursed my bourbon half to death, and he offers to buy me another. I say why not. We sit for a while and don't say much. The air is heavy with a mix of stale beer and the cheap cologne the young guys seem to bathe in. Curtis pushes back the damp hair that sticks to his forehead. He looks tired. I'm feeling a little bold, not just from the bourbon, and lean into him. He presses into me a little, too, smiling, not exactly looking at me but not looking away, either. I haven't felt this good in a long time. I could stay like this all night.

Jimmy comes flitting from the other side of the bar, all sweaty from dancing with some guy, the little-brother type he's so fond of, in tow. He walks up and leans his sweaty self against Curtis.

"And this is my Protector," he says to the young-looking stranger, who remains at a distance, looking cautiously at Curtis and, really, everything. Jimmy pokes Curtis in the arm. "Tell my new friend how you saved my life."

"Shit, Jimmy!" Curtis waves the air between him and Jimmy. "How many shots have you done?"

Clearly too many, not that Jimmy needs booze to act like a little asshole.

"Come on, tell him the story, Daddy."

"You told me you were going to watch how much you drank." Curtis shakes his head and stares at the empty glasses behind the bartender. "Why don't you go sit down or something?" His voice deepens yet softens as he speaks.

"Ooo. He'th tho butch, ithn't he?" Jimmy's voice squeaks. He's really performing for his new friend, whose wide eyes make him look both appalled and bored. Now that he's closer I can see the guy's face is orange and leathery. He has crow's feet and a crease across his forehead that makes him seem burdened by life.

Curtis stands up and takes a few steps away.

"I don't know what all the fuss is about," Jimmy says. "Those guys probably just wanted to fuck us." He starts laughing at himself. His strange friend joins in.

Curtis stops and turns back to Jimmy. He takes Jimmy by the arms and shoves him against the bar. The jolt knocks over Curtis's empty bottle. What's left of the beer dribbles out. The bartender stands frozen on his side of the bar as Curtis grabs Jimmy by the throat. All any of us can do is watch.

"They wanted to fuck you, all right! With a knife!"

Curtis is right down in Jimmy's face. If I'd just walked in, I might think they're about to kiss.

Jimmy looks confused, not entirely because he's drunk.

"People think you're so tough. But you don't do much besides take up a lot of room." He stares at Curtis with his unblinking green eyes as he says every word. "Worthless." He blows a burst of air in Curtis's face. Curtis winces, pulling away enough that Jimmy slips down to his knees and escapes between Curtis's legs. Jimmy's friend follows him through the doorway to other side of the bar. A strobe light sets them ablaze, then goes out suddenly, as if they disappear.

Curtis has his hands on the bar and his legs apart. Without Jimmy there, he looks like he's about to be frisked. He pushes off and starts walking toward the exit.

I'm not sure if I should, but I run to catch up with him. I have to go all the way outside to find him. He's standing right there on the sidewalk, looking around like he isn't sure which way. I put my hand on his shoulder. He whips around, ready to fight. When he sees it's me, he takes a step back.

"Where you going?" I ask.

"Home."

"Let me drive you."

"It's okay." He looks around. He doesn't walk off.

"I wasn't going to stay long anyway."

I'm parked at the end of the block. Curtis sits hunched down in the passenger's seat, his head touching the ceiling. He looks straight ahead and says nothing. I pull out from the curb, and he tells me where to turn.

"What's up with Jimmy tonight?" I ask. I can't help it. He's usually rude, but not this bad. And I've never seen him bother Curtis so much.

"He's a scary little shit, that's what."

"I'm sorry. I shouldn't have mentioned—"

"Everybody wonders." Curtis gives me the side eye. Maybe I'm about to get a lecture, but that's fine with me. "Everybody's sure there's something going on between us. That we're fucking. That's all anybody can think about—who's fucking who."

He isn't drunk, I know. His voice booms inside the tight space of the car. I can't tell if he's pissed or what.

"I wouldn't even want to think about fucking Jimmy," he says. "He treats me bad enough as it is. He only acts worse to you after he's had you."

I try to keep looking at Curtis while I drive. I want him to know that I really want to know.

"He's become an asshole, and this isn't the friendship I signed up for." He sighs hard and speaks more softly. "And yeah, friendship is all it's ever been, but sometimes it was great, you know? He's been like the little brother I never wanted." He chuckles to himself, but I can see tears glinting in his eyes. "He's easy prey, and they're out there, you know? Fucking creeps just waiting to pounce. I've gotten used to worrying about him. I just have to get over the fact that we're done."

Soon, he is full-on crying. I don't know how to get to his place, so I pull over and let him go at it, making sure to park under a streetlight. One of the regulars at the bar got jumped a block down from here. Even though they took his wallet, they beat him up pretty bad. Everybody knows they were looking for a faggot to bash. I keep the engine running, just in case. I lean against the wheel and watch him in the dim light, wondering if he's ever told this much to anybody else. He spreads his big wide hands on the dashboard, ready to shove out through the front of the car. The cords in his neck contract. I take him by the shoulder, but he feels too sturdy to budge. He turns to me slowly, eyes wide, maybe wondering what I'm about to do to him. I lay my palm on his dark hair, which looks black in the blue light.

Curtis closes his eyes and rests his head against my hand. Seemingly under my spell, he doesn't notice the approaching voices. Whoever they are, their laughter sounds sinister. If we hold still, maybe they'll walk by, but then again, maybe they won't. I can't see if Curtis's door is locked. I lean over him to press the auto-lock button, just in case. The sturdy clunking sound reverberates throughout my car as I watch the blur of legs pass by. The figures move through the bright center of the streetlight's glow and into the darkness beyond.

The emergency brake digs into my hip. I realize I'm lying on Curtis. He wraps his arms around me. Sprawled like this, I have no choice but to let him bear the weight of me. I rest my head on his chest. I feel my body rise up then yield with each breath he takes as I keep watch on the night.

on the moscow metro and being gay
dmitry kuzmin
translated from the russian by alexei beyer

IN THE CATALOGUE OF SINS IN HIS *DIVINE COMEDY*, WHICH IS AS RANDOM AS it is insanely detailed, Dante found room for the sin that "dared not speak its name" long before Oscar Wilde's trial—one of which Dante's beloved guardian and tutor Brunetto Latini was also guilty. (He placed such sinners in the Seventh Circle of Hell, near the suicides and usurers, but above thieves and bribe-takers.) I always wished that Dante had added another sin, one which probably couldn't have even occurred to the great Florentine. In my opinion, a separate circle, or at least a special place in the very last circle next to the traitors, should be reserved for those who hurt others for sheer pleasure, without deriving any tangible benefit for themselves.

This thought comes to mind every time I take the metro late at night, returning home from a poetry reading. To get to my not-so-distant suburb, I need to make an unusual transfer for Moscow, crossing a platform to the opposite track. There, a short shuttle train awaits arriving passengers. In nine out of ten cases, the doors of the shuttle close the moment my train comes to a stop, cleverly timing the shuttle's departure to let arriving passengers kick a car as it pulls away. I don't for a second believe that the shuttle has a schedule so tight that it's coordinated with ten-second precision. The problem is that nine out of ten conductors rejoice at the thought that they momentarily hold the fate of a few dozen countrymen in their hands. The best way they know to use their power is to make the lives of others more difficult, even if only a little.

It is the same metro station that is mentioned in a ditty by the excellent Russian poet Nina Iskrenko:

The train is moving speedily
To the Kashirskaya platform
Don't you dare cling to me
You filthy passenger scum

In contemporary Russian poetry (including my own work) the metro is often featured as a perfect place of communication. How people who accidentally find themselves side by side interact with one another is indicative of the state of human interaction in society at large. As a writer, I tend to focus on strictly private lyrical emotions, and for me it is a place of possibilities of communication. (It stands to reason, then, that twenty-two years ago, having exchanged fleeting glances, I met there the man with whom I have been living happily ever since.) For Iskrenko, on the other hand, since all her poetry is, in one way or another, a social commentary, the metro is a space where no communication is possible. The metro turns human beings into passengers who are engaged in never-ending warfare of all against all.

In its Soviet and post-Soviet form, such warfare doesn't allow for a winning outcome, at least not a meaningful one. It owes nothing to the relentless competition of capitalism but is patterned instead on the struggle among thugs at a prison camp, based on the notorious principle of the underworld: "You die today if I can live to tomorrow." The role of prisons and prison camps in shaping the post-Soviet mentality is enormous and not fully understood. For example, for many decades one of the most beloved genres of popular music in Russia has been the so-called "Russian chanson," cynical or maudlin ballads, always sung in a hoarse guttural voice, relating the lives of thieves or gangsters. It is sad to admit that this half-witted genre has its roots in the work of the honest and talented balladeer Alexander Galich, who wanted to give a voice to the innocent victims of Stalin's purges. How did this mutation occur? Perhaps it can be explained by calling to mind Varlam Shalamov, the greatest of those who wrote about Stalin's labor camps, who was always overshadowed by the much flatter and more pompous Solzhenitzyn and who never got the audience he deserved either in Russia or abroad. Shalamov thought that nothing of value could come of the prison-camp experience and that everything that comes out of a prison camp is inherently negative.

The social model of a Stalinist and post-Stalinist prison camp is based on a caste system. However, its strictest taboo does not relate to interactions between inmates and guards. On the contrary, in the official Soviet worldview, thieves and gangsters were classified as workers' allies in the class struggle, whereas the commanding officer at the camp was known in criminal slang as "the cousin." At male camps, the role of untouchables was reserved for those the slang described as *opushchennye*, "the low ones," i.e., those who, because of some character weakness, the type of crime they committed (not necessarily homosexuality, for which convictions were actually rare), or some fatal confluence of events, were reduced to the position of sexual slaves. They were so isolated from the rest of the prison population that anyone who entered into any form of interaction with them that was not sanctioned by the unwritten prison code (for instance, accidentally using the same towel) automatically joined the ranks of their lowly caste. Can there be any doubt that the camps' administration relished this kind of caste divisions? And not only because it released the convicts' overpowering sexual energy. More importantly, it was a way to channel hatred and disdain. Those who themselves were treated as nothings by the system of state-sanctioned violence suddenly had an opportunity to treat as nothings others who stood below them on the social ladder.

Today, our current All-Russian "cousin" and his entourage suddenly came to feel that the level of hatred and disdain in society has risen too high and that they are risking a social revolt. Is it any surprise that the small fry of the ruling party, who could never be accused of acting independently, suddenly proposed to find a channel for this hatred and disdain? The seeds fall on fertile ground. A cursory review of readers' comments to news items describing how some obscure elected official in yet another Russian region has hit upon the original idea of banning "propaganda of homosexuality" reveals a near-unanimous response, namely "our shitty government for once has done something right." Regardless of how such laws are justified—be it to protect the kids (against the backdrop of the state's systematic dismantling of the remnants of primary and secondary education), to raise birth rates (even though few young couples can afford to get home mortgages), or to promote the spirit of Orthodox Christianity (even as time and again church officials become embroiled in scandals by erecting country palaces for themselves and kissing the ass of the authorities)—they are really based on a simple sociopsychological principle: citizens are presented with an opportunity to look down upon another person and gratuitously make that person's life miserable.

The gay rights movement around the world has promoted a basic idea: we want to show society that we are human beings like everyone else. The problem is that the train driver at the Kashirskaya train station doesn't necessarily think that those few dozen passengers in whose face he closes the doors are a *priori* inferior and deserve such treatment. He feels that he becomes superior to them by means of using his power over them. This sense of superiority can be trumped only by some higher superiority.

I used to know a wonderful woman, the late Maya Dukarevich. Born into the family of a prominent Soviet military commander several months after her father had been executed by Stalin, she grew up in orphanages and became a psychologist, founding the first support group for attempted suicides in the Soviet Union. She also inspired the early Soviet and post-Soviet movement for the rights of lesbian women. Many of those who stood at its foundation in the early 1990s were her younger friends. She once said something to me which I have been thinking of again and again: Russia lacks the concept of respect for another person simply because he or she is another person, a unique, independent individual. It is therefore useless to say here: "I'm gay and I have rights." What you can say instead is "I'm a well-known writer and, besides, I'm gay and I have rights." Or "I'm a prominent scientist, and, besides, I'm gay and I have rights." Or else, "I'm a famous athlete, and, besides, I'm gay and I have rights," and so on.

During the 1990s, when I was an active participant in Russia's LGBT movement, as well as in the 2000s, when I began to feel that the forms and methods it had adopted no longer made any sense, I was always surprised by how few people there were who were willing to come out and say something like that—not just inside the movement but in Russian society in general. I remember meeting a highly respected philosopher, who in his old age obtained a transfer for a very good-looking graduate student from a provincial teachers' college to his department at the Academy of

Sciences. (Once his mentor was dead, the graduate student immediately surrounded himself with a bevy of undergraduate female admirers.) A casual lover of mine was once courted by another respected elder, a highly acclaimed St. Petersburg theater actor. And one of my poet friends had a short-lived but splendid love affair with a brilliant composer (before the latter became a worldwide sensation following a controversial staging of his opera at the Bolshoi). I often wonder what keeps those men from ending the charade—since their close associates are all in the know, anyway—and declaring openly: "I'm gay. I'm gay, and every attempt by the authorities, the press, and society to denigrate gays is directed not at some exotic prancing queer, whose image has been drubbed into mass consciousness by the skillful splicing of footage from Western Pride Parades, and not at some browbeaten 'low one' at a prison camp, but at me personally." What are they risking? Would the philosophy professor lose his chair, or the actor his roles? Would the audiences stop going to the composer's concerts? I do not ask a long-serving member of the Moscow City Council with whom in our student days some twenty years ago I used to chat casually at Moscow's early gay clubs that so much resembled village Houses of Culture why he doesn't raise his voice against the law banning the mythical "propaganda of homosexuality" in the capital after similar municipal laws have been passed in St. Petersburg, Archangel, and Ryazan. Because if he ever did, his party, Russia's program-free ruling party of power, would toss him out like a useless pawn from a chess board. But why do men whose achievements are beyond doubt, and depend, in the final analysis, on them alone continue living the lie?

An excuse or a justification can always be found. In any case, any public action can have private consequences. When I published my first book, my mother, who had long known everything about me, was torn between the desire to brag about me to her friends and fear that they might open the volume at some particularly explicit poem. Finally, one night, after several days of acute torment, she had a revelation. She cut the particularly compromising pages from the book. Then, in the morning, realizing what she had done, she called me to ask for a new copy. I was probably more touched than upset, even though I wasn't deaf to the special pathos of this scene, either. Nevertheless, preserving the peaceful sleep of one's elderly mother and her friends must not be the main driving force for the actions or inaction of a Russian intellectual. On the other hand, what would one's elderly mother find it easier to say: "My son is gay" or "My son has just published a book in the best Russian poetry series and it includes many poems about him being gay?" Who knows, perhaps in a different conversation about some other gay man, a kind elderly friend of my mother might say one day: "Well, you know, Mrs. Kuzmin's son is also gay, and yet he is a famous author, he has just published a book of poetry."

Of course the prestige of poetry and the respect for it in today's Russia is by no means overwhelming, so that my own personal openness means very little in the context of the country. But at least in a certain segment of Russian literary circles, among some readers, anti-gay rhetoric has now become unthinkable—in the public domain, in any event. Everybody understands which specific individuals will become targets of such rhetoric. On the other hand, the opposite is also true. Those who want to attack me always have an additional argument at their disposal. Some time ago, a certain panel comprised of respected literary elders refused to include *Air*, the poetry journal I founded, in the consolidated electronic library of Russian literary journals. They did not, of course, favor me with any official explanation for their decision, but I have been told in confidence what provoked their indignation: at a poetry reading, I had once dared to allow my lover to read his work. I'm very sorry none of them had the courage to say this to my face. I would have dearly liked to ask them what they thought of Nikolai Klyuev, who was instrumental in attaining recognition for Sergei Yesenin's poetry; John Cage, who wrote ballets for Merce Cunningham; Benjamin Britten, who wrote operas for Peter Pears; Jean Cocteau, who cast Jean Marais in his films, etc.

I always mention this story, along with several equally awkward ones, when I'm asked what kind of discrimination I have experienced as a gay man. But if among Moscow intellectuals and in bohemian literary circles discrimination is felt mostly in such innocuous forms, it doesn't mean that outside the capital, or in more traditionalist social groups, or among teenagers or, on the contrary, among older people there is no real, far more damaging mistreatment. For me, the anti-gay hysteria that is being currently revived and fanned in my country has strong personal implications. It forces me to cling to my gay identity. As long as the image of the enemy is being concocted out of gays, I must make all my public statements exclusively as a gay man. My small reputation thus protects a section, however small, of the battlefield in this war that has been imposed upon me against my will. But sooner or later this war will be won—perhaps when today's boys and girls grow up, get smarter, acquire a reputation and are able to demand their rights from a position of strength. (They have already shown readiness to go to the barricades for their convictions, but they have not yet learned that convictions must be defended by different means.) When this happens, I will gladly set aside the classification system which divides people into gay and straight and will fall in love with a beautiful man (or sometimes, for the sake of variety, with a beautiful woman) not because we are gay (i.e., belong to a certain category of people) but because of what brings two (or three, or four) people personally and immediately together. In our attraction for each other gender shouldn't matter. I once read in an Edmund White interview that "in the future... maybe it would be a mistake to embrace a gay or straight identity. I think it would be more amusing and mysterious and interesting and coquettish and seductive to leave everything kind of vague." I hope that this future is not very far. It will surely be followed by some other kind of future, when today's heated arguments about who can and who can't sleep with whom will come to seem incomprehensible nonsense, the way we now regard Medieval disputes on how many devils can fit on the tip of a needle. But for now I simply want to live to see the time when I can smile at someone beautiful in a metro car without having to think of the gender of that individual.

lloyd
michael thomas ford

LLOYD HANDED THE WAITER HIS EMPTY GLASS AND ACCEPTED FROM HIM HIS fourth gin and tonic of the evening. Although his dinner was inedible (the steak overcooked and the asparagus the opposite) the drinks were surprisingly good, particularly for what was obviously a tourist trap of a restaurant. The lobster buoys and fishing nets offended his sense of aesthetics, and the wooden seagulls suspended from the ceiling as if in flight made him positively ill.

What kind of idiot thinks this is classy? he wondered.

His eyes wandered to the waiter. The boy couldn't be more than seventeen or eighteen, he thought, probably a high school kid on summer break earning money for college or a new car. His hair was a little long for Lloyd's taste, but he could ignore that. Blue eyes and blond hair had a way of making up for a lot, and the boy's pug nose and lopsided grin were endearing.

He looked across the table at Brian. When he'd first seen Brian he'd felt the same tug of attraction. At the time Brian had been a steward with American, working First Class on a New York to LA flight. Lloyd had been the handsome passenger in seat 5F. Although twenty-seven, Brian had looked much younger then, and when he'd smiled at Lloyd and asked if there was anything he could do for him, Lloyd had felt himself stiffen in his pants.

Traces of that boy still lingered in Brian's face. His hair was still blond, his eyes still blue, his body still thin and toned. But middle age had worn away the youthful shine that Lloyd found so appealing, that newness of flesh and spirit that was impossible to retain after a certain age, no matter how many moisturizers were applied to the skin or how many crunches were done to keep the stomach firm.

He heard Brian talking, but he had long ago stopped listening. Brian's topics of conversation seldom interested him, focusing as they so often did on the past: vacations taken, holidays celebrated, meals eaten, movies watched, and pets who were no longer alive. "Remember when" was a phrase Lloyd detested. It made him feel old. He didn't care for reliving the past; he wanted to think about the future, about possibilities. That's why he was so attracted to youth. The young seldom said "remember when." Instead they talked excitedly about what they could be and what might happen. With them there was always another day. With Brian there was always the feeling that the days were running out.

He didn't feel old. It was true that when he looked in the mirror he saw a man with silver hair, but he'd had that hair since he was in his early thirties and it looked good on him. People often told him how distinguished he looked, how put together and stylish he was. Young men—men only slightly older than the waiter—frequently flirted with him. Palm Springs was of course notorious for the hustlers who came there looking for wealthy older men, but Lloyd could tell the difference between their empty flattery and the compliments paid him by those genuinely appreciative of his charms. Also, if they ever asked him for money he just laughed and told them to find someone willing to pay for what he could get for free. Word got around pretty quickly that he had no interest in being anybody's sugar daddy, and for the most part the working boys avoided him.

He sometimes wondered why he hadn't yet left Brian. There was no cruelty behind the thought, simply curiosity. The sex between them had ceased to be exciting some time ago, but that was to be expected in any long-term relationship and didn't particularly bother him. He assumed that Brian satisfied himself elsewhere, and although he himself rarely felt the need to go beyond flirting and fantasy, when he did indulge in the occasional flesh-on-flesh encounter it was always done discreetly and never twice with the same partner. This was his form of fidelity, and if Brian was bothered by it (or even thought about it), it had never been spoken of between them.

The waiter approached and asked if he wanted another cocktail. He did, but he declined. He could tell that Jay was watching him, had been watching him since the third gin and tonic. And although he knew that *he* would be picking up the tab for dinner and should be able to order as many goddamn drinks as he liked, he wasn't going to give Jay the opportunity to judge him.

He'd never really liked Jay. Adam and Jay were Brian's friends, not his, and he'd always felt that Jay didn't think he was good enough for Brian. Never mind that he was the one who brought in the money, or that *he* was the one with the degree from an Ivy League university. What had Brian accomplished with his life? He'd been a stewardess (to Lloyd all flight attendants were stewardesses, regardless of gender) and he'd married well. That was all. Lloyd was the one who had worked hard and succeeded. Yet he had never been able to shake the feeling that Jay felt Brian could do better.

He'd never gotten that impression from Adam. Of course, Adam was from the South, and with Southerners it was almost impossible to tell when they were lying because everything they said sounded as if it was wrapped in honey. His first lover, a lawyer, had told him that the most successful defense attorneys were all from below the Mason-Dixon Line. Juries believed just about anything they were told by them because they always sounded so polite that no one could imagine they were lying. The lover, a Harvard man with a strong Boston accent, resented this deeply.

Not that it mattered now. Adam was dead. That was why they were there, to honor his memory, although Lloyd had little interest in memorials. Like looking at photographs of a vacation, it was an exercise in hanging on to what was instead of a step forward into what would be, only it was worse because the photographs were of a vacation taken by somebody else. He would have stayed home but Brian had insisted he come. He had agreed primarily to put some distance between himself and a certain young man who had shown himself to be a little too eager to earn Lloyd's affections.

He once more considered the waiter, who was delivering desserts (it looked like chocolate cake of some kind) to a table of six on the other side of the room. He wondered what the young man looked like naked. Was there hair on his chest, or was it smooth save for a sprinkling around and below the belly button? Were his nipples flat, or did they stick out, ready for a gentle tug?

He was considering these questions when he realized that both Jay and

Brian were staring at him. He gathered that a question had been posed to him and that they were awaiting his reply. That he hadn't heard a word made it all the more difficult to know how to respond.

"Sorry," he said. "I was thinking about something."

"I asked you how your dinner is," Brian said. "You haven't eaten very much of it."

"It's fine," Lloyd said. "I'm just not very hungry. You know how I am when I travel."

Brian made a noncommittal noise. "I think it's past his bedtime," he joked to Jay.

Jay laughed. Lloyd ignored both of them. In truth, he was tired. The nap earlier in the day had been nice, but not enough, and even though it was only six thirty back in Palm Springs it felt closer to midnight. He was anxious to get out of the restaurant and back to the house, where he would announce that he had a headache and was going to bed. Brian and Jay could stay up all night if they wanted to. He didn't care.

"Stan and Sawyer will be here tomorrow," he heard Jay say. "They're going to meet at the airport in Portland and drive up together."

Lloyd tried to remember if he'd ever met Stan or Sawyer. He didn't think he had. Adam and Jay seemed to have a lot of friends, more than was necessary. How could you have meaningful friendships with more than one or two people? He'd never managed it, and he really doubted anyone could. *Maybe it makes them feel better to know so many people,* he thought to himself. Less lonely.

He wondered when Jay would start dating again, and how long it would take him to find another lover. He wasn't Lloyd's type by any stretch of the imagination—the bear look did nothing for him—but he was a handsome man. He wouldn't be alone for long. When had Adam died? He tried to remember. Brian had been very upset. Of course—it had been around Christmas time. Brian's mood had put a damper on the holiday spirit. He hadn't wanted to go to any parties or even to the Follies, despite the fact that Susan Anton was that year's guest star. Lloyd had gone alone, resentful, and had taken some small measure of satisfaction when he got home in telling Brian that Carol Channing had made a surprise appearance to sing "Santa Baby."

He counted forward. It was eight months since Jay had been made a widower. That seemed to Lloyd to be a suitable amount of time to grieve.

He knew men who had taken up with new lovers even while their current ones were in hospital beds dying, he supposed for the same reason people with elderly dogs so often brought puppies into the house when they sensed the end was near—it eased the pain of loss. What the departing loved one felt about it never seemed to be of much concern. Maybe the approaching meeting with death made such things irrelevant to them.

It occurred to him that perhaps Jay was going to be one of those men whose identities became inextricably tied to their lovers' deaths. Lloyd knew several such men. In his youth these were men whose lovers were lost to accident or heart attack or some other unexpected event. Generally such men eventually recovered and chose new partners, but occasionally one would realize that he was far more interesting as someone who had lost his true love to, say, a brain tumor than he was simply as himself. One man of his acquaintance, a timid and altogether unremarkable man who worked as some kind of a clerk, gained instant notoriety and became the subject of much fascination after his lover was killed when a tornado touched down outside their home, knocking down a utility pole which in turn fell on the lover, who had come out to see what was happening, and broke his neck. The surviving partner was forever after known not by his name (which Lloyd now recalled was James) but as the Guy Whose Lover Was Killed by the Tornado.

With the dawning of the era of AIDS the gay widower took on a far more sinister connotation, of course, and those who had lost lovers were no longer novelties but were both pitied and feared. The uninfected offered condolences from a distance, afraid of getting too close, and prayed for the safety of themselves and their relationships. The survivors were left to re-pair with one another or, as was more often the case, to remain alone.

This too changed over the years as those with the virus stopped looking like the walking dead and succumbing within days of diagnosis, and instead became indistinguishable from any other men and in some instances (thanks to the steroids used to combat the virus) far more attractive and desirable. For most gay men under thirty-five the AIDS widow was a relic of the past, something to be viewed under glass in a museum, like the Declaration of Independence or Jacqueline Kennedy's pink pillbox hat.

No, playing the widow was not a performance that would last Jay through more than a couple of seasons. At some point the audience would lose interest and he would have to reinvent himself as something else. But he could easily get a year or two out of the part, especially if he got his friends to play supporting roles. This get-together was a good start, Lloyd thought, an excellent way of cementing his status as a tragic figure all alone in that big, empty house with nothing but an old dog for company. Seeing him this way, his friends would undoubtedly offer Jay all of their love and support for as long as necessary, or until they grew bored with not being the stars of the show.

"Honey."

Brian's voice startled Lloyd. "What?" he snapped.

"I asked you if you wanted any apple pie," Brian said.

Lloyd shook his head. "No," he said. "I'm ready to go."

Brian looked at Jay. "I guess we won't be having any either then," he said.

"That's okay," said Jay. "I have a peach pie at home. I went to the farmer's market a few days ago and came home with a bag of peaches. I didn't even remember buying them. Peaches were Adam's favorite. I guess I just saw them and picked them up thinking they would be a nice surprise for him."

"Oh, sweetie," Brian said, giving Jay a sad smile.

"No, no," said Jay. "It's not a sad thing. It made me happy, actually. Like he was still around."

Lloyd took out his wallet and removed his American Express card, setting it inside the small black folder the waiter had at some point brought and left beside his plate. Why had the boy assumed he would be the one paying? Was it because he looked the oldest? The thought annoyed him, and for a moment he considered suggesting they split the bill, just to remind both Brian and Jay that he couldn't be taken for granted.

"Thank you, Lloyd," Jay said as the waiter picked up the check. His hand reached out and covered Lloyd's, giving it a gentle squeeze.

Lloyd nodded. "It's my pleasure," he said.

He felt the headache coming at him like a freight train. He badly wanted to be out of the restaurant. As Jay and Brian continued to talk, he closed his eyes and waited impatiently for the boy to return, bringing him his ticket to freedom.

ma tu sei pazzo?!?
notes from a southern
italian queer activist

tommi avivolla mecca

WHENEVER SHE HAD AN AUDIENCE, MAMMA WOULD SOMETIMES TELL THE STORY of how she believed I got my start as a queer activist. She was proud of what I had done, and gave it that old southern Italian flair, meaning lots of dramatic inflections in her voice and, of course, her hands dancing wildly as if they were doing an aerial tarantella.

The story takes place in Catholic school in the heart of South Philly where I was born and raised. It was the early '6os and the Immaculate Heart of Mary nuns ran our local school like a blue-robed Gestapo. Repressed is an understatement. Their concept of morality was firmly entrenched in the Middle Ages.

One particular nun, I don't remember her name or what grade I was in (fourth or fifth, I believe), liked to tell stories and spent a lot of time, when she should have been teaching us about geography or history, gossiping about the people—particularly those of Italian extraction—who lived in the neighborhood. It was more than gossip, she trashed them, particularly this one poor soul, a widower, who never went to Sunday Mass, she claimed, but instead stayed home to stir his tomato sauce. God didn't take kindly to the slight, and eventually burned down his house. Which then prompted an editorial about how horrible, and what lousy Catholics Italians were.

One day, as Mamma told it, I stood up and shouted, "Basta!" If Puccini were directing it, I would have gone into a very loud and intense aria. Though I vaguely remember what I said, Mamma's version had me reading that nun the Declaration of Guinea Rights.

Incidentally, that was the same nun who told my mother at the annual open house that I draped my sweater over my shoulders like a girl. In front of a line of other parents and kids standing behind us. She once admonished me for staring at a boy in class: "someone might get the wrong idea," she cautioned.

Note to Sister: the wrong idea was the right idea.

testa dura

I think it was actually Mamma who inspired me to be an activist.

We were dirt poor during those first ten or so years of my life. Then we moved on up to the working-class. Papa ran a gas station with his brother, my Uncle Jack. They managed to eke out a modest living. For Uncle Jack, the money stretched further because he and his wife had no kids. For Papa, there were four young mouths to feed and sometimes more (as when my Nonno and Mamma's sister, my godmother, whom I suspect was a friend of Dorothy's, lived with us).

In order to make ends meet, Mamma aggressively haggled with the neighborhood merchants. A little bit off here, a little bit off there. Every tiny savings helped her put food on the table with the small allowance Papa gave her.

Mamma was a spitfire. Her family was from Avigliano in the region of Basilicata in southern Italy where the people were reputed to be stubborn and strong-willed, full of testa dura. She fought with everyone, especially Papa's famiglia, which hailed from Monteroduni in the region of Molise. Papa's sisters had married men who made enough dough to move them into Upper Darby, a suburb of Philly. They weren't rich, but they enjoyed middle class life, '60s-style. They even had a real garden in the back with the most incredible rose bushes. My garden was a rectangular cinderblock enclosure that Papa constructed and filled with dirt from the dumps on the outskirts of the city.

Papa's sisters wouldn't even come to our house, it was beneath them. Which made Mamma livid. She spent her life trying to prove to them, and to herself, that she was just as good as they were.

She also fought with the local clergy. One year, when the priest arrived at the door for the "Annual Visitation," she greeted him with a string of southern Italian expletives. He had come for a donation, ten percent of Papa's income was the suggested amount, but she didn't have that much to give. She said she had it "up to here" with our name appearing at the bottom of the list of contributors (from highest to lowest) that the church published in the monthly bulletin they sent to all the parishioners.

Years later, in a final act of defiance, she refused last rites from my cousin, the priest, when she lay dying.

sexual awakening

By the time I was sixteen, I was an avowed atheist and had come to doubt all that I was being taught in Catholic school. I was sneaking off to civil rights and anti-Vietnam War demos. My descent into skepticism started with a brush with gay sex in a dark alley one summer night after a neighborhood boy and I stole a copy of *Playboy* from the local drugstore. We were bored. He suddenly decided he simply had to see those big-breasted, pink-fleshed women the magazine splattered all over its shiny pages.

I could have cared less about those women, but he was another matter altogether. I had been drawn to boys since I was about five. I used to stare at the olive-skinned boy next door from a hole in the yard fence. Even at that young age, the sight of him aroused a feeling in me I couldn't comprehend. It also set a pattern for the rest of my life: I still drool at the sight of black hair and olive skin.

It was easy enough to get *Playboy* out of the store without being seen. Kids got lots of five-finger discounts there, usually candy. My friend was ecstatic. As he hungrily paged through the magazine, he began to grope himself. Then he asked me to get down on my knees.

It was no secret that I was queerly disposed. I jumped rope with the girls in the neighborhood. I was sometimes seen out on the stoop with my sister playing with her dolls. It didn't take a rocket scientist to figure out what I was. Kids in the neighborhood and at school had names for me. They all stung.

I couldn't sleep that night. I knew God was going to strike me down for what I had done. It was a mortal sin of the absolute worst kind. I said my Act of Contrition several times. It didn't help. I could sense that God was gunning for me. He was going to make me suffer the most agonizing death possible. Like those poor slobs who burned to death in Sodom and Gomorrah.

When I woke the next morning to another beautiful hot summer day, I felt a crack in the wall of fear the nuns instilled in me. I didn't become an atheist right away, but the seed that was planted that morning grew to full maturation by the time I was sixteen and reading those subversive queer writers Jean Genet and Allen Ginsberg.

One day I simply decided that God belonged in the same discard pile as Santa Claus and the Tooth Fairy. I was content to be "condemned to freedom," as Sartre put it. Then I met someone and fell madly and irrationally in love (olive-skinned, black-haired Sicilian boy, no surprise there). Sartre would have approved.

gay liberation

Two years of an "affair" with that classmate ended rather abruptly a couple nights before Halloween 1969 when he suddenly told me he didn't want to see me again. I still don't know why. I'm guessing that our relationship had gotten too intense for him. Since the night we first met, we had been joined at the hip. We had even decided to go to the same college and live on campus together.

I wanted to die. I contemplated ending it all with a razor blade, but not knowing what I was actually doing combined with a fear of facing the unknown kept me from harming myself.

Luckily, I had just started classes at Temple University in North Philly. That first semester I discovered two amazing organizations that helped me forget that boy: the campus chapter of SDS (Students for a Democratic Society, an anti-Vietnam group) and the Gay Liberation Front (GLF). I didn't feel much affinity for school, so I spent a lot of time being an activist rather than a student. I was only in college to avoid the draft. I was too cowardly to do what friends had done: walk into the neighborhood recruitment office and declare that I was queer. I knew instinctively that the news would spread throughout the streets of Little Italy within seconds of the words leaving my lips.

After I walked into a GLF meeting one Friday afternoon, gay liberation became my obsession. Within weeks of joining the group, I was elected "chairperson." We only appointed leaders because, as an official student organization that received funding from the university (how we pulled that off is another story altogether), we were required to present the Office of Student Affairs with a list of officers and a copy of our constitution. I was basically the person who had to answer for anything controversial we did. We managed to do a lot of controversial things during my time there.

One was opposing Aversion (or "Shock") Therapy. The school's counseling department was routinely referring gay men to the Eastern Pennsylvania Psychiatric Institute (EPPI), where they were subjected to a form of "therapy" in which they were shown slides of cute naked guys and then jolted with electricity through electrodes attached to their dicks. It was supposed to "shock" them into heterosexuality.

It didn't work, of course, but regardless, it was a barbaric practice and we pledged to stop it (we eventually succeeded). Our campaign got the attention of a very popular late-night talk show host.

Big trouble was brewing.

Puccini would have a had a field day.

When the talk show representative called and asked if one of us would debate a shrink from EPPI, everyone pointed to me. I was doing most of the grunt work on the campaign, anyway. I reluctantly agreed.

Ma tu sei pazzo? (Are you nuts?) I asked myself several times as I headed home that afternoon. How could I appear on television when la mia famiglia didn't know I was queer, let alone a big gay activist on campus?

Nonetheless, I went to the taping. I was so fired up with a newfound gay militancy that nothing could have kept me away. I was so obnoxious during the program that I wouldn't let the rep from EPPI get a word in edgewise. At one point the director held up a card telling the host to "shut him up." It didn't work.

I told Mamma the day before the program aired. She was hysterical. Not only because I was gay, but because Papa would find out. No one wanted to deal with the raging bull. When he went on a tirade, we all ducked for cover. Usually a gentle soul, Papa got out of control when faced with something that challenged his conservative political beliefs. Like the sight of hippies or antiwar demonstrators on TV. Or the Beatles on Ed Sullivan.

I disobeyed Mamma. I didn't tell Papa before the show aired. I figured, he'll never see it, he goes to bed early, the program airs at one a.m. Papa didn't see it. My uncle, the cop, did. And he called Papa to let him know that his youngest son was a finuck (from "finocchio," fennel, southern Italian slang for fag).

All hell broke loose in my house. Papa went on a tirade. I had never seen him so angry. My godfather, Uncle Johnny, called to say that he was never talking to me again. He never did. In fact, when my father died, he snubbed me at the wake—and that was seventeen years after I came out. Another uncle suggested to my oldest brother that they take care of me *Godfather* style. My mother's family, on the other hand, continued to treat me as if I had not "shamed the family," as Papa's kin charged.

When the dust settled, I was banished from la mia casa and Papa didn't talk to me for about fifteen years. Mamma remained in touch with me, stopping in at work to see me. She became my staunchest supporter, defending me to family members and neighbors alike. My godmother, Mamma's sister, the unmarried one who used to live with us, also visited me at my job to make sure I had enough to eat. My siblings were fine, too, they rolled with the punches they were no doubt receiving from Papa's family.

My oldest brother ultimately performed a miracle: he got Papa to agree that I could come along when he and his girlfriend visited for Xmas one year. It was a strange reunion, Papa didn't say much, he asked if I had enough money, and, as we were taking off, offered me an old coat.

"That one you're wearing's not warm enough," he said. It was. He just didn't like the style of the jacket. The one he gave me was far too conservative for me to be seen in. But I accepted the olive branch, tears flooding my eyes. We had finally made peace.

A few weeks later, Papa was dead.

Puccini would have a field day with my life.

giving voice

I beat him to it. In 1985, I decided to put my own life on stage. I was a well-known queer activist in Philly. I wrote for the *Philadelphia Gay News* and other publications. But I had a lot of demons with which to contend. Confessional art was all the rage. So I wrote "Giving Voice," a performance art piece that utilized dance, song, poetry and prose to tell the story of a sissy growing up in South Philly's Little Italy, an effeminate boy who still bore the scars of having been tormented and made to feel that he was the problem when clearly his bullies were. It was cathartic to say the least.

It wasn't just about being gay, "Giving Voice" was ultimately a celebration of being a queer Italian/American man. As such, it was, as far as I know, the first of its kind. At a time when most Italian/American queers were still content to remain in their closets, I was going where no wop had gone before.

"Giving Voice" received rave reviews and played to sold-out audiences, which was a complete shock to me. The work was so personal that I had no idea people would love it so much. When paesani from South Philly came up to me and told me I made them cry, I knew I had succeeded.

"Images of a war unfought" was my next theatrical work. It took "Giving Voice" to another level. Focusing on a gay man with AIDS who holds hostage two college jocks, his former neighborhood tormenters, it was the ultimate revenge fantasy. The *Philadelphia Inquirer* critic got it right—he found it provocative and "wish fulfillment." At the end of the play, as lights blacked out, the gay man shot one of the jocks who refused to repent for his bullying.

The '80s were a dark decade. As more and more friends died of AIDS, the anger in me grew and grew. I was tagged the "angry performance artist" by a national arts magazine. I founded Avalanche, a multi-racial queer theatre troupe collective that did cutting-edge material about our queer lives. We struck a nerve. All of our shows were sold out.

In the '80s, my Italian politics became more radical. I read about the history of southern Italy, how after Rome fell the land of my ancestors was conquered by so many different countries. I also learned about the discrimination Italians faced when they emigrated here: NINA (No Italian Need Apply) signs in shop windows, lynchings in the south, and negative stereotypes in movies and on television.

I wrote a piece for the *South Philadelphia Review Chronicle* (the neighborhood paper serving the Italian/American community) calling on Italians to reject Columbus and, instead, celebrate the legacy of Sacco and Vanzetti, two anarchists from southern Italy who fought for the rights of workers. They were falsely accused of murder, I believe, and executed by the state of Massachusetts in 1924, despite international cries to spare them.

It was like yelling "dago" in a crowded Italian restaurant.

hey paesan

I moved to San Francisco in October, 1991. Too many friends had died. Philly felt like a graveyard. The realization that I desperately needed a change came when, at an exhibition of the AIDS quilt, I broke down in tears as I was reading a list of names of those who had died. I just couldn't stop crying that night.

Before I left, I penned a memoir for *Philadelphia Magazine* ("Memoirs of a South Philly Sissy") that received tons of responses, including many from young Italian/American queers thanking me for my courage in being so out of the closet. I didn't see most of those letters, I heard about them from my editor, Lisa DePaulo, after I moved.

Lisa and I became friends during the Anthony Milano murder trial in 1987. An Italian immigrant who was a closeted gay man, Milano had his throat slashed by two homophobic guys in Bucks County, outside of Philly. I was covering the trial for the *Philadelphia Gay News*, Lisa for *Philadelphia Magazine*. Neither of us was prepared for the horrific details of the murder that would emerge during the weeks of the trial. I had very vivid nightmares and couldn't sleep. The sight of his sweet Italian parents, so frail and frightened, was too much. Every day, I fought to keep from sobbing in the courtroom.

My first contact with the Bay Area's Italian/American community was in 1992 when thousands took to the street to protest the quincentenary of Columbus' arrival on the shores of the "new world." I joined the "Italians against Columbus" contingent.

In the next few years, I would meet two amazing Italian/American lesbians, Giovanna Capone and Denise Nico Leto, and we would edit the first anthology of Italian/American queer writing, *Hey Paesan: Writings by Lesbians and Gays of Italian American Descent*, and inspire Anthony Julian Tamburri of the John D. Calandra Italian American Institute to put out *Fuori: Essays by Italian American Lesbians and Gays*, a smaller version of our anthology. We co-founded the annual "Dumping Columbus" poetry and prose reading that had its kickoff at a cabaret owned by an Italian gay man and now occurs at City Lights Bookstore in the North Beach area of the city, once a solidly Italian/Sicilian neighborhood.

a Halloween blowjob

There was other work, too. I found a great and affordable place in the Castro two days after I arrived. You could do that in those days. I got a job on Castro Street at A Different Light Bookstore, then a three-store gay bookstore chain owned by two gay men. Life in the Castro was wild and wonderful. It was bouncing back from the devastation that the neighborhood had suffered during the '80s AIDS crisis.

On weekends, the corner of 18th & Castro was hopping with political activity. Activists set up ironing boards with literature or stood with petitions in hand. There was always a gathering in Harvey Milk Plaza to protest something. On Halloween, it was like a coming-together of the many tribes that made up our community.

My first Halloween in the Castro, I joined up with a group of Radical Faeries a block from the bookstore. We stripped down, painted each other's bodies, and then marched through the crowd to 18th & Castro where we formed a circle. At some point, someone grabbed my dick and then went down on me—in the middle of the street as some in the crowd applauded. I felt as if I had reached the Emerald City.

The feeling was short-lived. When the dot-com boom hit in the late '90s like a tsunami, sending rents through the sky, many young queers, fleeing here as they have since the '60s, found themselves unable to afford an apartment. They started lining the Castro asking for change and sleeping in the doorway of shops. Many merchants and neighbors went ballistic.

The Rev. Jim Mitulski, then minister of the Metropolitan Community Church, and I organized three winter shelters, a free meals program, and a place to get a shower.

The other negative effect of the boom was that greed became epidemic among landlords. Desperate to rent to the dot-com workers who preferred to live in San Francisco rather than Silicon Valley to the south, they used every trick in the book (some legal, some not) to get long-term tenants protected by rent control out of their apartments so they could re-rent them for more money.

In the Castro, scores of gay men with AIDS, long-term tenants who had been in their places since the early '70s, were pushed out. Talk about class warfare. While the mainstream AIDS organizations stood by and did nothing, a group of us organized protests against the realtors and landlords doing the evictions.

Unfortunately, we lost the battle. Today, the Castro is upscale, not completely queer, and unwelcoming to poor and homeless folks. There's no more Halloween celebration, no more weekly activist tables at 18th & Castro, and far fewer protests at Milk Plaza. Queer organizations don't rent office space above the stores, it's far too expensive.

Instead of "ACT UP fight back," people typically wear Abercrombie and Fitch t-shirts.

It feels like history is repeating itself.

price of the ticket

A hundred years ago, Italian/Sicilian radicals mobilized in much the same way that queers did in the gay liberation movement of the early '70s or in ACT UP in the late '80s. These sovversivi, as they were called, were active in all of the major labor strikes. They helped organize workers such as those in the garment industry in New York. They had an analysis of oppression and class, setting up discussion groups and publishing newspapers in Italian to spread the word about their revolutionary ideas. They understood that this country to which they had come was not a land of the free. There were no streets paved with gold, but instead with the blood, sweat and tears of immigrants and other workers. Speaking out meant being persecuted, executed or deported, but they were brave and kept up the fight even when the odds were against them.

Their names are mostly forgotten, but we need to remember them: Carlo Tresca, Arturo Giovannitti, Luigi Galleani, Maria Roda, Angela Bambace, Mary Nardini, Bellalma Forzato-Spezia and Virgilia D'Andrea, among so many thousands of others.

There was Camella Teoli, a girl barely in her teens when she had the top part of her head cut off after her hair became tangled in a machine she operated in a textile mill in Massachusetts. At fourteen, she testified before Congress about her experiences as a child laborer.

There was the New York's most progressive Congressman, Vito Marcantonio (a member of the American Labor Party), who championed black civil rights in the '30s and '40s and pushed for federal anti-lynching laws. He formed a coalition between Puerto Ricans and Italians living in East Harlem, which was the center of his district.

In the queer community we have an incredible history of resistance as well. On four occasions that we know of, street queens and hustlers, many of them of color, all of them people at the bottom of the totem pole in the queer and straight communities, rose up to say No to the unrelenting homophobia and transphobia with which they lived every day of their lives: Cooper's Donuts in Los Angeles in 1959, Dewey's restaurant in Philadelphia in 1965, Compton's Cafeteria in San Francisco in 1966, and the Stonewall Inn in New York in 1969.

After Stonewall, radical queers from many other left groups (anti-war, civil rights, etc.) came fleeing out of their closets to form the most progressive LGBT movement ever to emerge in this country.

Now that gay marriage is becoming a household word and gays and lesbians can serve in the military, not to mention be elected to public office and selected as a spokeslesbian for major corporations such as J.C. Penney's, it's beginning to feel like that moment in Italian/American history when the sovversivi faded into the background and the desire to assimilate took center stage.

Will forgetting our radical roots be the price of the ticket to acceptance for the LBGT community as well?

If history repeats itself, it probably will be.

the country of dead voices
sam miller

THE DIAL TONE CALMED ME DOWN. ITS PURR WAS COMFORTINGLY ETERNAL, a freight-train whistle forever coming from far away. My windows let in the noise and cool air of early summer city night. I shivered, bare toes clenching against the wood floor. Friday night and I was home; I was safe; I had survived another week.

Bodies were everywhere. They filled the streets and leered at me from television screens, living breathing men of skin and muscle who made eye contact and grinned and sent me into a panic of desire. Every subway ride or trip to the gym was an expedition into enemy territory, for there was always one or many bodies trying to taunt me into a terrible mistake.

I punched in *976-HEAT*. As always, I felt sad to leave the dial tone behind. A gruff automated voice asked if I was *looking for action* and chuckled and said *of course you are* and promised that *hot horny men* were only a moment away.

Then came the silence, the most terrifying part of the whole process, black empty ether and the click of unimaginable machines, a silence like dark churning river water that anything could float up from. On phone sex lines I'd found trolls and old racists and scatophiles, but even these monsters were nothing compared to the ones that lurked in the real world. The ghosts and demons I faced on the phone could be banished by pressing my finger into the switchhook. In the real world, the most beautiful men were the most dangerous. They smiled at me and I lost my mind. All those hours in Marcus's hospital room, watching a beautiful man's mind and body fall to purple weeping blotchy pieces, had made real sex too terrifying.

And a phone call never gave you anything to feel guilty about.

"Hey," said a living voice after only a few seconds, a single syllable of pure manliness, so young and butch I could have come right there.

"Hey. What's happening tonight?"

"Man, I'm beat," the man said—but he was a boy, really, a year or two into his twenties tops, his voice rich with all the energy and seductive confidence of my long-ago crushes, college summer boys, working-class guys who washed dishes or hauled tackle in my waterfront home town.

"I'm—"

The script demanded names, even fake ones, but if I shared mine then he'd share his, and I wanted to keep him in shadow for the moment. The better to let him be...anyone.

"I'm exhausted," I said instead, sinking into the chair by the window, startled by a squeak from one of hundreds of orphaned rubber dinosaurs that Marcus bought for when my nephew came over. A month after his death I was still finding the fucking things everywhere. "Must be the weather, because early summer always makes me so fucking horny. I was at work trying hard to keep from jerking off in my cubicle."

"I hear that," the boy said.

Phone sex was an anachronism, a lightweight type of time travel. The world had changed to accommodate man's constant need for sex with strangers, producing apps and websites to tell the precise geographical coordinates of the man who was into exactly what the seeker was into. Phone sex was for old men, for whom it held nostalgic value of the time when technology limited your options, or men like me whose fear of actual sex had become pathological.

I asked "What do you look like?"

"*Five seven, black hair, twenty-something, pretty fit. Good ass.* They tell me. You?"

"Pretty similar, except for thirty-something instead of twenty." The thirty-part was a lie. "Italian."

"My lucky night," the kid said. "I got a thing for Italian guys."

"Is it a big thing?"

Boy X chuckled. Ice broken. Goose bumps climbed my spine.

Phone sex was the only truly safe sex. For my ego as well as my health. Friends claimed internet and street-corner hook-ups were anonymous, citing your freedom to use fake names and extravagant lies, but their momentary lovers could still see exactly what they were getting. They saw you, in its most fundamental form, stripped of the clothes and social context that you hid behind. How big or small your belly or whatever else was. On the phone I could still be thirty-something with all my hair intact. I could still communicate confidence, still be a sexual being. I sniffed the rubber dinosaur, looking for a trace of Marcus, but there was only the stickiness of apple juice.

"Top, bottom, versatile?"

"Total top," the boy said, almost apologetically. "You?"

"Bottom only."

"Well then. We got us somewhere to start."

I stripped in darkness, looking down at my city, although I was not in a hurry to get to the sex stuff. The boy's voice was calming, reassuring in its gruffness, flashing me back to the older boys of my adolescence whose attention was like sunlight. Maybe it was just the fact of a friendly voice. Maybe I was lonelier than I thought, since Marcus died.

But something else was happening. This man's voice didn't just vaguely evoke many voices; it precisely evoked one specific voice.

Cameron. Five seven, black hair, twenty-something, pretty fit. Good ass. The one who cut me the deepest. The most damaged one, the one I fell hardest for. The one who haunted me still, awake and asleep, the one whose name I chose when my sister asked me to be godfather and name-selector for my third nephew. "Talk to me," I said, unwilling to take the lead but knowing how fast my phone-sex comrades could lose interest.

"Shit," the boy said, and laughed. "This afternoon I spent eight of my last ten dollars on a pint of scotch, and then got home and remembered I don't have a single clean piece of clothing, and it'll take five bucks to do my laundry. So. I fucking stink."

Cameron. Cameron the drunk, two years ahead of me in college, who often, to be honest, stank, but in a way that I found intoxicating.

"Tell me how you stink."

"Heh. You ever wear the same pair of underwear two days in a row? In summer? Like that."

I clenched the dinosaur in my fist, slowly so the squeak was a dying wheeze, and then hurled it out the open window before I could think better of it.

Cameron, who gave me my first STD. Crabs, as it happened, one of the more manageable ones, causing only insane itching, requiring the thrice-daily application of a thick stinky goo that I was sure everyone I met could smell and identify immediately. I had never before felt the frustration of being trapped inside a damaged body. Such sad irony that it should be Cameron, he of the lazy physical perfection, who first brought home the horrors of the human body, how much potential it had to go wrong.

But this could not be Cameron. Cameron would be approaching fifty, his voice destroyed by smoke and drink, except that Cameron was dead.

"My shirt's off," the boy said.

"Let me unbuckle your belt," I said. "Unzip your fly. I want to smell you."

"Be my guest."

The whole thing was ridiculous, of course: two grown men playing a filthy game of make-believe. Normally I had no problem shutting my eyes and vanishing into it, but now I could not stop the icy conviction that I was talking to a dead man. Silence thickened. I had played this scene a thousand times, so why couldn't I think of what came next? It felt rote and wrong when I finally said "Smells like you had a rough day at work."

"Heh. Yeah."

"What do you do?"

I thought *Don't say dishwasher* several times.

"Dishwasher," the boy said.

Cameron. Poor, working-class boy, born beautiful, cursed with it and little else, who learned young to barter and trade with it, first at fourteen with the older men whose supermarket groceries he bagged, later with the teenage girl classmates whose strength and friendship fed him, and so on, each year bringing a new crop of men and women for whom he was plaything or accessory, a long line leading up to his last year in college, when he met freshmen me. A long line in which I was only memorable for being the last.

Cameron. For years I'd been telling myself that my guilt and my grief were ridiculous, exaggerated, self-important. Who the hell was I? Just one of dozens of boys and girls who failed him. How could I have played a role in his death? But there, then, hearing his voice, I knew I had never believed it.

"It's big," I said, almost against my will, knowing somehow that if the boy on the other end hung up my life would lose all meaning. I had been given something, an opportunity, although I did not know what it was or what I should do and it was already slipping through my fingers.

"Uncircumcised," the boy said, clinching it, for Cameron's was, and Cameron took the same kind of pride in this peculiarity that now edged this boy's voice.

My mouth would not open, for fear the questions would come tumbling out. *Are you dead? Am I talking to a ghost? Do you know that you're dead? Or are you alive, and some cosmic phone-sex-line glitch has connected me with the real live Cameron of twenty years ago?*

But either way, there was something I desperately needed to say to him, and I didn't know what it was.

"I haven't come in what feels like forever," he said, wind whistling in the background.

"Me either," I said. "I been—"

And here my voice broke, going high and then bailing out entirely, and out came a sob I didn't know I had been hoarding, for Cameron but mostly for Marcus, and for that matter for everyone else I loved who died or suffered or did dumb irrevocable things that I could not protect them from.

"Hey," he said, alarmed. "What's up, bro? You okay?"

"I'm sorry," I said, imagining his finger grazing the switchhook. "I just lost someone, and he—"

"Don't even worry about it," Cameron said, his authoritative voice now calming and warm. "You don't have shit to be sorry for. Go, man. Talk. I got nothing fucking better to be doing."

"I." I shut my eyes.

"Tell me about him," he said.

"I loved him," I said, trying hard not to think about Marcus. Instead I focused on Cameron: his initial tolerance of my hero worship, the way I carried a notebook with me whenever we hung out, and was forever scribbling down names of bands and obscure movies he'd mention. We were young then. Our bodies obeyed us. With their help we drove rickety old cars down midnight highways, drunk after crummy concerts in the big city, or we smoked cigarettes and argued about music with other young men and women like the fate of the world depended on it, or I blew him on the roof of the parking garage for so long that my knees and jaw ached marvelously for the whole next day. When we behaved too badly, our bodies punished us like stern but forgiving parents. A morning of hangover agony, a day of diarrhea, and then all's well, we're ready to go again, what shall we do tonight.

I tried to think about Cameron. But Marcus kept coming back.

"I loved him a lot," I said. "We were together for eight years."

"You said you lost him. That usually doesn't mean a break-up. How'd he die?"

Marcus died like the man went broke in Hemingway: slowly, and then all at once. He died and I couldn't help him, because I couldn't handle how terrified I was. I flinched, at the thought of Marcus, and backed away, but not before one image burst back into my head. My nephew, five years old, screaming when we went to leave, refusing to leave the body behind. *Uncle Marcus!* he bellowed, and I thought *Welcome to the world* as I picked him up and carried him out, as his shockingly strong legs kicked hard at my gut.

"AIDS," I said, finally.

"Fuck."

"Yeah."

Cameron died coming back from the Melody Bar, driving drunk down the 'pike like we'd done a hundred nights before, except he was alone this time, and he had asked me to come to the concert that night and I'd refused, because I didn't like the girl he was bringing, because I never liked his girlfriends, because I could see from the smile in his eyes that he cared about them in a way he'd never care about me, and it was winter, two days after Christmas, and he was drunk when he left and I gave him a half-empty bottle of whiskey as a joke present.

Marcus was older than me. Marcus knew what a mess I was when we met. He'd tolerated so much, and when I wanted to hurt him and said he was an ugly old queen who only kept me around because I was younger and hotter I truly believed it. Years would go by before I realized what was wrong with attributing all my self-worth to being young and hot—when I became less and less of both. Marcus was wise when I was not.

Cameron was sexy because he was stupid. Cameron said "Fuck it, man," when someone told him smoking would kill him. I let him drink and drive. I got in the car with him willingly, stupidly, dazzled by his own ignorance of the possibility of death. Like all his admirers, I clapped and cheered for him when he did dumb things. I cheered him all the way to the grave.

"Did you ever have it happen, where you loved someone so much, but you still hurt them?"

"Yeah, sure," he said.

"Tell me about that person," I said.

He breathed, in and out. I think he was really trying. "It was a long time ago."

Do they lose their memories, in the country where dead voices go? Do they forget their waking lives? What is left , when everything else is lost?

Standing there, looking down on my city, its lights and its sounds, I wondered whether I'd know it if I was dead. What would remain of me. How much there was to start with. Marcus was gone and I was unmoored, insubstantial.

"At least you had something," Cameron continued. "With someone, for a while. You know? Lots of people never have that. Fuck, *I've* never had that. Of course it's my own fool fault."

"Tell me," I said, my voice small. "Tell me why."

"I don't know, dude. Something's wrong with me."

"What do you think it is?"

Silence.

"I don't know."

"We always fuck it up, don't we?" I said.

"I guess."

"I fucked it up," I said. "I fucked everything up."

Easy to beat yourself up over things that happened ages and ages ago. When you talk about twenty years ago you're talking about someone else, some other you. Marcus was one month dead, and in all that time I still had not looked myself in the eye and accepted what I had done.

I didn't give Marcus AIDS. We found it separately, before we found each other. But I did cheat on him, even after so many happy years, while he was in the hospital, and I don't know why. Man, subway car, eye contact: as simple as that, two bodies sparking like dry tinder.

A siren or woman wailed faintly from the other end of the line. "Where are you calling from?" I asked.

"Y'know," he said, "Around."

There was a hopelessness in his voice now, a false note of cheer masking something. Like he really didn't know where he was. More questions I couldn't ask: *Is it cold there? Is it dark? Is it hell? Is it heaven?*

"You ever cheat on anybody?" I asked, not meaning to, not sure why.

"Yeah."

"Why?"

"What do you mean, why? I guess I'm just an asshole."

"Yeah," I said, feeling stupid for expecting insight from a ghost or alternate-reality twenty-something drunk. Again the sound, clearly a siren now, but wrong: different, higher-pitched and with a choppier rhythm, like a siren from a foreign country. "It's like, on the one hand we all know it's like the evilest thing you can do. On the other hand it's the most rational thing on earth. We're mammals, after all. Animals."

"Hard to argue with sex," Cameron said. And he laughed. "For real, now that you mention it, I've done a ton of dumb-ass shit for sex. I mean, girls, boys, I'll take whatever I can get. But sometimes it's like, Jesus Christ, Cam, get your shit together—"

—and I missed it in that moment, and laughed, and kept listening, and only when he came to the end of the story did it sink in:

Cam.

Cameron the First scorned nicknames. My college crush never allowed anyone to shorten his own name, and he never referred to anyone else by anything other than their full name. He was no Cam. The only Cam I knew was named by me in honor of my long-dead lover: my nephew, whose mother incessantly shortened it from impatience.

"—and I never had a problem yet with a dude calling me up six months after we fucked to say I'm gonna be a daddy."

Cam: currently a kindergartener, incapable of keeping a secret, ardent lover of chocolate ice cream and vehement despiser of vanilla.

"That's funny," I said.

Cam: whose favorite thing was tyrannosaurus and not Scotch—for now, and whose fine black hair grew hot in the sunlight when I pushed him on the swings.

Silence lengthened, hardened. My body was one big goosebump. I could hear him breathing. New questions churned in my head, things I would ask a version of my five-year-old nephew who happened to be twenty-something years in the future. *Who is the president? What's up with the ice caps? What do you have cures for? What mistakes are we making now without knowing that we're making them?*

Am I still alive?

"I'm sorry," I said. "You called this number looking to get off , and instead you got a fucking sob story."

"Ain't no thing," he said, the words gilded with laughter. "Shit, a night this big? Plenty of ways to get off in a city like this."

The siren dopplered off into nothing. I listened to the sounds of his city and tried to imagine . Only the choppy tremolo of the phone connection itself gave anything away, hinting at a future falling apart faster and faster, the telephone grid disintegrating, subject to terrifying glitches that exposed the past to the present with gut-curdling clarity.

"Cam, listen," I said—

—but what would I say to him, this man my nephew would become? How could I help him steer clear of the horrors that lay ahead? *Your uncle loves you? Be a good boy? Don't drink and drive? Wear a condom? To be born is to die? When you love someone, you absolutely must tell them how you feel, over and over, every day, until they believe it, until it changes them, until love gives them what they need?* But he would hear these things, a hundred times, and probably never truly comprehend what they meant until it was too late. His world would be full of voices he could not heed.

"Take care of yourself." The words were flimsy but I prayed my voice was not. I prayed I could project all the love and the fear that I felt for him.

"Thanks, man. You too. And chin up. Life ain't all ugly."

My first thought was *You have no idea how ugly it is*, but for the thinnest fraction of a second I was shivery and frightened enough to say to myself instead: *Maybe he's right and I'm wrong, and life is only as ugly as we choose to see it.*

"Sleep tight," I said. "Pleasant dreams."

"I'll see you later," he said, and I knew I would.

A click, then, and I was alone again with the dial tone. The wind felt colder.

I spent a long time listening, trying to blot out every thought and become one with that sound. Surely if I tried hard enough I could board the dial tone like a boat, leave my body behind for the country of dead voices. But when I opened my eyes I was still rooted in me, in my forty-first year, in the apartment I could not afford on my own for much longer, chained to a dying animal. The dial tone purred in my ear, as big and all-knowing and useless as God.

lay-by
l.a. fields

BRUCE STILL TIPS THE SCALES AT AROUND TWO HUNDRED AND NINETY POUNDS. It was an event the day he fell under three hundred, albeit a low-key one, and it mostly took place in his head. He did not want his aunt, who he'd been living with since he started his first semester at college, to know that he had ever been over three hundred pounds. She could probably tell regardless; she's incredibly weight conscious and measures out all of her food based on a large chart on the fridge. She makes Bruce feel helped and harassed at the same time, when nagging and reminding start to sound like the same thing.

Aunt Leena (short for Leeanna) keeps sugarless candy stashed around her apartment to curb her appetite. She knows how much food is in the fridge, and can usually tell if Bruce has eaten a portion of something, and how much, just by eye-balling it. This had once been part of the incentive to living with Leena as opposed to paying for a room on campus. No cruel city kids to room with, no lines for laundry machines, and Bruce would have someone around to keep him on his diet and monitor his exercise. He asked for all this. He moved in here especially, like it was a good thing. But he's since learned that the kids at college aren't even mean. In his computer classes, the ones only majors take, Bruce has actually found some friends. It isn't like high school at all; they don't make fun of him, and Bruce knows it isn't because he's skinnier, like Aunt Leena says. Bruce is still huge, he has a long way to go before he's not considered repulsive by many, but still the kids talk to him, and invite him to parties, and seem to genuinely like his personality.

In fact, Bruce has even met a lesbian at school. He only made it to

Raleigh for college; he didn't make it out of North Carolina, and he didn't get out of the South at all, but something about the university culture made it okay, somehow, to be such a thing. A gay, as Aunt Leena says. One of them.

Bruce has told no one about himself, not even the lesbian, just in case it's some sort of trap. She might be a secret agent for the school, posing as a student, trying to trap Bruce into admitting what he is so they can throw him out. He tells Aunt Leena lies about all the pretty girls, and certainly they are very pretty at his school, not that it matters either way to Bruce. But Aunt Leena is still Aunt Leena; she already finds his fat disgusting, he can only imagine the look on her face if she found out he was gay on top of it. He'd be nothing more to her than a big fat, flabby faggot, and who wants to be that?

The guys are pretty on campus as well, though no one is so gorgeous that they're worth the risk of approaching. There were hot guys back in high school too, but Bruce wouldn't talk to them either. Even if by some strange chance those pretty guys were actually gay, they'd just fuck each other, wouldn't they? Or be celibate for a while. Bruce imagines most guys would rather abstain for the rest of their lives than have anything to do with him.

But that is not true about everyone. There was one guy, Wade Anderson from back in the Mile, as the town is nicknamed. He was interested in Bruce, or at least he had sex with him a few times. After months under the relentless attention of his aunt, Bruce feels sure that Wade was just desperately hard-up, that he only chose to be with him because there truly was no one else around. Never mind that Wade was always kind to him, that his eyes would travel the great distances over Bruce's body without the critical wince that Aunt Leena and even perfect strangers get; but surely Bruce remembers it wrong. He didn't yet understand the subtleties of disgust. He knows them better now.

The last time he saw Wade, Bruce packed a bag to go with him on one of his hitchhiking adventures. Wade takes off all the time, no roots to hold him down, no money to carry him, he just goes out in the world and exists with no plans or support, every once in a while showing back up in town to crash on his mom's couch. He's her only son, and she lets him get away with all that. Bruce doesn't have anyone so tolerant in his family. He packed his bag one night to go with Wade, but he unpacked it the next morning, and starting planning for college instead. The idea of running away had grown like a bunch of grapes in his heart, each aspect of the fantasy branched out from the others like a plump, glistening opportunity. But Bruce let the ripeness pass. He thought he'd have to content himself with a handful of shriveled dreams, the sensible raisin snack that wild imaginings age into. But instead his fantasies fermented. Something bloats in Bruce still, even as he is slimming down. Something buoys him.

The day Wade calls is a terrible one. Bruce is accused (fairly) of eating the last yogurt, a decision he made after nearly an hour of late-night agony, pacing next to the refrigerator, opening it over and over to stare at the tiny cup, pulling himself away, and then coming back again, until finally he just ate the thing in a rash attack with his spoon. It wasn't that he was hungry, or that a shot glass of yogurt is all that tempting, but once it occurred to him to eat it, he couldn't stop thinking about it. If he wants it, and it's right there, why shouldn't he eat it? His aunt says it's a question of his willpower, but if it takes that kind of gargantuan will to avoid eating one tiny snack, then his life must be a torture of longing and shame and obsession if he wants to be skinny. But hell, his life is like that already.

The phone rings in the middle of the fight, and Bruce runs to answer it as he would rush to an escape hatch.

"Hello?" he says, and it's Wade, calling from a pay phone, asking for directions, wondering if he can stop by. They haven't spoken in months, Wade has been MIA from his mother's house, and Bruce had been pining for him, or so he realizes, as he tells Wade the way to his building. Aunt Leena perks up when she hears they'll have company. She enjoys showing off, though she probably won't like Wade, as he's not impressed by nice things or polite people. He's an underwhelmed sort of kid.

Wade comes to the door as Bruce is changing, trying to find some clothes that aren't too tight or too big. He can hear Aunt Leena falter in her greeting, which means Wade is not what she expected, and when she shows him into Bruce's room, Wade is not what he expected either.

His clothes are filthy, and there's a hole in his shirt with blood on it. There are burgeoning bruises on his face. His hair is matted to his neck with sweat, and his fingernails as he waves hi to Bruce are dark and ragged, like he just climbed out of his own grave.

"What happened to you?" Bruce asks as Aunt Leena snaps the door shut on them both, most likely wanting nothing to do with it all.

"Just some guy robbed me," Wade says, sort of collapsing carefully against the wall. "It was kind of funny actually. He only got about twenty dollars off of me, and he seemed disappointed that I wasn't more scared." He closes his eyes in a long blink, like it's a lot of trouble to open them back up again. "Let me keep the wallet though. Mind if I sit down?"

Bruce looks at his daily-made bed, then at Wade's clothes again.

"Aunt Leena's really picky about stuff getting dirty. Maybe you better take off your clothes first."

Wade snorts and starts yanking at his clothes. He is a little younger than Bruce, but has always seemed so much older, worldly from all his daring travels. Back in the Mile he was just the grandest thing around, at least to Bruce. He went where he wasn't supposed to, he'd had sex with strangers and lived to tell about it, though Bruce was the only one who cared to listen.

Wade gets down to his underwear and Bruce tells him that's good enough. He wanted to help Wade undress since it looked like a struggle, but he did not want to be too presumptuous. Wade might have met anyone, done anything, while he was gone. He always comes back so mysterious.

Wade sits down close to Bruce, too close, and lays his head on Bruce's abundant shoulder.

"You don't have a concussion or something, do you?" Bruce asks.

Wade rocks his head back and forth. "All he did was pop me in the mouth a few times. I'm just tired. I had to bum change, and find a phone, and try to remember your aunt's name, and it's just been a long day."

Wade puts an arm around Bruce, and kisses his sleeve, but Bruce tries to slide away. Wade picks up his eyelids heavily again.

"Sorry," he murmurs. "You got a boyfriend or something?"

"No, it's not that," Bruce starts to say, but his aunt's voice interrupts him from the living room: "Bruce? Can I see you for a moment?"

Bruce makes a face in the direction of the door, hopefully communicating all of it, his aunt, his situation, his recurring fear that something is different between them now, too different to be comforting.

He closes the door behind him and walks down the hall to find his aunt in a huff .

"I called your mother," she says. "I wanted to know just what kind of boy shows up looking like that." She watches Bruce, her nostrils flaring, and he can only imagine what kind of gossip she's heard.

Wade has a terrible name in their home town, and he earned it fair and square being such a loafing, conspicuous queer, but it still seems lame that his reputation should precede him, that his past should follow him here. "Just what have you allowed into my house?" Aunt Leena asks.

Bruce cowers before her. "He's my friend," he mumbles.

"Some friend! Your mother said he almost got you fired, hanging around all the time, being a useless leech."

Bruce grimaces. Wade did almost get him fired from the McDonald's once, but not just for hanging around. Everyone hung around the McDonald's, there wasn't a lot else going on. Bruce thinks his manager suspected what they were up to, what Bruce and Wade did behind the dumpsters after close, on the nights that meant everything to Bruce.

"I can't ask him to leave, Aunt Leena. He's got nowhere to go." Then the clincher: "It would be rude."

Aunt Leena swells at the very suggestion. "Oh, don't worry about that!" She grabs her purse and heads to the door. "I'm such a Christian I'll let you force me out of my own home, but he better not be here when I get back from Sue Ellen's." Her friend Sue Ellen lives in the building. They sound like screechy birds when they get together, talking crap about everyone, including Bruce, knowing full well when he's in earshot but also knowing that they're untouchable.

This latest event with Wade should fuel tons of gossip. She might be gone for hours.

"I better not even see the back of him going down the stairs," she says, and sweeps from the room importantly, enjoying her own show.

When he gets back to his room, Bruce finds Wade fallen asleep in a slump on his bed. Mouth open, arms dangling, his feet still clad in socks. Bruce tucks him in, noting a scrape on his chest where the hole in the shirt was, which looks like it's from being shoved down on gravel and rocks. Wade's socks smell, and his hair isn't just dirty, but has actual dirt and sand in it, and even so, Bruce still sees something marvelously worth staring at. He wants to wake Wade up, not knowing how much time they will have at Aunt Leena's discretion, but he just can't do it. Wade looks too finished, and by now Bruce is used to this kind of yearning anyway; it's become sweet to him.

Wade doesn't wake up until evening, after Aunt Leena's called to say she will be spending the night with Sue Ellen. Bruce had been watching him sleep from the doorway, and he scurries away when Wade stirs, afraid of having his desperation exposed. He made Wade a sandwich anyway, which he holds up wordlessly as Wade emerges from the hallway.

Wade seems grateful for the food, like he just remembered he was painfully hungry and had been for a while. Bruce watches him build up his humanity again; eat, stretch, breathe deeply, like the tin man oiling hinges. Wade takes a shower, and Bruce washes his sheets and remakes the bed, he thinks because of Aunt Leena, but maybe also to have clean sheets for something else. He meets Wade in the hallway, steam billowing out of the bathroom and crawling across the ceiling like smoke from a house fire. Wade is in a towel, suddenly clean, and pink with flush, and his eyes are awake finally, and it's good to see him again.

Wade smiles at Bruce, and leans suggestively against the wall. Bruce is slightly sweaty from wrestling with his bedding. He had meant to change his shirt, comb his hair, put on cologne, but Wade doesn't care about any of that. He takes Bruce's hand and tucks it between the panels of the towel. For a moment Bruce is able to palm Wade's soft , dangling cock, still moist and warm like the inside of a kiss, but the front door opens with a bang and Aunt Leena announces, "I'm just here to pick up my things!"

Wade disappears quickly back into the bathroom, and Bruce is left standing in the hallway with a guppy face, his hand cupping thin air.

Leena catches him just standing there, then notices all the steam.

"He in the bathroom?" she asks, her face pinched up around the question. Bruce nods stupidly. "I guess we can disinfect it later." She gets some pajamas and her not-so-secret stash of booze and leaves again. Wade comes back out of the bathroom fully clothed, breaking Bruce's heart.

"I gotta go out for a while," Wade says.

"No you don't." Bruce follows him around as he finds his shoes and slicks his hair back in the reflection of the microwave. "Leena's already gone again. You can at least stay the night."

"Don't worry about it, I'll be back," Wade smiles. "I wouldn't say no to a bed, especially if you're in it. I gotta see about making some money though." He heads for the door, Bruce still trailing behind him.

"What can you do to get money?" he asks, but Wade just tips an imaginary hat and leaves. Bruce hurries to the window to see Wade emerge from the building, and he falls asleep on the couch waiting for him to return, which he does eventually, a few hours later, well after dark.

"How'd it go?" Bruce asks, wiping drool off his chin.

"Pretty good," Wade says. "I made almost two hundred bucks."

Bruce hesitates, wanting to know how, but he thinks he knows already. He's seen skinny kids like Wade hanging out on the bus line but never actually getting on the bus, and he knows what they do.

He's thought about going to one of them before, he has plenty of money saved, but the thought that even they might reject him was too terrifying.

"Do you want to go straight to bed?" Bruce asks instead. "I know it's still early and everything, but I figured you might be tired."

"Yeah," Wade says. "Just let me clean up first, you know?" Bruce nods. He follows Wade to the bathroom but continues past the door and into his bedroom with his mind purposefully blank as he listens to the sink run, to Wade swishing and spitting. He isn't in there long. Wade comes to him. He stands in front of Bruce, his crotch at eye level since Bruce is sitting on his bed. Wade's wearing only jeans, but not for long as he unbuttons them. No underwear. Bruce puts his thick hands on Wade's skinny waist, assuming that he should start sucking, but Wade stops him by holding his chin.

"Don't do that," he says, cocking his head. "Kiss me."

Bruce stands to obey. He holds Wade's face as he kisses him, his fingers exploring the bone structure and tucking back his hair. Wade keeps his hands at his side and allows himself to be felt, and it's a shift in their dynamic, as if Bruce has enough confidence now to act, rather than be acted upon.

He can see he's making Wade hard. He touches Wade's dick coaxingly, and feels Wade's hand describe the arch of his belly beneath his shirt. There is a moment of frenzied stripping, and they end on the bed, Bruce lying back on his pillows and Wade tearing a condom he must have pulled from his pocket. He rolls it on and works himself into Bruce, and it's like pressing a reset button, and suddenly Bruce feels just the way he wants to feel, comfortable in his body.

Even better, with all the weight he's lost, it's easier for Wade to kiss him while they're doing it, and Bruce gets to fulfill a small fantasy of his. First he comes while Wade is still inside him, and then Wade finishes off while they kiss, tongues pressed deep together, and the way Wade nearly chokes on his own orgasm is a thrill to feel.

They settle into a post-coital stupor, Bruce trying hard not to snuggle too much, under the strange impression that it would make him a nerd. They sort of nap and fuck throughout the night, not saying much until Wade sits up at dawn and starts getting dressed.

Bruce, miring in the two extreme emotions of panic and depression, puts on his clothes as well. Probably they don't fit like they used to, because Wade says, "How much weight have you lost?"

"Thirty pounds," Bruce says sheepishly.

Wade hmms, noncommittal. "Is that because of you, or because of your aunt's regime I saw on the fridge?"

"Both," Bruce says, more than a little hurt. "Don't I look better?"

"You looked fine before." Wade pulls on his shirt, covering up his skinny ribs, and it's easy for him to be so casual, since he doesn't even have so much as a single stretch mark. "I don't know," Wade continues. "Your aunt just seems a little Reich-y, you know what I mean?"

"Oh. Yeah." Bruce does know what he means, but he feels like anything must be worth it if it makes him thin. He has thought about moving onto campus sometimes, into the gay dorm, which they unofficially have over there. "I can't really leave though," Bruce says, following his internal line of logic. "Aunt Leena and my mom and everyone, they wouldn't let me."

Wade snorts. "Let you. Dude, you could have them make you leave. Just let your aunt walk in on us spooning on the couch. You'd hardly have time to pack."

Bruce is still thinking. "So you're saying I should come out?"

"I'm saying you should get out. If you want to." Wade looks sagely at Bruce, his elbows resting on his knees, his hands folded together, and he reminds Bruce of Jesus right now, and a lot of the time really.

He seems so wise and doomed.

"Are you leaving?" Bruce asks.

Wade nods slowly. "I should." He gets up, starts moving with purpose. "And you should think about it too," Wade says, and to Bruce's questioning stare he adds, "Leaving."

Bruce feels like they've had this conversation once before, when Wade offered Bruce the chance to go with him, to leave town and never come to college in Raleigh, but this is different. He isn't saying come with me out of pity. He's telling Bruce to go on his own, for his own sake.

werewolf
michael carroll

AFTER A WHILE, I GOT SO TIRED OF GOING BACK TO FLORIDA NOT BECAUSE
I didn't miss it but because each time I returned I got more and more
disappointed by my life, and by myself. Plus I couldn't afford it. I'm not
talking about the disappointment of the suburban nature of it. I missed
driving around the old places but even renting a car for a week was way
out of my budget. In New York I was getting poorer just staying alive,
while my friends who'd had the good sense to stay behind owned houses;
they had pension funds and investments, as grown-ups were supposed to.
They'd thought that my living in New York, where the rents are obviously
insane, meant I was rich. And I was single and gay and you know what that
meant. Champagne cocktails before the opera. I'd lost touch with most of
them. I just assumed they were all flourishing down in the palmy 'burbs.

Then my best friend from high school got sick. He was living in a
boxy apartment off the expressway not long after his second divorce. His
kids, one from each of his two marriages, had been living with him, and
it sounded happy until he'd gotten the diagnosis about his liver, and so
they'd gone back to their mothers. He had insurance from his job, but
it didn't cover everything. He'd had to take a leave of absence and go on
disability. When the insurance ran out and he was scheduled to go into
hospice, he would be depending on Medicaid. And I think there were
debts, although before I left New York to see Phil I asked a friend who'd
been on disability for twenty-plus years with AIDS if anyone would be
liable for paying the debts and he said he believed not.

"But who knows," this friend of mine in New York said with his
patent kooky, wild-eyed foreboding (since New York bred just as many

kooks as suburbia had), "between all the different dumb laws in all the different fucked-up states, and what the Republicans are planning to do..."

Still, Drew, with AIDS, appeared to flourish. He swam five miles a day at the Fourteenth Street Y in Chelsea and traveled a lot. He was a good saver. He had a BlackBerry full of friends who took him out regularly and bought him dinner, gave him tickets to see the sold-out shows at BAM and let him stay in their country houses in upstate New York or out in the Hamptons while they were in Europe or Southeast Asia or India (they were all Buddhists, it seemed)—and they'd leave him "expense" money so he could buy himself groceries and the food for their pets he was sitting. In May, just ahead of tourist season, he somehow scraped together enough cash to fly to Spain where Drew had more friends. He'd had his Paris and Berlin periods and he spoke French and German and was working on his Spanish. He was from Houston and had the withering habit of making fun of Texas and the big-haired rich ladies he'd grown up around, wearing the prestige of knowing it top-to-bottom while beaming an assurance that he'd been smart to get out. He was a snob—and I took it as a moral failing, in his eyes at least, that I should want to return to Florida at all. He had a sense of entitlement all the more devastating and annoying to me because he had nearly died three times, which should have made him more empathetic but didn't—since, I guess was his reasoning, as an eternal patient he had a spiritual outlook that didn't punish him for being apathetic to the point of offensive preachiness. He'd had every opportunistic disease in the book: viral and bacterial meningitis, pancreatitis, kidney failure, a heart attack, gout, bloody-puke bouts with severe ulcerous reflux...and the list went on. Given his two decades of living with HIV, I suppose I thought of him as something of a testament to modern medicine, an inspiration capable of shaming me out of my own silly hypochondria. Around Drew I swung violently, but covertly, between admiration and a perhaps slightly misplaced pity. Drew was intelligent, and had wowed them briefly as a student of classics at Columbia before dropping out. He knew everybody—and from his stories that I didn't necessarily trust, had slept with most of them. Cosmopolitan Drew!

With Drew, the world was imperfect except for wherever he was at the moment or he was headed next. Drew was always in a good mood. But with my old friend Phil, who did not have rent control in Florida, and who'd been told he had only a few more months to live, there wasn't going to be any world by the end of the year. Phil and I were both agnostics, and didn't have the comfort of a poetic, onion-layered nothingness. Our neither believing nor disbelieving but being sure of a horrible nothingness had kept us loosely in touch for more than thirty years—and meant that I had no idea what to do when I finally saw him again after maybe two decades. Only that I had to leave New York right away to see him, wet-eyed, nostalgic and with even greater self-pity.

The day before I flew off, I was meeting Drew for lunch and told him about the situation, giving him the background of my friendship with Phil, then shading in some of the finer nuances.

"Oh, no question about it," he said with a tenderness that was unlike him (and all the more frustrating because I'd always had a crush on Drew, those flashing blue eyes): "You have to go."

My anecdote took up most of the meal—at the end of which I hastily grabbed the check, despite my personal financial straits. Nor did my volunteering to pay the tab disarrange Drew's usual Zen composure. He smiled handsomely and nodded semi-brightly. How I hated him then!

It went like this, and in spite of the fact that Drew was into Eastern medicine and loved to use disease horror stories to spank Western doctors and form object lessons out of them as quick, hard-to-follow advertisements for nontraditional practices (starting with acupuncture, which had helped relieve me of a nasty few months of GERD), he sat by and listened, drawing me out at the right moments, touching my hand when I almost blubbered, and telling me it would be okay. (A rather different Drew, I was seeing. And stupidly I wondered if we could still be lovers after all.)

I knew it wasn't going to be "okay," but I took comfort from Drew saying my loyalty was sweet. "It really goes to show how important old friends are," he said, but I also noticed a glazey look in his eyes that made me think he was really just trying to contain himself and not show that he was getting a tad revved up for his trip to a private island off St. Martin, paid for by a designer friend. Drew was getting on a plane the next day, too: "No, darling, it's a sweet, sweet story."

At the door of the bistro he kissed and hugged me, saying, "Best of luck to Phil, okay?"

Which wasn't much like Drew, either. I felt jealous, envious and, as always, unsatisfied.

I went home to pack, and as usually happens I completely forgot about

Drew within a few hours. I wondered if this was generally the case with foul-weather friends. Was I one of those to my old flame Phil? It occurred to me that time got behind the best and the least of friends—that only in times of crisis did we rise to the occasion and remember ourselves as loving familiars.

For a long time Phil and I had only exchanged a few, scant emails to stay in touch—until, of course, those recent, terrible back-and-forths by email between us. I hadn't directly spoken to Phil in years. But we'd been talking a little in the last week or so. I was ripped by the news, and suddenly I was back in his life, and he was back in my mind. So I flew the fuck back to Florida.

Although he was basically straight, Phil and I had slept together in high school, two or three times. One night when most of our classmates were at junior prom and my parents had driven up to the St. Mary's for the weekend to fish, I asked Phil to stay over. He confessed that he was part werewolf, and said that he believed this meant he was a bisexual. He was open to trying it out. I blew him and at first I thought it was going to take too long. We went to sleep in my bed holding each other. The next morning I scrambled him some eggs while he colored a sketch of a satanic-looking superhero he'd created in his sketchpad. We didn't kiss, he didn't talk. I looked at what he was doing and touched his shoulder as I was serving him. He growled, ate, then went home.

And I hated myself for that stupidity of having touched him like a lover, like a girlfriend.

Someone, not our friend Cindy, told me that Phil was getting into drugs with some of the other kids in gifted, the ones he played Dungeons & Dragons with, and I seethed inside. I was a priss who would never finish even one beer at pool parties if the teen host's parents were not at home. In fact, I disliked the taste of that stuff, so who was I? Since the night of the blowjob we spoke less, and I was hurt—and before school was out for the year and summer began I told him in the hall in front of our lockers that I couldn't be his friend if he kept on getting high.

"That's your old-tomato?" he said, sniffing, sneering. *Old tomato* was one of our jokes.

"That's my ultimatum," I said steadily, nodding, then waited and watched as he slunk off.

That summer I went to Memphis for a couple of months to be with relatives and to avoid growing up, I think. I helped out in my grandmothers' gardens and read books in the AC. I was not gay. I kept telling myself that. But I knew I was the gayest person I'd ever met—so in love.

I got my second chance with him during our senior year. Phil lived in my neighborhood. And one night while my parents were in bed he scratched on my screen and I opened my window and helped him wriggle over the sill into my room. We whispered. He said he'd missed me. I think I was crying but in any event I told him I'd missed him and could we start over. I was a snob and an idiot, I said, and then he quietly growled and we kissed for the first time, deeply. We took off each other's clothes and kept kissing and also for the first time he went down on me. I wanted to keep the lights on and he settled for a desk lamp. He asked me if I had any Vaseline. I put a robe on and crept into the hall, stopping to hear my father's snores, then I hurried to the bathroom and opened the cabinet carefully, found the Vaseline. In the bedroom he kissed and licked and bit me some more, quietly growling, then he put the Vaseline on both of us and I crouched on my bed in front of him on all fours and he slowly entered me, which didn't hurt at all, only at the beginning and then exquisitely as my head went numb and white noise bristled in the canals of my ears and my vision went blank. Somehow he knew to tell me to take deep breaths. I pushed back against him and it was over in two or three minutes. He pulled out and let himself into the hallway. He was dirty and needed to wash up. I held my breath and led him through the den and let him out through the French doors. He sprinted across the backyard and scaled the fence. There I was in my sweat pants, shirtless and feeling delicious, my naked arms folded across my chest, taking in the night air. I must have smelled the air carefully. I must have thought, Now just let me sleep.

The next morning I got out of bed forgetting about the bites and my mother said to me in the kitchen, "Did you have a date last night that you failed to mention to me? My God, you have hickeys. Hickeys! You sneak out and see some girl? You're all marked up with hickeys!"

"I was scratching at these mosquito bites and I guess bruised myself," I said, yawning.

"Bullshit. That's a hickey, that's a hickey and that's a hickey. Can't fool me on hickeys."

"I just mostly miss my sweet little Gretchen and my big cool Pops," he was saying, and looked cadaverous yet pinkish—and I could see some of Phillip's old contours. "My big sweet Pops."

I smiled encouragingly and said, chuckling foolishly, "Why do you call Derek Pops?"

His daughter was the senior in high school, I remembered, and his son, the oversized gay kid everyone picked on because of his effeminacy and his autism, was a sophomore. Derek was half-Asian; Phil's second wife was Cambodian. He'd met the first while they were both working at the Wal-Mart out on Beach Boulevard—when Phil was working as a pharmacist's assistant and "between things," as he put it, finishing his degree, getting sober, about to get his first divorce, as it turned out. I was trying to keep the chronology straight. It seemed clear, Phil preferred Derek.

Phil was sitting up in his crushed-velvet swivel La-Z-Boy in his robe and sweats and said, "I call him Pops because he's more mature than me in some ways—except when other people are around. He can laugh at me in a way I take fine, but only from Pops. Kid's really hilarious when he wants to be, so I give him that—figure it's his due. Those bratty fucks give him enough shit."

In school, Phil had never bullied anybody, even after tenth grade, when he'd gotten taller and had more muscle. It was his father who was the bully. But when we had first met, in middle school, Phil still looked chunky in his dark cords and Black Sabbath t-shirt and gray hoodie with the drawstrings—the hoodie even on warm days to help hide what he called back then his blub.

I said, "Does Pops come over a lot? Does your mom or Pops's mother bring him over?"

"He's too scared. We're close, and if I'm not with him I guess in some ways he can miss me less, not think about me. But I'll have him come see me in the—y'know—when I'm..."

Phil must have been determined to be the dad, but with a lot less money, that his own dad had never been to him. Phil had been artistically talented. He drew series of comic books when no one else I knew was into reading them even. He worked on the covers he'd like them to have with oil crayons with far more dense detail than the frames on the pages inside. He read Tolkien and played Dungeons & Dragons with the gifted druggies. The only thing we did together was go to the movies or swim in his pool. His father snickered and said flat-out that if Phil wanted to go to college and wanted him to pay for it, Phil wasn't studying anything artsy, he was going into a practical area. Which luckily my father had never said to me, just wanting me to go to college.

"What do you want Pops to do?" I said. "I mean, what's he interested in doing in life?"

"Anything he wants. Look, he's got long, black-painted nails. He says he's going to be a dress designer and do everything for Madonna, from her apartment to her clothes. Pops plans on marrying Madonna. He can't decide if he's going into architecture, fashion or musical theater."

"That's great. Jesus, Phil, you're the best father he could possibly have. So incredible."

He half-closed his eyes and said, "It's nice of you say that. It's really cool, so thank you."

He was evidently tired. I imagined he was like that all day, of course. I'd dropped over by appointment, texting him. He'd said he was too tired to talk. We'd talk when I came over. The apartment had clean walls and overall clean-but-flattened-down tan carpet, and there was very little furniture in it. In the living room, just our two crushed-velvet swivel La-Z-Boys. Mine was wobbly on its axis. I had to sit still not to pitch left or buck suddenly forward. He was already getting rid of most of his stuff, parceling it out to his younger brothers, keeping a dresser and the bed in the bedroom, minimum kitchen utensils, towels, linens. The fridge held his meds, some uneaten fruit and several individual-size bottles of Ensure nutrition supplement drinks, like instant shakes. When I saw those, getting myself some cold distilled water, I prayed stupidly that he could get better and beat the cancer just from having a pure infusion of vitamins and minerals. Not even for the two kids, for me. Not because I was still in love with him. I wasn't. He wasn't yellow, and I thanked my stars for that. The last time I'd seen him he was a bit overweight again, tan and vivid. This was back at Wal-Mart when Phil was finishing night school after flunking out of college in Gainesville. His parents were helping to support him because of his DUIs, and his wife had to pick up the daughter Gretchen from daycare then pick Phil up at work and drive him to his AA meeting. Knowing none of this, I had come in to buy soap and toiletries, right there in front of the pharmacy counter, and he called down from his perch, calling me Mr. West, and we'd stopped to talk, me dazzled, him full of "pressured speech" and epic confession. He knew, and I knew, that it was another brief encounter for us (like that time in the school hallway), and that we were about to say good-bye and not see each other again for a long while—the tendency of ours.

I remember feeling awkward, out of place. I'd wanted to travel, be free. And I knew that he knew this about me, too. "Wow," I'd said, taking in his slightly beat-up appearance. "Wow!"

"Some fucking anecdote, right?" he'd then said, looking right at me, not looking off. I had stood there and said he looked great, then wondered if this wasn't uncool, smiling at him longingly and not acting impressed or stricken by what had happened to him. The truth was, I was still surprised by everything—our running into each other, the sordid details that frightened me, made me wonder what I should say. I was gay, single, and had no real direction in my life.

"Well, you look terrific," I said, and he frowned. "I'm glad you're getting it all together."

"You're the one who looks great," he said. "How do you do it? Clean living? Hope so."

"I'm just here for a little bit," I said, "passing through, actually. But you look and sound great. I'm still just so shocked. I didn't think you were in town. You were really the last person I'd expect to see for some reason. I mean, there's never any time. I just miss you, but you seem like you've got this one, like you've got it together, and I'm glad. Married! Child! So cool..."

I told him I was just in town between grad-school years, and was headed back to Ohio. I hated my graduate program and wondered why anyone should do anything but live a real life. I was lying, though: I wasn't going to finish grad school at all. I didn't want to teach, no way.

"No, man, I really fucked up," he said. "All I do's work and go to meetings and go home and fall in bed. But Laurie's a saint. I know it's bullshit to say that, but I'd be in jail without her. My asshole dad doesn't want to see me, he just writes checks and my mom brings 'em the over."

"God, tell them hi for me then, okay?"

He made his way toward the counter, touching things along the way as though attending to them, accounting for them as a good employee, and I was making moves to go, too. I'd been surprised in my funk, hating the old home haunt, hating myself, wanting to chase the past away.

Worse, I had the self-loathing feeling that we never should have fooled around. We might still be friends if we hadn't fooled around, good friends, the kind who kept up with each other.

Finally I waved my purchases at him and he said, "Stay in school, dude. You got that?"

Then I was mad at him. Jailhouse Joe wants to go avuncular, scare me straight, I thought. I walked away knowing I'd misunderstood him. And I thought of Mr. Johnson bawling a great son out over the rim of his Scotch glass, the old man's eyes looking boiled. I went overseas a year later, though, and heard that the old man had died suddenly of a heart attack. I thought of Mr. Johnson jiggling his scotch and ice and getting worked up over something Phil had said and keeling over, the way I'd actually imagined for years would happen. I'd seen too many movies, I thought when I heard about this from Cindy.

Even more than for Phil I'd felt sorry for his mom.

Mrs. Johnson came in, first knocking on the hollow construction of the apartment door, then unlocking and pushing the door right open. Of course she looked older, but not a whole lot older than Phil. She'd moved out to the beaches years ago, away from our neighborhood, and played a lot of golf and tennis, but she was carrying a lot of weight that I supposed was appropriate to her age, and she still had a girlish laugh and a bright smile. She set down her plastic shopping bags, in the middle of the carpet, managing not to seem embarrassed by the sparseness and sordidness of the room, and went to kiss Phil on the forehead. Phil smirked and didn't get out of his chair.

I got up and she said, "Well, well, always the gentleman. Always the gentleman and hey, looking so good. So handsome, like always. So what do they put in that Manhattan water?"

"We probably don't want to know!" I said hugging her, then we pecked on the cheek.

"Right you don't," she said, and she pinched my arm, and when I withdrew it she lunged in and got another snatch. "That's right you don't, mister. How are things in New York City?"

"They're fine, I just don't have any money is all."

"Hey, but you can't have everything," she said, and winked. "Can't have everything, can you, Phillip? Phillip can't have everything, I can't have everything, but you've got Manhattan!"

They were originally from Ohio and Mrs. Johnson was too tanned to dream of New York. Once Phil and I had dreamed of getting out of Jacksonville together and heading to New York as writing partners. We were going to write sci-fi and horror books. Phil said, "Mike's a writer."

"That was always the dream, right?" she said, looking adoringly on.

We'd always had this flirty rapport, this quick flame to friendliness and intimacy, in their kitchen or on the screened-in porch next to their pool. Phil knotted and knotted a rubber band. I said, "But hey, Candace. Take my chair. I've been sitting all day driving."

"Driving in this hellhound heat and traffic?" she said. "Thank you, I will. I bet you don't miss the Jacksonville traffic. That's one thing. Don't miss that. And Dick died, you knew that."

"I did," I said. "Cindy Cross told me. She wrote me a letter not long after it happened."

"Well, not a day goes by. Nothing changes, he's still sort of here. But I swear, the traffic. And how is she, Cindy? Phillip—I'd nearly forgotten all about her—you guys been in touch?"

Phil said blandly, "She came and saw me last week. I told you that, Mom. Jeez."

"That's right. I stay so busy, Mike. I'm all awhirl. I have five freaking grandkids!"

I was sitting on the floor to the side and I said, "It doesn't seem possible."

"Thank you, but should it seem possible that your best friend from high school has a pair of kids in high school, when you've hardly changed?" She pitched it to a holler: "Hardly at all!"

I felt this power again which I'd felt back then. I'd been a pretty boy, once I'd dropped a lot of weight from dieting and running, lost the zits with the help of the burning cream and gotten the braces off. I had been sometimes happily in love with her son: did she have any idea? Moms of the world had to be as randy as the rest of us. We were now the age Candace had been then.

A moment of quiet passed, unnervously, wherein she and I kept smiling at each other.

Phil said, "Mom, did you remember Dickie's card?"

"Oh, damn it," she hissed, then smiled at me for sympathy. She rolled her eyes.

"I'd like to be able to describe it when I call Dickie up and thank him for making it."

"It's in the glove compartment," she said, clapping once, and hitched left in the chair.

I offered to go out and find it so she wouldn't have to get up out of the tricky chair yet. Her car was right out front. I opened the passenger-side front door and the inside smelled like cigarettes.

I found a manila envelope curled and crammed in the glove compartment and undid the brass clasp and slipped out the homemade card. It was done in Magic Marker, which made me think of Phil's earliest colored drawings in sixth grade. It read, "Dear Uncle Phil, I'll come see you real soon, okay? Before that I hope you get better and better. Love, Dickie (the Third)."

It was a picture of a man and a boy in the basket of a hot-air balloon, a close-up, which I thought clever. (Whenever my father made photos of anyone, he backed up so that expanses of a brick-veneer side of a house dwarfed the human figures he'd shunted to the lower right corner of the picture, their faces obscured by shadow or erased in strong sunlight.) On the card, the man's spidery hand rested lightly on the boy's shoulder. Only the bottom section of the colorful striped balloon was shown. The sky was streaked a cloudless pale blue, banners flapped from the tethers attaching the basket to the balloon, and the boy waved at the viewer with a frozen poker howl.

Before I left I made Phil a pan of rice, which he said he'd take with a little parmesan. He said just to give him the Kraft container and he'd sprinkle it on. He called from his chair while I was lifting the lid to check the rice: "Hey, are you planning on seeing Cindy while you're here?"

I stirred the rice, waited, then replied, "I guess so. I thought I'd give her a call at least."

"Cool."

He asked me to bring him his meds in from the kitchen counter. And when I sat carefully down in the chair again and he swallowed the pills with wads of rice and distilled water, he told me things—not about his fears but about his kids, how he regretted that they didn't live together, even though they had two different mothers. I settled in for a while longer and enjoyed myself.

"I'd already decided to wait her out, and you know how much I always liked Candace," I said.

Phil's and my friend Cindy was a married mom of two, and I wanted to give the moms of the world a shout-out, although since I'd realized I was gay I'd never wanted to be a parent.

"That was your time to be alone together," said Cindy. "Candace is sweet, she probably thinks it's partly her fault—or more than partly. Moms just naturally will. I feel sorry for her."

I said, "I told him you and I would come together one time. You know what he told me?"

I didn't tell her about when Phil had said of Candace, "I kept wishing the bitch'd go."

Cindy and I were sitting on the deck of the top floor I'd rented of a beach house, which had fallen into my lap at the last minute, and it felt propitious. We were drinking Riesling.

"So what did Phil say?"

"Well, that his mom was an alcoholic. That it was all over the family, all of his brothers, his mom, and that it was what killed his dad. That and the Kents. And then just before I left, he was mixing his rice around and dropped this bomb. Maybe it's not a bomb. You never left, you were the one who always gave me the updates. He had hepatitis twice, from using needles."

"Habitually? Like a lot?"

"I didn't ask. See, I made a vow never to ask him questions like that ever again." Phil had mentioned trying everything once, and according to the Oscar Wilde dictum or whatever given it a second try just to be sure. Smoked crack, injected things. My puritanism I'd had to push into the back of my mind. Who was I? Maybe it was Mae West who'd said that.

She fretted her brow and the frets stayed up there a bit. I smiled at her and lit a cigarette.

She said, "God, can I have one of those? I could get myself into so much trouble."

She did an imitation of her daughters mewling judgmentally, "Mom, Mom! God, Mom!"

I slid the pack her way across the glass of the little outdoor table, its wicker frame starting to rot and wobble on the deck. None of our families had come from here, we'd all migrated from different cities, hers from Atlanta. This was a clear, windy March day. The owner had rented the three floors to people planning to go to the races at Daytona, but those weren't happening, they'd been violently stormed-out. The bad weather had passed, but I was alone and spent the evenings when I wasn't running to the pharmacy or grocery for Phil driving back down the coast, stopping at Publix for supplies, then heading home and out to the deck to see the moon squat on the ocean.

My father had called Phil and me the Gruesome Twosome, and when Cindy came into the picture the Gleesome Threesome, then more and more the Three Caballeros. It was Phil who not long after Cindy and I started dating in tenth grade told her that I'd already confessed to him that I thought I was gay—but that I was in love with her and another guy I hadn't specified. Now she was a mother who was probably grateful that she didn't have to pretend not to be glad she didn't have boys. In time, she'd learned everything. We weren't the Three Caballeros for nothing. She had asked me, around graduation, just before we all went our separate ways, if I thought Phil was jealous of her and me, and I'd acted angry and asked her why in the hell he should be, Jesus.

I'd told her, "It's all right if you want to date him instead of me, I'll be fine. Honest."

"I like him but I don't want to be with him," she'd said. "I like being with you."

"I like it, too."

"But who are you more in love with, Phil or me?"

"Neither. I love you both the same," I said.

And she'd made a fart sound with her mouth and looked evenly at me, saying, "Bullshit!"

Which was one of the reasons I'd loved her. This and the fact that she had liked being a virgin and never had any qualms about not having sex. I'd told her I wasn't great at it, anyway.

It was agreed that next time, a Saturday, she'd pull a shift with Phil at his apartment then drive him down to the beach and we'd sit out on the deck and I'd cook. Then she'd drive him home.

"Only it pisses me off," she said, "that we shouldn't drink in front of him. You have no idea how good you have to be as a mom! It's bullshit, acting the role model. It's restricting, it's like a slow suffocation. Since you told me that about Candace, I've thought a lot, Good for her!"

I thought not wholly tragically about the aging of our childish generation—gone youths.

"I can refrain," I said. "I can tie one on while I'm cooking then chew breath mints. I can smoke, can't I? I mean, I'll shower before you guys get here, then sneak one surreptitiously..."

Cindy was an OR nurse and she said, "Not such a hot idea, actually. Not the secondhand smoke part, but what if he gets tempted and begs us? There's liver portal hypertension and Phil's vulnerable to a sudden complete organ shut-down. We'll just have to be good little bunnies."

"Then I guess I can wait until after y'all go," I said, "and all the good bunnies are in bed."

We held hands watching the moon that was partially melted down tonight. I was glad she and I had this time together. I thought we'd never have it again, though we said we would.

"Now that the kids are in middle school and junior high, thank God," Cindy said, "I can swing it so I've got afternoons and evenings while they're doing all their extracurricular junk."

She and Todd had considered getting a divorce, but recently he'd gotten promoted and his workload eased up. He was good about taking turns with her watching the kids on weekends.

"This is just so nice," she added, a little slurry on only her second glass, and I nodded.

I said, "You know, it won't ever be often enough, me coming. I'm just way too poor."

"Where'd you get the money this time?"

"I told my parents, and they'd always loved Phil, always loved the sight of the three of us together actually, so they fronted me. But I hated taking it, even though now they have more."

My parents had retired comfortably and had no debts, no mortgage, but I'd been raised to be independent once I'd gotten through college. I had a problem with debts. But at least I didn't have a family to bankroll. Secretly I had my first book on contract to edit: stories of growing up, the debts I'd incurred to people for providing me with my material for it awkwardly alive in me.

Cindy said, "If I got sick, would you do the same and ask your folks for the money?"

"Absolutely and unequivocally yes," I said, and hated myself for sounding so literary.

She didn't say anything, and I was proud of her for that, too. We had to deal with this, I thought, as honestly as possible. By my next trip Phil would be long gone. She expected me to take off before Saturday, the way I'd run from my "bisexuality"—the issue less important at the time than how much you loved someone, or what your HIV status was, back when the virus was raging uncheckable. There was one question I'd evaded over the years, but Cindy had asked it of me over and over: "Did you ever think you were really bisexual?" Inevitably it was followed by, "Did you ever want to sleep with me? I mean, did you ever want to, out of sheer physical lust?"

She'd put that last part different ways, sometimes drolly, over the course of years during a bunch of long-distance calls and with a hint of falsely shared conspiracy, of queasy complicity.

You didn't ask those questions then, not when you were eighteen, nineteen, twenty. But I was still evading them when I was thirty-five. She'd stopped asking around my fortieth birthday. She said now, "My mom told me to tell you hi, and that she'd like to see you."

"Why don't you invite her out on Saturday," I said. "Is she doing anything Saturday?"

She was trying to finish her cigarette without gagging or coughing. She tamped it out in a way that reminded me of noir movies, those films we'd gone to see sometimes with Phil in the museum's vintage movie series. She said, "But wouldn't Candace say she was being excluded?"

Her voice was rough and low and I nodded and we laughed and I said, "Good point."

I lifted her hand and kissed it. She'd always been so real to me, the way my mom had.

"There's never enough time," she said, and I knew she needed to get ready to motor out.

My parents had hoped I would marry her, and she knew this. She'd married the guy who in college had gotten her pregnant and derailed her education for a while. They'd stayed together and she'd gone to night school, then she'd started her career and now they had this nice family. I couldn't fathom it but I'd started to see the point of it while knowing I didn't have the stuff for it.

She mashed the butt out in the crock ashtray, extinguishing just some evidence of her sin.

Later that evening, when I was comfortably tipsy reading Stevenson, my New York friend Drew called, having returned from the Caribbean, and said, "How's tricks, sweetness, you good?"

"Sure."

"You don't sound that all right. That would make two of us, bloody fucking hell!"

He liked to make fun of Brits while co-opting their idioms.

I said, "If you want to know the truth, I'd like to be life-flighted out of this entire deal."

"Your buddy Phil, if he wants to get better—and look, I'm not saying he doesn't want to get better—but if he wants to, he needs to get off those meds. His liver qi's in a rage. That's the story on his liver. It's shot. The drugs and pharmaceuticals, they're only making things worse."

He sounded like he was well into the Malbec, like he was giving his own liver qi a zap.

I waited and then said, "How was St. Martin? All tropical paradise and great splendor?"

"Oh, you know," he said, "those freaking airlines, they have us where they want us in this corporate-hostage country. All the corporations have us. Listen, I know of some herbals..."

Drew was a coddled, welfare-aided brat, I flattered myself, and right now I was a victim.

I listened, lying in my bed holding my book open and upside-down on my chest.

"You need to get him to an acupuncturist, get him some Chinese herbs. The acupuncture is one thing, the Chinese herbalist another. But go online and look, you might be surprised..."

We hung up finally, leaving the topic at nothing, and I went back to *Treasure Island.*

"I can't do this," Cindy called and said into the phone on Saturday morning.

I was just having my coffee on the deck and steeling myself up. I couldn't do it, either.

She said, "Todd thinks I've gotten obsessed, and the girls all have colds. It's cold and flu season and they're all sick and Todd has to go into work all of a sudden. But I called Phil."

"Uh-huh?"

"He got it. He just hopes you'll come up and see him."

"Obviously. Hey, sweetie, no problem. It'll be all right. Double-pinky promise, okay?"

She said, "My mom's mad."

"At whom?"

"I couldn't tell."

"Will you tell her I miss her, and that I'll see her, like, really soon? Promise?"

"Are you mad at me, Mike?"

"Not in the least. I couldn't possibly love you more. I never could."

I drove up. I'd been up too late the night before on the deck drinking and smoking and thinking. Adolescence had been just an embarrassment and it locked you into making too many romantic, silly statements you lived with forever if you thought about it. You couldn't overthink it. That way you'd go crazy. You'd had no idea you'd live to feel tired and defeated all the time.

He came to the door and seemed energetic. He said, "Man, all I can think about's pussy."

"I get it," I said, stepping past him. He was wild-eyed from the meds, I guessed.

"I'm supposed to be sick and I'm not supposed to last, but that's all I can think of. All I ever think about is hard, horny sex, doing nasty things with girls mostly. I never did it with her."

"You didn't?"

"Because of you, asshole, and because she was never in love with me."

"But she was. Cindy was always in love with you."

"But not like she was with you, man. You were my best fucking friend for a long time."

They had him on mood elevators, and maybe they counteracted the opioid dosages.

He said, "And it's not your fault that I'm dying. Obviously. No fucking shit there, too."

"I didn't say that. I hate this. I hate knowing it. I loved you more than I did myself."

"We were a team," he said.

I nodded and said, "We were."

After a while, sitting there with him, thinking about the sex, and thinking tenderly of him in bed with Cindy, should that have ever happened, I said, "Who says you can't beat this, man?"

He'd been crying but now he got quiet, smiling, then said, "I thought I'd lost my mind."

There were only so many extra livers, so many motorcycle casualties to provide livers.

Finally, no laughing, no crying, just smiles between us.

I said, "And I always loved you."

Then he wouldn't look at me, though after a time he gave me the thumbs-up.

"I hear you," he said.

Later when I learned he'd passed after a botched excision I had some more things to say, but he was gone finally, and there was no reason to say them, and no one to say them to.

left on monsignor o'brien
michael alenyikov

STORROW DRIVE ENDED IN A CONFUSION OF SIGNS. One read: *If You Lived Here You'd Be Home.* To its right rose grimy white apartment towers: sorry grave markers they might as well be. It was the West End once; Samuel'd read of its demise back when he still made the effort to read the *Globe* to keep up on home, to follow each August's swoon by the Sox; the gossip of politics; the accounts of who'd died. Bits of news for conversation with Peter and Ma via letters and the occasional phone call. But the *rawness of* seeing the West End gone, the rawness of it; the East End alone now, he knew, stranded across the harbor on the far side of the Callahan. Samuel admired an East End true to its past, reminding the world—which, he knew, didn't give a good God damn anymore—that, once, east and west were two; like brothers, one could say. One could, thought the brother who still lived.

Samuel and his Subaru (dusty, grimy, and insect splattered after the journey from San Francisco) arrived none too gently at a crisscross of streets and signs, a buzz saw it felt to him. A din of ratcheting sounds. This town will have its revenge on you; and *better late than never* they screamed to the elderly prodigal, better late than never signaled the flash and blur of traffic lights, headlights, streetlights. I'm not ready, he thought, not ready, not ready, the thought refrained as if the city would take pity if he acted the part of a frightened child.

A long red light allowed him to gather his wits. Then a trusting to instinct guided him through streets that seemed not to have changed in fifty years he'd been away, though their names had been erased, rubbed clean from wherever it was they had set up camp in Samuel's memory, and the buildings that lined the streets were new and old, old and new, no pattern to the urban madness. He had no use for what he's offered: Government Center, Downtown, Faneuil Hall, Callahan Tunnel, Logan Airport—and what a laugh: the way to the *Freedom Trail*. That passes through home's turf, and he laughed out loud at the idea that the irony was intended for his amusement. Had there ever been a sign that pointed to Charlestown? Wasn't that the point? His heart pounded in the glare of lights. Can a person die of panic? But there—yes!—it's a left on Monsignor O'Brien, he recalled with a rush of blood to his head. A sense of direction he still had. And over the river he drove to find a Charlestown Avenue familiarly dingy and neglected. Over the river? He'd forgotten that home was on the Charles' north side, apart from the city itself. It had migrated in memory as if by small quakes. Oh, how they'd thought themselves the *heart* of Boston, the bloody pumping heart and soul of the old town. So many fist fights to prove it.

Over the river, then it's a right for sure. How quickly he found his way in a maze of narrow streets. And there, rising to its modest crest, Charlestown's crown jewel, Bunker Hill. No Beacon Hill for sure, though now he saw homes spruced up: sand-blasted bricks; clapboard hard-scrubbed and painted, hands hired by yuppies, but still a *ghetto*. The word brought a smile to Samuel. Not once had he ever thought it so and proud he was for seeing it clear this ghetto.

He turned from Warren onto School, past Sheafe where School transmigrated into Mystic. Two houses beyond the church (still standing, sprightlier than in memory). And there it is: the old house still there. He double-parked in front, pulled back on the hand brake and looked up.

So small.... So small it was.

Samuel sat in his car and stared at the house in which he'd been born. Three floors, three flats. They'd had the top and access to the roof, hot tar in summer. And Peter's last address—before the nursing home—was only just down the street. He'd stop there next. Was the cemetery from colonial days still there, with its jagged row of tombstones that tilted one way and the other? Surely they've not razed it! It had looked to him once like an old man's mouth, but now it was a child's proud grin of new grown teeth he imagined. Is it that we see what we want to see? Or is it all changing like the weather in New England and determined as much by the sausage we had for breakfast or the rise and fall of blood sugar from a jelly donut, the flapping of a butterfly's wings in China?

No, it came to him: he did not want to see the cemetery. He did not want to see the flat where Petey'd lived when he'd faced those long years alone. Petey, the brother he'd lost touch with, *let slip away*, let die alone. Petey, the sort that needed family, its sounds, its comforts and irritations; its dailiness. Poor Peter. He'd never wandered far. It was a tough Irish neighborhood and proud they all were of its separateness. Samuel's tongue played with the word—*ghetto*. An oddity of history that tickled his fancy: how an Italian word forced on Jews can hold a collection of poor Irish in the New World. He took out a pint of Dewar's he'd saved over a continent's drive for just the right moment and permitted himself two swallows.

Rain began to fall. Slowly. Large drops of it. How long had he been sitting here? He shook his head to wake his wits. Now a red-haired woman with a child in each hand rushed out the door of his old home, then stopped and looked to the sky, in anger, before darting down the street. "Hurry," she shouted, hands empty of an umbrella, the weather no surprise at all, except to Samuel, too long in the west. Once all life revolved around this square mile. History, now. But Peter had stayed, through two lost marriages. Bedrock to him, Samuel supposed.

Samuel watched the patch of red make its way down the street and disappear around a corner.

The surprise of weather. What was this outrage? When did clouds sneak into a murky night sky? Samuel felt aggrieved, for no worthy reason he could identify. It was only rain, after all.

Swish, swish, the wipers turned on again. How dare the weather interfere with his view of home! But then, on impulse, he opened the car door. A smell so fresh, seasoned with a touch of sea and salt, rushed in. And in a moment he's out and standing. He had no umbrella, no raincoat. A baseball cap he wore. Shame on you, Sammy, his mother's spirit—if it had chosen to haunt this street, to stay close to home—would scold. But his senses were alive to weather, not ghosts and spirits; so Samuel, head up, neck stretched, mouth open, stood swallowing what to him were heaven's tears. The rain fell faster now and Samuel in shirtsleeves grew soaked to the skin. A wind gusted and stole the cap from his head quicker than his reaching hand and twirled it a time or two then plopped it into a rain-filled gutter.

Where was the red-haired woman? And where are all the people he once knew? He swallowed more Dewar's. How wise he was to know it would be needed. *Come back, he implored her, and we will dance.* Samuel's rain-slicked head swells with joy. Come back and I will dance with you and, yes, meet my Da, my Ma, my brother, Pete. Join us, sweet lass.

But the locals had sense enough to stay in when such weather strikes. A loose top to a garbage can was sent banging down the street by the wind. "Can you no longer recognize a Nor'easter?" the well-bred voice awoke in him scornfully; that damn homunculus who'd taken residence in his mind for days and days. "The ocean, I fear, has moved to the other side of your brain. The Pacific's your reference now." Piss off, Samuel thought. But rain is rain and Samuel now recalled the routine, retreating into his car—a kind of home it's been—to consider a hot meal as the sensible what next.

Yet he sat, hands resting on the steering wheel, eyes fixed on the two small windows of the top flat, the clapboard, grayed by years of soiled air, now growing darker, stained by rain, forming fingers like the shadows of stalactites in a cave.

He thought: I am winding down.

Samuel stared at the two top-floor windows and they stared back, dark beady eyes, suspicious of strangers...and stranger he was. Piss off, their message. Piss off to strangers in the eyes of all he grew up with.

He'd fled five decades ago. And presumptuous it was to expect a glad-to-see-ya shake, a slap on the back, a hearty embrace.

So small, the windows, so much smaller than in memory. And where were the steps? Five and a small landing he'd carried in memory; but before him the house was near-flush to the street; two steps that were hardly deserving the name, cracked and chipped; and where was the landing he remembered sitting on with Pete and Mickie those long summer nights, their words about Sammy's feats on the mound hurling baseballs as if they were their own.

Charlestown Sammy he was in the neighborhood...and at Boston Latin the name stuck; the stare he'd perfected on the mound silenced any who mocked.

Samuel sat in the darkness, aggrieved again at the rain, the wind, the swish, swish of the blades, the surprise of weather.

A knock on the window to his left. Outside the car, a face, but no features.

A glance up at the rear view mirror: a startled old man who's seen a ghost looked back. The window was rain-wet on the outside, fogged on the inside. Samuel of the once-nimble fingers searched for the knob to roll the window down, cursed himself at the second knock, remembered it's electric; the soft whir as the window opened, like a man's final exhalation, he thought; and the face: freckled, pale, pink, the red-headed woman close to him, breath a sour smell.

"You lost or something?" she said. "Are you from around here?" He'd expected his mother's voice, faint from hunger as he was. What had he eaten all day? Chinese, too many miles back; later a muffin, blueberry, crumbly at Dunkin' Donuts—no, it was a cardboardy bran, fitting for an old man, he'd thought. "Mister, are you okay?" But this woman's voice is raspy, the words hard to discern; why is she speaking so fast, he thought, and felt again aggrieved, then: it's the townie accent, playing musical chairs with their r's. Oh, how hard he'd worked to lose it at Harvard and then in California.

"You looking for someone?" she said, talking slower now as if to an idiot child, and he forgave her raspy voice, which wasn't his mother's—smooth as syrup she'd spoken—aspirations to something higher, better, his father accused when he'd passed the fourth bottle of beer.

"Mister, you've been sitting here for all of an hour. If you're not looking for someone, maybe you'd best go home." A touch of threat now added.

"Who lives up there in the third-floor flat?"

"Me and my kids and my husband, who's a cop and will be home any minute, if you must know."

"I used to live there."

Her face grew blank. "Well, isn't that nice." Her accent thickened so Samuel couldn't tell sarcasm or if it's just the way the young talk to the old.

She's pretty, he noticed. In a weary sort of way. Shadows under her eyes, the color of which he can't make out in the dark, but he knows are blue; the pale blue of a red-headed Irish girl.

Little Orphan Annie, he thought, and fought back a chuckle. Little Orphan Annie, that's who you look like, he struggled against saying because then her decision on him would land on the word loony.

"Look, mister—" she began, but he pressed the button and the window rolled up.

Samuel moved the stick into drive and put the pedal down hard, burning rubber; just like the time he and Peter and Mickie had stolen the Chevy. Fled from the scene, they had, and had not been caught. Ditched the car in some sorry end of Somerville. "You're running away." The words Ma'd hurled at him when he said he was leaving for the west came back to him. "Leave and you don't come back," she said and swore in her first letter she'd never meant.

A few blocks later, he stopped at a light. Just one truth he'd hoped to find in the old neighborhood, but he was hungry for something hot now—beef stew and a beer to chase it; and there's the nursing home to find, hidden away in Dorchester's depths; and a place to stay for the night; he'd forgotten essentials—bedrock: hot food and a bed for the night. Foolish to expect more from life, old man, he thought and let go with a laugh and some gas. He pulled out his pint of Dewar's for another sip and reflected on how the muscles of the mouth and ass grow loose in time—and that, yes, this nugget, this truth, hard-earned, will have to do.

The air was misty now. The wiper blades helpless. Street lamps were on, blurred yellow stars distorted by the glass. A tinge of pink in the light. Samuel drove, crawled his way crab-like through the maze of narrow streets, pulling around cars double parked. He was tired, hungry. A horn blasted. Shrill. A man's head—stuck out the window—inches away, traveling in the opposite direction. A hand motioned. Samuel lowered his window.

"Ya got eyes, old man? Don't ya got eyes?" He stared at Samuel, waiting for an answer. When none was forthcoming—Samuel wanted to say, "I've come home"—the man spat in his direction, then drove off.

Samuel worked to steady his hands. He swallowed and felt the dryness of his mouth. He ran his tongue over parched lips. Samuel turned the corner and pulled into an empty space by a fire hydrant. He inhaled deeply as he was taught in a yoga class. Ten deep breaths. He placed himself in a darkened redwood grove. He looked for his wise inner guardian, as he was taught. Yoga for Seniors. He'd swallowed his pride to go. He evoked the smells and sounds of a redwood forest—pungent, whispery—but there was no inner wise man. He was alone among the giant, ancient trees. They've seen too much to know even where to begin, was what he imagined. I'm as important to them as the snails that scavenge their roots or the moss that covers rocks and tree trunks alike. The dew that forms, he'd like to think, is their pity for him. Just now, he would settle for pity. Too late, he thought: maybe I should have gone back, not quit after three classes. But growing old was bad enough. Don't need to be surrounded by mirrors, he'd thought at the time.

He looked up at another three-floor relic of a building. Same as the one he'd grown up in—but not the same. He stretched to roll down the window on the passenger side. Mickie's house. On Chappie, across from old Doherty Park. First floor flat. Samuel crimsoned. All by himself. Five decades and then some, after the fact, he was blushing. Mortification and lust. Mickie was his first. They'd been a trio, he and Peter and Mickie. Inseparable. Grades one through nine. In school. After school. After church. Even after Samuel'd made it to Boston Latin—*The Academy*, Mr. Rourke, his guidance counselor in junior high, had called it with a bit of a sneer—they stayed best of friends. He'd overheard Ma saying to Aunt Peg, "They've gone and separated the wheat from the chaff," and it had made him proud in a sad sour kind of way that had him trying harder to act with Mickie and Pete as if nothing had changed. But there was more to his missing them than the hours lost in travel to Roxbury, hours lost to serious baseball drills, his long left arm and high leg kick his ticket out. And there was a difference in the way he missed his friend and his brother, strong as he missed the easiness of time spent with both, there was that shade of difference that crept up on him, that had him wishing away a feeling that lacked a name even as it twisted his insides. Always one for naming things was Samuel, the university historian, the scholar of Grant's failed presidency.

His first.

Whose idea had it been? Samuel couldn't remember. What he can remember: the fumbling with belts and zippers. Peeling Mickie's shirt off, the shock of seeing what he'd seen before, seen anew. To feel his body with intention. The dropping of pants. Touching what was a sin. They'd both touched at the same time. On a dare. No one's fault that way. Each on their knees in turn. Who first? It can't matter now, thought Samuel. Surely it can't. But the historian needed to know if Mickie wanted it as bad as he. To pin down that truth.

Where? Not here. In Samuel and Peter's room. Da was at Malone's. Ma out to visit Aunt Peg. The bitter taste. He'd spat it out. And Peter walking in. Accounted for at football practice, he'd been sent home with a fever. How could he stand there and gape?

Framed in the doorway. Staring at them. Green eyes blinking, dumbstruck's the only word that'll do. "He's your cousin, in the name of Christ," Petey said, in his eyes, the set of his face, Samuel saw what he'll see again, sometimes real, sometimes imagined—in the face of the cop in the toilets, the night the bar on Polk was raided, strangers on a trolley if he crossed his legs, knee over knee, and in his own face reflected—yer no man at all. How does a stranger's face shape this message? Eyes narrow to a slit, the mouth goes crooked, as if the very sight of you makes them want to puke.

And in Samuel's mouth: the bitter taste takes up residence; and words: "Don't tell. Don't tell." But Peter's gone. He runs. Door slams. The pope and Roosevelt rattle in their frames.

They dressed quickly in silence, and after, Mickie had gone his own way. Samuel steadied his hands, which trembled, still, these many years later.

He held tight to the wheel. He'd never forgotten the craving he'd felt— lust such a poor word; but considered now if it was a kind of love that was there too.

Samuel made a fist and pounded the steering wheel. Softly pummeled it so as not to make a sound.

seven days of poe
richard bowes

Monday

I HAD BEEN PASSING ALONE ON HORSEBACK, THROUGH A SINGULARLY DREARY tract of land and at length found myself as the shades of the evening drew on, within view of the melancholy House of Usher.

I read those lines for the first time in the stacks of the Boston Public Library on a summer day in 1960 when I was sixteen. Sunlight came through skylights and I sat cross legged in what someone would later tell me was a yoga pose.

The book was *Terror by Poe*, a slim popular paperback at a time when even straight boys still read stuff like this and Poe was kind of hip. I had seen the movie *Usher* with Vincent Price lisping madly.

Life for a gay kid fifty-plus years ago was a series of half open doors, whispered secrets, stories you had to find within the stories everyone else told each other.

Edgar Allan Poe was part of this. Price's campy performance introduced me to the suspicion that Poe spoke to queers. And a narrator going to visit a childhood friend of whom he says, "*Although as boys we had been even intimate associates...*" had to be talking about something beyond friendship.

So involved was I in the tale that a voice whispering in my ear, "We have put her living in the tomb!" made me drop the book and half jump to my feet. I'd just read those words!

It was Charlie Gains, the stacks supervisor; tall, queer, dressed in sneakers and chinos like he was one of us stacks kids but old, twenty-seven he'd told me.

"Richie, your break is long over. There are trucks of books waiting down in Sorting." Gentle reminders: Charlie never ordered anyone around.

My trips to the Sorting Room always included a detour out of the stacks and into the public areas of the Copley Square Library. The building was a classic Italian palazzo, an ornate, impractical anomaly way more alien in that northern city than the House of Usher in its bleak landscape.

Down the marble stairs I trotted. Overhead lighted glass chandeliers shone. High on the walls were John Singer Sargent murals.

I loved the grandiosity, imagined myself booted and spurred, with hair in ringlets to my shoulders and a sword at my hip. A cavalier with a secret both exciting and dangerous.

In fact, because leather shoes were too noisy, stacks kids had to wear sneakers, which were entirely unhip back then. And I was spending my summer in a short crewcut because I'd flunked French.

These were the visible aspects of my lack of cool. But this city at this time held no place for gay kids, even ones like me who somehow thought we were kind of straight. Either we got shoved into niches where we didn't quite fit or we tried to carve out ones of our own.

The nice, polite boy making deliveries for the local drugstore, the high school hall monitor, the kid who sang in the church choir, the tame-looking teen hitting the bottom of the marble library stairs in his black PF Flyer Hi-Tops and slipping through a door marked "Personnel Only," were each trying to find a way to make sense of his life in the fierce hetero world.

And any one of us could also be the kid who went by the bus station to use the men's room even when he didn't need to. And maybe that boy made it a point to walk at night past the nameless bar to try and glimpse through the darkened windows the guys he'd seen slipping in the door.

The back areas of the library were dim and dingy places. I swung down the small circular metal stairs that were like something from a submarine movie and went past the basement men's room.

The Poe book in my back pocket was pulsing against my ass. This had started a couple of days before after I'd read "The Telltale Heart," with an obsessed narrator and the corpse he murdered and concealed.

True!—nervous—very dreadfully nervous I had been and am; but why will you say that I am mad?

I crossed the hall and opened a door into a large, badly lighted region. The Sorting Room lay a bit ahead, a light in the dark. Otherwise to the left and right all was black recesses—the boiler room, storage vaults. I saw nothing moving. This wasn't always so. The shadows were a meeting place.

The door of the men's room opened and closed behind me. I heard that as I took a slow, deliberate step into the dark. Then I jumped as a pair of hands had my shoulders. I turned enough to see a guy, old, grey haired but big. I nodded and found myself propelled through the door and into the dark.

Last September just after I started in the library I had seen a pair of guys disappear into the dark. In the previous couple of years I'd had enough encounters like that to know what I saw and what it meant for me. Several times since then I'd let guys lead me into these shadows.

Mostly, though, I did this at night when nobody much was around. And the guys who picked me up were nervous and jumpy. The ones that wanted kids who still looked like they were thirteen usually were. With them I could be a bit removed like this was a movie or play I was in. And I had some control over the action.

This one kept his hands on my shoulders and guided me into the darkest corner. He stuck a bill in my shirt pocket before I could even say, "Five bucks." Taking money meant you weren't queer. Everyone knew that.

I started to unzip my fly, wanting not to be too exposed. But he yanked my belt open, hauled my pants and jockeys all the way down. I heard the paperback fall on the floor. Then he had my shirt unbuttoned like he could see in the dark.

In seconds I was half-naked, vulnerable if anyone really looked and the guy crouched down, grabbed my ass with both hands and pulled me towards him.

Usually I stayed mostly clothed and managed to imagine I was with some kid I'd seen on American Bandstand or some rookie just brought up by the Red Sox.

With this guy working me, all I felt was him, me in his mouth, his hands pushing me into him. The danger excited me. I was panting loudly and when I came I heard myself cry out.

As he stood he smacked my ass hard with each hand like he was spanking me. He spat into a corner and went out the door as I pulled my clothes back together in the dark.

Then I had to walk into the Sorting Room. There Eddie and Hal, two older full-time workers, straight and fat, worked without shirts in the stifling cellar, took books out of dumb waiters, off a conveyer belt, sorted and slammed them onto old wooden library trucks.

They saw me, said nothing, pointed at two loaded carts. They stared like I disgusted them. Understanding they'd heard what had happened outside and knew it had to be me, I got out of there fast.

Pushing one heavy cart, pulling the other one, I left the Sorting Room and went into the dark. I must have remembered to pick the Poe book up because I felt it beating against my butt like a pulse and thought of the line from the story:

What you mistake for madness is but over-acuteness of the senses.

Moving the trucks onto an elevator was a struggle. I wasn't a big kid. The books were for the reading rooms—the large lending library within the reference library.

Charlie was there when I hauled the trucks into this public area which had lots of people around. My shirt was out of my pants and my expression, I guess, was dazed.

Shaking his head he got me into a quiet corner and made me pull my clothes together. "Had a bit of a dizzy spell did we?" he asked in a cockney accent. "Bit of oopsy-daisy, was it?"

I caught his amusement and was horrified to realize that any queer or even any straight who knew anything could guess what I'd been up to.

But Charlie sent me up to a quiet balcony that ran around the main reading room. I straightened books, sat with my head in my hands, recovered from getting raped.

When I felt a little better I looked down and saw some of the other kids shelving and Charlie standing at the information desk talking to Mrs. Lord, the boss, and a couple of the other librarians.

Charlie knew a lot for a guy who'd never quite connected with college, had never really got past being a stacks kid. The librarians were always telling him, begging him really, to go back to school. He'd just shake his head like they were asking too much, or he had something better to do.

That seemed to be what was going on. It didn't occur to me that I was the subject of conversation. When it was over, he spotted me, beckoned and I joined him in a corner.

"Feeling better?" I nodded. "Okay, I want this truck shelved before you leave." Then he said, quietly but very seriously, "No more fun in the building, understand? The vice squad has that men's room targeted. Stop squirming and looking so embarrassed; anyone seeing us is going to think I'm propositioning you."

When I signed out, instead of taking the subway home to Dorchester, I made a little detour, walked up Boylston and past the Common. I looked up and down Arlington Street to see if I could spot my friend, a kid named Ty.

I even looked into the Greyhound terminal at Park Square, taking a bit of a risk by going there. But he was nowhere to be seen and I didn't have a lot of time.

At moments like this when I couldn't find him, Ty seemed more an imaginary friend than a real one. We were Boston Irish kids, a bit undersized, looking cuter than we were, with the same brown hair and blue eyes. We seemed enough alike that I sometimes thought he was me but me without parents or school, a scary life but a tempting one.

When I finally hit the subway, I was already late. A couple of tough kids stared at me like there was going to be trouble. But they got off at Broadway in South Boston. I played a game of looking and not looking with this old guy who had combed-over hair. But I was careful after what had just happened.

Mostly I finished "The Fall of the House of Usher," read about Lady Madeline's interment, saw her with the blood on her robes, heard her brother's shrieking, "*Do I not distinguish that heavy and horrible beating of her heart?*"

Reading about the destruction of Usher, I pictured the Public Library falling down and getting sucked into the ground. Imagined standing in a suddenly desolate Copley Square.

In my neighborhood, guys my age gathered in the playground and around street corners. I'd drifted apart from them in the last couple of years. I came across not quite as a sissy but as someone whose parents ran his life too much.

The neighborhood had its sissies, boys who giggled and wore short pants to church well into their teens because their mothers insisted. I made it a point not to be seen with them.

When I got home my parents wanted to know where I'd been and why I wasn't back in time for dinner. They weren't happy with me but it seemed like they never were. They said I couldn't leave the house that night. I had no place to go.

My little brothers and sisters watched television while I read "The Masque of the Red Death" and sympathized with Prince Prospero defying the plague, imagined myself as a reveler in the colored rooms. Then Red Death appeared at the end, "*And darkness and decay and the Red Death held illimitable dominion over all,*" and I identified with the specter and had to read it all again.

Getting undressed, I remembered to take the five dollar bill out of my shortsleeve shirt before that went in the hamper, and stick it in the book.

Tuesday

Tuesday was a late day at the library. I went to work at four in the afternoon and stayed till eight. I'd told my parents that I worked until ten. In the morning I went to summer school, took French, and learned to type.

Then I came home. To please my mother I wore short pants around the house but nowhere else. To keep my tan that's all I wore as I mowed the backyard and trimmed the hedges. Then I lay in the sun reading and dreaming. Not quite a sissy.

Afterwards, I got dressed again, put on my sneakers (like T-shirts worn as outer clothing and jeans, these were forbidden in school) and went to work.

The library was full of odd legends and odder people. One of the librarians sent me on an errand and going up the main stairs I imagined myself as Prince Prospero in his palace. In a perfect coincidence I then saw the one Charlie called Red Death.

A queen with outlandish long scarlet-dyed hair, penciled eyebrows, thick makeup, given to shawls, parasols and flowing pants that could almost be dresses, he was someone with whom every man gay or straight was afraid to be seen.

And as I saw Red Death, he saw me. He'd spoken to me once before, affixed me with his bloodshot eyes, asked my name and age. One of the librarians had shooed him away.

Now he stood right in my path. "There's a legend of kidnapped children in this place," he told me. "They take boys like you, ones that can't grow up, and keep them here forever."

"It's what happened in my case," a voice said behind me. It was Charlie.

Red Death smiled. "Saving him for yourself?" he murmured. "That's *adorable*! It's his little friend I want. Or is that other one your brother?" he asked me. "A tough boy, not a fairy." Red Death must have seen me with Ty.

Charlie guided me away, shaking his head. "Sooner or later Red Death comes to each of us!" he said. Then he asked, "What friend was he talking about?"

"Just someone I know."

I shelved books, talked to one of the girl shelvers who was going to college in the fall, did odd jobs for the librarians.

Just before eight o'clock I looked up and Ty was there. Ty was a smart, cool kid who knew lots of stuff . His hair was how I wanted mine to be: combed back like a greaser but with strands flopping over his forehead. His T-shirt, pants and tie-shoes were all black.

Maybe we were similar but I was the clueless twin. I looked to make sure Red Death didn't see us as we left and walked up Boylston Street. It was sunset and lights were on in the stores.

I told him about the guy in the cellar getting rough. "You gotta carry a knife or something," he told me. "Otherwise they're gonna get you where first you do it for free and pretty soon you're doing them and you're a fucking fag."

Ty had done a stint in a halfway house and a couple of months in reform school. I still got hit at home and had been punched around a few times in gym. Ty had gone through much worse stuff.

I bought us both ice cream cones since I had that five bucks and had to spend it where my parents wouldn't see. Ty just gobbled his down and asked me for another one. His parents weren't dead but they weren't around. He was staying with some relatives. But that was it. Staying. They didn't feed him.

He mentioned wanting to get dexies and said, "First we need some money. I gotta see the Collector." I liked doing speed.

He wouldn't tell me anything about where we were going, took me to the other side of Beacon Hill near the hospital where it wasn't so nice. It was an apartment house where you had to buzz to get in.

A voice said, "Yes?"

Ty said, "It's Tom." He shrugged when I looked at him.

"Oh, Tommy!" and the buzzer sounded.

The Collector was right on the first floor at the back of the building. He was a thin guy with a grey mustache, seeming not really creepy.

Until we went in his place and all I saw was underpants. Some boxers but mostly ones like I wore and most kids did. White briefs were displayed on top of cabinets, laid out on bookshelves, hung on the walls like paintings.

"Amazing isn't it?" the collector said. "I have the shorts of half the teenage boys in Boston. What do you have for me?"

I shook my head but Ty said, "I want to sell," and pulled down his pants. He was wearing red boxers. Old guy clothes, big and flowing around him like he was wading up to his waist in blood.

The Collector looked offended. "Those aren't yours."

"I'm wearing them. What more do you want?"

"I'll only buy those if you get your friend to sell me his. Five for both of them together."

This was super creepy. "My mother may notice if they're gone." The Collector found this wonderful, I could tell.

But Ty kicked off his shoes, dropped his pants and the shorts. His t-shirt didn't cover him. I looked at his dick. He noticed and flicked it. Here we were different in a couple of ways; his was more impressive and he'd been circumcised.

He said, "Come on, do it. We got places to go."

If my mother noticed I was going to have to say I must have left them in the gym locker or something and get in trouble. I sighed deeply, untied my sneakers, kind of trembled as I pulled off my khaki chinos. You had to do this in front of the Collector.

"Oh, nice and white!" he said when he saw my undershorts, "Your mother buys Sears and Roebuck briefs. Size sixteen, boys, I'll bet." So it turned out to be when I handed them over. He gave Ty/Tom the fiver as I got dressed.

"Mine's bigger," Ty said when we were outside heading away, "even though part of mine got cut off. You need to ditch those faggot shorts. Hustlers don't use underwear. Sell them to the Collector."

"Where did you get the ones you had?" I asked, like I hadn't noticed his prick or seen him looking at mine. My balls and cock bounced around inside my pants and I kept checking to make sure my fly was zippered. Until now I hadn't been much interested in guys my own age. Mostly sex was just older guys interested in me. Now I spent a lot of time imagining myself as Ty with his hair and clothes.

"They're my aunt's boyfriend's. He's too fat and dumb to notice," he said. "Guys like you got it easy. Mother to take care of you."

We stopped and we got hamburgers at a diner, ate as we walked, shoved it in our mouths as fast as we could.

My time was running out and Ty hadn't found any dexies. We headed for the bus terminal.

At school there had been a kid in the year ahead of me who sometimes had Benzedrine. He'd gone in the navy. But over the last couple of years I'd gotten in the habit of doing speed when I could find any, which wasn't often enough. Like sex, it got me around bad days and boring adults.

And looking for drugs and sex gave me the tang of danger which was part of the excitement. Being in the bus terminal was part of that. Looking around I didn't see anyone who seemed like a cop. Ty was a step ahead of me and he saw nothing either.

The light in the restroom and in the waiting room made the people slumped on benches look like hopeless plague victims awaiting Red Death.

A bus was leaving for Worcester and the few people kind of stumbling towards it reminded me of refugees fleeing. There was one dark guy, Italian maybe, standing near the big entrance. He was there for some bad reason but not speed. Ty saw him and shook his head.

We left fast because it wasn't wise for either of us to hang around. This was where we'd met maybe a month before:

We were both loitering on a Saturday when I didn't have to work but had told my parents I did.

In vain I'd visited my usual spots for getting picked up, the Y, the far side of the Public Gardens, the bad stretch of Washington Street. Then I came here and spotted Ty.

He caught sight of me out of the corner of his eye, I could tell. Each of us, I think, recognized in the other the good-looking Boston Irish boy with the nice smile when he chose to use it.

Then I noticed a guy who spotted Ty and moved toward him grinning. As he did, Ty broke and ran out the terminal door. I was so stupid I stood staring and the vice cop turned and grabbed me. Did it very quietly and walked me out back to a parking lot.

He asked me what I was doing there. Said he could run me in. I was going to tell him I had an uncle on the force which legend had it would stop them arresting you. But he slapped me and said not to let him see me there again.

Walking away, I was scared, relieved. Looking real young was a pain sometimes if you were a kid trying to grow up but an asset at moments like this. My face stung where I'd been hit. I wondered if I should go home.

Then I saw the other kid across Arlington Street. He saw me, stood blank faced. When I stopped and looked his way he made a little gesture. I crossed the street. We introduced ourselves, told our names, where we lived. He was Charlestown, which meant hard; I was Dorchester, which was boring. Immediately I thought his hair was great, his clothes cool.

When I told him some of what had just happened Ty said, "I can't believe we're the exact same age—you're like a retard. Why didn't you run when I did?"

I couldn't stop staring at him. We were about the same height. We could have been brothers. That first time Ty and I walked together around the Common and he told me, "I'm on my last chance. One more bust and I'm going away for good."

On the night a month into our friendship, I needed to head for the subway and home. We walked down a side street past a place I'd seen before, the bar with darkened windows and shadowy guys you could glimpse slipping in the door.

It had nothing on the neon sign but the word BAR. "Queer bar," Ty said when he saw me staring.

"Guys call it the Sugar Bowl. Queens go there. We could get in, I bet. And someone will have speed."

I'd been in a queer coffee shop over on Washington Street. Kid hustlers hung out there. I was curious but I needed to get home.

Two figures crossed the street, a tall guy and what I thought at first was a woman. I looked again and saw it was a guy in a pink shirt, loose pants and sandals. He had short hair. But something about his walk, the way he leaned towards the man with him, was feminine.

The other guy was a bigger shock. I didn't know if Charlie Gains had seen me. But I saw him go in the door of the Sugar Bowl.

It was late when I waved goodnight to Ty, wanted to touch him, to hold him. "See you Thursday," he said. "We're gonna sell all your shorts."

And I went down the subway stairs at Washington Street and caught a half-empty train to Dorchester. That night, though, I paid no attention to the passengers, to the talk around me or to the lights playing on the water when we came out from under the ground at Columbia Station.

I was reading "The Cask of Amontillado" imagining myself in a red cape, black velvet doublet and hose and knee-high boots, my hair like Ty's, smiling a smile only I could see as Fortunato ran his ridiculous schemes.

When I got home it wasn't real late and I said I'd already eaten so things weren't that bad. I remembered to throw a pair of clean briefs from my drawer into the hamper.

Wednesday

I sat cross-legged in the library stacks, aware of my cock loose in my pants, re-reading the "The Cask of Amontillado" as a succession of guys, the vice cop from the bus terminal, the man who assaulted me in the dark, assholes who'd pushed me around in the high school gym, my father, Eddie and Hal from the Sorting Room, pleaded naked and in tears, "*For God's sake, Montresor!*" And I walled them in.

Right then Charlie appeared. "Break's over, lover boy: the Lord has summoned us." I knew the Lord was Mrs. Lord, head of Public Service. But as I stood I looked at Charlie like the first part made no sense. He was smiling the same way he'd done when he saw me after I got mauled by that guy.

"Spotted you and your friend last night," he said.

"Just a kid I know. What about your friend?"

"Larry/AKA Lauren? My *roommate?*" he said turning the word over a little bit. What's your friend's name?" I told him. We descended circular metal back stairs, reached the basement and went along a dark corridor. The Sorting Room was down another passageway.

The whole place reminded me of Castle Island. Just that day I'd learned that Boston, like most East Coast cities, had a Poe connection. In this case it was the old fort on Castle Island in South Boston. Poe served there when he was in the army.

Learning this struck me as a major coincidence. I'd been inside that fort. A causeway connected the island to the mainland now. Picnic tables were set up on the grass. But the dark grey building itself, all stone and mortar, was sealed.

When I was maybe ten, I was there on a family picnic. A bunch of guys, government surveyors and engineers, had pried open one of the entrances to the fort.

I was curious and in the slaphappy way of that time and place I got to follow them and their flashlights through dark passages inside the walls. Doors were jammed closed. Rooms smelled of stale water and decay. It was scary and I was glad the guys made sure they didn't lose me.

Now in memory it felt like Usher, and Montresor's wine cellar and the basement that held a Telltale Heart all at once. And the stairs and passageways where Charlie and I had just walked could have been in Castle Island.

Ahead of us light came from a room. Mrs. Lord stood in the doorway with an expression of mild disgust. She turned, "Charles, go up and get discard tickets from Preparations—lots of them, if you would. And pens."

Charlie hesitated but went. I wondered why she hadn't sent me. Mrs. Lord didn't come up to my shoulders. She wore a dark blue jacket and skirt and a ruffled blouse. She had grey hair and in this stifling heat did not break a sweat.

She looked not at all like anyone's idea of a librarian. Mrs. Lord's husband had died long ago. He'd been the mayor's lawyer and the library job was said to be a political plum. Nobody had ever seen her read a book.

She indicated the room and its shelves crammed with volumes. "These need to be weeded out: damaged books, duplicates, things not read in twenty years, must go. Charles will show you what to do.

"He suggested you as his assistant on this project. I've seen you about and you seem a good worker. Do you plan on going to college?"

"Yes, ma'am."

She looked me in the eye. "Keep to that plan. For boys of a certain kind libraries become a trap. They lose their ambition, fall in with the wrong companions and fail to grow up."

She nodded her head in the direction of the Sorting Room. "I loathe accusations with no proof. But if someone is accused too often I must act. Understand?"

A chill ran through me. I'd been reported. "Yes, ma'am."

We heard Charlie returning. "Very good. This should take you today and tomorrow." She walked past Charlie with barely a nod.

He asked, "Did she talk to you?" I hung my head.

"I guess so." He sounded amused. "And did she tell you to go on to college—like I didn't?"

I nodded, glad to change the subject. "Why didn't you?"

"I found other things. Like Larry." I thought that over. He showed me how to make out a discard ticket, stuck it in a book and put the book on a truck.

It was hot and stuffy and there were thousands of books. He took off his shirt. "Better do this," he said. "Otherwise it'll be a stinking mess at the end of the day." He had body hair and was better built than I would have guessed.

Everyone wanted to get my clothes off me. I made a face. "I'll turn my back," he said and did. We worked on opposite sides of the room. I looked at him each time I put a book on my truck.

I had almost no body hair but I had somewhat of a tan from sunbathing and the beach. His skin was white. I started to sweat and took my shirt off.

We both turned to put books on a truck at the same time and I asked. "Why do you call him Lauren?"

He said, "I'll have to show you. Bring your boyfriend by. I'll give you the address."

Hearing Ty called my boyfriend made me feel exposed. I covered my chest with my arms like I was cold. But after a while I asked, "Why is Red Death the way he is, scary and everything?"

"When you're a queer kid and everyone hates you for stuff you can't help, you can either die or make them afraid."

Somehow being shirtless and our not looking directly at each other made it easier for me to talk. Charlie told me how Larry, his boyfriend, sang at the Sugar Bowl and how the bar's management paid off the cops.

I talked about guys who gave me money, the first time I ever told anybody. It made me feel less alone. I wished Charlie had been my big brother or older cousin or something.

At the end of the day the job was more than half done. We washed up in the restroom and got dressed. Charlie said, "I meant it about you and Ty visiting us."

Thursday

Had the routine of our life at this place been known to the world, we should have been regarded as madmen...

I'd read "The Murders in the Rue Morgue" before I saw Charlie and Larry/Lauren's apartment and not thought much about it. After being there, I realized the story wasn't about murder, detection, Paris and weird apes, it was about two strange men living together.

Charlie and Larry even blotted out the sunlight like Poe's narrator and the French detective had.

Made a counterfeit night until the real thing came along.

Then we sallied forth into the streets, arm and arm, continuing the topics of the day or roaming far and wide until a late hour...

Charlie and Larry lived on a shabby street near the Back Bay. Their place had drawings up on the walls of naked guys with their dicks displayed, and clothes piled on the chairs and the half-made bed. On a bookshelf was a row of wigs on stands.

Larry wore a dressing gown and selected a wig. He'd just washed his hair and I guessed he was being Lauren right then. He and she changed back and forth.

Lauren started singing "Right from the Very Start," like some night club singer. But my two musical beacons at the moment were Sam Cooke for his voice and his smile and Beethoven for the heart-thumping rhythm, so I was a little removed.

"I'm in a bad mood," Lauren said. "I need some happiness pills if I'm to perform Saturday."

Looking at Ty she said, "And I'll bet you know how to make that magic happen."

Ty smiled like he knew how.

I'd thought Larry/Lauren was going to wear the wig. Instead he leaned forward and put it on my head. It was so sudden I didn't know what had happened. Charlie stared and smiled. I put up my hands to take it off.

Larry grabbed them and was stronger than I'd imagined. "Stand up and take a look," he said.

Ty with a half grin nodded that I should do this. Charlie opened a closet door and revealed a full-length mirror. In it I saw a figure wearing my clothes. But the face framed with blond hair and looking out at me was a young girl's.

I took the wig off and no one stopped me. The kid in the mirror became a crewcut boy. But I couldn't stop seeing the girl.

It was as if Ty couldn't either. Outside, he kept looking at me like he'd never seen me before. I had to get home, was already late. We walked through the Common and when we got to the subway he said, "Meet me here, tomorrow at six. We got some business to do." He'd agreed to cop speed for Larry/Lauren. I waved, watched him turn and walk away.

A line kept popping into my head.

"Have I not indeed been living in a dream?"

I needed to sit down and read and think. I'd found out the library was Usher, discovered a book that could beat like a buried heart, a crazed queen who was Red Death, Montresor's Vault in Boston, and Charlie and Larry in the Rue Morgue.

Now I'd found Ty and me in a Poe story.

That evening, after Charlie and I finished working in the cellar, before going to his and Larry's place, I'd started to read "William Wilson." It's a story about a man haunted by his double. The difference was Wilson hates his double. I had a crush on mine so big it frightened me.

I thought about that as I walked from the subway station, thought how Ty was part of a world I could never show my family.

Friday

In the back of French class in summer school, on my breaks at work, I reread "William Wilson." I stood with the narrator as he looked down on his sleeping double: *"The same name! the same contour of person! the same day of arrival at the academy!"* And wondered why Wilson wanted to kill him.

At six p.m. I came out the library doors and there he was. "Hey, thought maybe you'd be wearing a dress."

"No," I said, "Just pants and no shorts the same as you."

Ty was amused. "The Collector's gonna be sad."

I'd just been paid so we got something to eat and he said over burgers and cokes, "I need you to front me ten bucks for dexies that Lauren wants. You'll get it back."

Ten dollars was a big deal in those days and would be a big chunk of the paycheck I was saving to go to college. But because it was him and because it was speed, I did it. We went to some place near Washington Street.

It was this narrow old building with kind of rickety stairs. This guy up on the third floor, real thin with intense, staring eyes, let us in.

Ralph was his name and I noticed he called Ty "Ted." "Who's this, your cousin?" he asked and looked again. "A brother?"

The place was kind of empty, a table and chairs and a bed in the next room. Not much else except that completely filling one window was this great big ancient iron birdcage with all these little sparrows chirping away inside. They had birdseed and a nest and everything.

The cage rested on the windowsill and the window was open but the cage blocked birds from flying into the room. There was this little round hole on the outer side and as I watched a sparrow flew in. They were all chattering and I saw eggs in the nest.

Ralph saw me looking at this and said, "I spend hours watching them." His voice sounded creaky like he needed to be oiled or something.

It took them a little while negotiating, but Ty (or Ted) got twenty pills for ten dollars. As that was happening, this seagull appeared in the sunset light, floated in front of the cage not able to get in.

"I had a hawk outside a couple of weeks ago. My birds all went crazy," Ralph said from behind me. All of a sudden there was one hand on the back of my neck then down my back, another touching my ass.

I jumped out of the way because you didn't let guys do that. "You should come by and watch the birds," Ralph said.

Ty told me when we were back outside, "He's talking about seeing a hawk and he's a chicken hawk! He goes for you, he'll give you speed. But the thing is you gotta go down on him. Of course, then we could sell the pills."

He gave me a couple of dexies. I put them in a pocket. Speed was better than booze, undetectable by parents. They thought I was just in a good mood when I took it. It even made it easier to study. I'd have taken it all the time if I could.

"Is Ty your real name?" I asked.

"Sure," he said and I wondered if that was true.

I took one of the pills. The other I saved for Saturday. On the train home which became this intense ride with blazing subway lights, I reread the story. The narrator wondered about his own alter ego.

Who is he?—whence came he?—and what are his objects?

I wondered the same stuff about the kid who obsessed me. That night at home there was a baby sitter who was an old family friend. She wasn't going to report me for showing up late and didn't think I needed to get told to go to bed like my brothers and sisters.

When my parents returned I pretended to be asleep. When all was quiet I looked again at the end of "William Wilson" where the narrator thinks he's killing his doppelganger but actually kills himself.

"You have conquered, and I yield...see by this image which is thine own, how utterly thou has murdered thyself," said the bleeding double in the mirror. And I fell into the kind of red-tinged doze that passes for sleep with speed.

Saturday

Saturday was a day off from school, from the library. I was awake and alert and busy convincing my parents that I was going to a Boston Pops concert on the Esplanade (they were playing Beethoven's Seventh—I'd checked that out in the *Globe*) with school friends and said I'd be back before twelve.

My parents were so busy wanting me back before ten that they didn't even remember I had no school friends.

That evening I wore my best tight black chinos, my blue polo shirt with matching blue socks and dress-up loafers with taps on the heels. I took the second pill before I got on the subway.

Ty was late and I stood for a while in the evening light on Park Street with crowds walking by, guys noticing me. Dexedrine made me good at spotting that.

When I saw Ty he was on the other side of the street and I knew he'd been watching me. When he crossed, he said, "Decided to go as a guy, huh?" But I was getting tired of being reminded of how I'd worn a wig for two minutes.

Like magic, Dexies let me take long remote looks into others. The opposite of William Wilson, I stared at my double and saw ways he wasn't me. Caught the furtive look of a stray and how it seemed like maybe he'd slept in his clothes.

When we stopped so he could get something to eat, I asked for another pill and he was very reluctant. "I gotta save these for Lauren. We need to go back to the Hawk tomorrow and you need to be nice to him."

He was looking for my reaction and I knew he thought I was as queer as Larry and Red Death. And that I'd go down for dexies.

Then it was after dark and we were headed for the Sugar Bowl. I'd never been in a bar, let alone a queer one.

"I don't think we can get in."

"They'll let us in but they won't serve us," he said. "Don't worry. They'll want to see you."

As we approached, I saw guys walk down the street and suddenly turn toward the dark windows and door. A big man with a bald head stood inside the doorway. He shook his head when he saw us.

Ty told him, "Lauren said we should see her." The guy turned and shouted something. Charlie appeared, smiled at the sight of us, nodded and the guy waved us past.

It was bigger inside than I'd thought, a long bar with dim lights behind it, a jukebox playing Sinatra, some tables, a low platform at the back with a mike and a piano.

Walking behind Charlie and Ty, I felt eyes on me like every guy in the place was staring at me. I couldn't raise my eyes to look back at them.

"I said they'd like you," Ty told me.

In the back room Lauren wore the gold wig. She had big breasts and wore a red sparkling dress and gold high heels.

"I need an empty stomach to do drag," she said in a hoarse, sexy voice to a guy who turned out to be the pianist. "It is most trying. Drink just makes me dizzy. But these cherubs have brought me relief."

She went into the bathroom with Ty. Charlie put his arm around me, gave me a hug, "So glad to see you." He took me back outside. On the jukebox a woman sang "The Man That Got Away" and guys sang along.

"Friendlier than the library," Charlie said. He brought me a beer and I knew it would be on my breath unless I chewed a lot of gum but I used it to wash down the pill. This made my blood pulse and the lights brighten to pinpoints. Someone pinched my ass.

"Don't worry about it," Charlie said. "It's time you got to see all this!" Time and Space began to slip. And when Ty came back, I thought it was me sitting down. He handed me a couple of bucks and, "One last pill. We need to see the Hawk tomorrow."

"You said you'd return my money when she paid you."

He looked like he couldn't hear me. Then he handed me another dollar and said, "This is all I got." I didn't want to think of what lay in store for me at home.

The place filled up. At some point the jukebox went off and the pianist sat on stage playing.

Lauren came out and there was applause, some whistling. She started singing "Right from the Very Start" again. Charlie looked at her like he was in a dream.

"So many men here I'd *love* to start with!" Lauren said when she finished, and a couple of guys stamped and cheered. I drank the rest of the beer and washed down the pill. She sang "Moaning Low" in this weird woman's voice.

The room rotated around me. All I could see were guys' faces in the dark. Charlie had disappeared so I moved close to Ty. But he was so busy pretending not to see a guy in a suit who was staring at him that he didn't see me either.

Finally, between songs I told him, "Let's get out." And he ignored me.

My mind raced and it seemed everyone in the place was staring at us. I realized I was chanting under my breath, "Want to get out; want to get out." But somehow I couldn't leave without Ty.

Lauren was ending her act, singing pieces of songs one after another. "Dear Marlene," she'd say, and sing "See What the Boys in the Back Room Will Have." Then it was "my older sister Bette Davis," and some other song.

Right in the middle of the applause, I heard something cold and scary outside. Sirens, shouting. "*Raid!*" someone yelled and then someone else.

Charlie jumped up on stage and escorted Lauren off and into the back room. Ty moved fast. I was right behind him. We ran across the platform and into a corridor. The bathroom was on one side, the dressing room on the other.

Lauren was tearing off her dress and wig. Charlie handed her Larry's pants and shirt. A back door was open, light came in, people were pushing me from behind, someone spilled beer on my clothes, someone else shoved me aside. Cop voices were yelling and someone was screaming back in the bar.

Ty yanked me through the door. We were in an alley, light came from the street and noise, police radios. He grabbed my arm, tried to hand me a few pills. "They won't search you," he said. I didn't take them.

Then the cops were there. One of them in plain clothes had Ty by the front of his shirt and smacked him up against a wall, asked his name and address.

Another had me, a uniformed cop. "What's your name? How old are you? What were you doing in there?"

I gave my name and age and said, "Just looking. I didn't know." My cop slapped me so hard across the face that my head spun. I tasted blood in my mouth.

I heard Ty give his name as Timothy Connors. The cop who had him was holding the pills he'd tried to palm off on me and yelling, "*Where did you get these?*"

When Ty just shook his head he got punched in the stomach. He doubled over. "A guy," he said. "What guy? Where?"

The cop who held me went through my pockets, found the book and tossed it away. Took out my wallet, used his knee in my stomach to hold me still and looked at my name and address. I got the wallet back.

"I'm running you in," he said.

"Please no." I started to cry. "My uncle's a cop," I said and gave his name and precinct and my aunt's name when he asked for that to make sure.

Larry, half naked, and Charlie in handcuffs were shoved down the alley to the street. Ty was in cuffs too. "You're going to Juvie," the cop who held him said.

"You know that one?" the cop holding me asked. I shook my head and he slapped me again and hauled me down the alley.

On the street outside the Sugar Bowl, the cop cars had their lights and sirens on and there were lights on the top of a truck. Photographers from the papers were there and a television crew.

They all caught Larry's face smeared with make-up. Charlie leaned over and kissed him. Ty was shoved in the back seat of a squad car. His eyes glistened with tears and his jaw was clenched. It was like I saw myself get arrested.

My nose was bleeding. I thought I was joining them in the light and that my life was over. But the cop said, "I'll tell your uncle about this and let him decide what he wants to do," and pushed me into the dark. "Run," he said.

Sunday

I moved as fast as I could, ran through the streets, guessing I'd never see Ty or Charlie again. Way after midnight I got the last subway train to Dorchester. People stared at my bloody nose and red eyes and torn shirt, smelled the stink of beer on me. Home was the last place I wanted to go but the only place left for me to go.

I felt the book in my back pocket and was too strung out to be surprised. I remembered a line.

"I was sick, sick unto death, with that long agony..."

The first story I'd read in the Poe book was "The Pit and Pendulum." Memories of the dark, the rats, the bottomless pit, the blade swinging ever closer had held me. That, I now realized, in the horrible clarity of a speed crash, was my special tale.

My picture wouldn't be in the paper or on television but the story would be everywhere. Would my parents, once they'd seen me, draw the obvious conclusion? Would the cop contact my uncle? Poe's Inquisition seemed like nothing compared to what was in store for me, the humiliations and ass whipping I'd suffer, the rights I'd lose.

Like prophecy, I knew there'd be no more Charlie to talk to and protect me at the library. No more Ty waiting for me. My first adult friend and my first love both wiped out.

Off the train, walking through the sleeping neighborhood, I tossed the book in a trash can. I wanted to lie down in the street and let a car run over me. But I knew I wouldn't.

In the story, at the last moment the French army storms the prison and saves the narrator. *"An outstretched arm caught my own."*

Nothing like that was going to happen for me. My parents would make me do whatever they wanted. I turned the corner onto my street and saw the lights still on at home. I felt the book pulsing in my back pocket as I went to meet my fate.

proem: how to read gay pulp fiction
james gifford

How can I take this book seriously?

After spending so much of my academic career in ferreting out gay texts of the past, looking for coded references to homosexuality in books that have long been forgotten, why am I even looking at a yellowing and brittle paperback from the 1960s called *Idylls of the Queens*? Such texts are disposable, I thought, the remnant of an era that trashed gay sensibilities by reducing them to the salacious writing that you'd find on a Forty-Second Street newsstand kiosk. And even if one *did* hide copies of the Marquis de Sade and *The Pearl* at the back of one's bookshelf—well, those are *old*. Are these relatively recent pulps really worth my time? How could they be? They could not say anything to me.

I was wrong.

The more I read in *Idylls of the Queens*, which is a 1968 Greenleaf Classics anthology of fifteen short stories by one "Charles Branch" (clearly a nom de plume[1]), the more I realized that something quite different is going on from what I had expected. And I should've known better.

Thanks to graduate school I am familiar with Steven Marcus's *The Other Victorians*, a study of nineteenth century pornography, not to mention Janice Radway's *Reading the Romance*, a close look at the phenomenon of the Harlequin bodice-ripping paperback that shows no sign of aging after decades of jaw-dropping sales. Both analyses dignify the bluest and trashiest (I thought) of genres by recognizing their success—for they were successful productions—as psychological and sociological if not exactly proper literary phenomena. So I took pause. Was I really labeling 1960s gay pulp as sub-literary because I had become an academic prig? I know all about canonicity, and the process of glorification of some works as good, over others, is really at heart a subjective thing. My own research involves the recovery of early American gay-inflected writing, so what right have I to canonize *those* texts as sacred and dismiss a very successful strain of gay writing—namely, pulp fiction—that was active from the 1940s well past the 1980s? After all, any Greenleaf title had easily outsold the meager five hundred copies of Edward Prime-Stevenson's *Imre: A Memorandum* (1906), which I idolize as the first great American gay novel. Both productions had their readership; and the story of American gay writing is far from complete.

Not to mention my own knowledge.

Back to *Idylls of the Queens*. The stories read easily and are mostly Westerns, with an occasional military-themed one. What brought my guard down and struck me at once, though, is that each story is far from the lascivious and oversexed text I had expected. In fact, all are instead optimistic, "proper," and even romantic. Two men meet, usually thrown together by the most arbitrary of circumstances, fall in love, forge a bond, and plan on staying together. When the cowboys in particular fall in love, the bond is often referred to as "marrying up," a term which reverberates to a reader in 2012 who has just married his life partner after a surprising marriage-equality victory in New York State. But more than that, it is the *tone* of these stories that proved an eye-opener.

Usually Branch's heroes find themselves adrift, to put it kindly, isolated as the stories begin in some kind of nowhere state, whether on a ranch or a road or even in a jail cell, and though often ambitious, set to live life woodenly. They are men in their mid-thirties who are stoically trying to deal with the hardships of life. Until love steps in. And that's *love*, by the way, not lust.

Imre was significant in its own day as the first known American novel where two men end up happily together; but by the 1960s it seems that there were dozens of homosexual novels where the same Hollywood ending was a given. Both Edward Prime-Stevenson and E.M. Forster, writing in the closet in the early twentieth century, foresaw an age when such unions would be acceptable, and these gay pulps from decades later seem a fulfillment of sorts. It is difficult for modern readers to imagine there was a time in gay literary history when the (rare) appearance of gay characters automatically assumed unhappiness and psychopathology, if not an unhappy ending, as the norm for them. Suicide or rejection or disgrace was usually their lot. Such is the example in *A Marriage below Zero* by "Alan Dale" (1889). Even when the gay relationship seems relatively stable and happy, the structural and cultural demands of the day insisted that two men could not stay together at the story's conclusion, as in Bayard Taylor's *Joseph and His Friend*, 1870, and Frederick W. Loring's *Two College Friends*, 1871. Indeed, after *Imre* up until the period after World War II, American novels with gay characters (excepting perhaps Henry Blake Fuller's ambiguous *Bertram Cope's Year*, 1919, and Forman Brown's roman à clef *Better Angel*, 1933, by "Richard Meeker") simply did not conclude with their heroes safely and happily in each other's arms.[2]

But the paperback boom that began in earnest during that war proved a boom for gay writers as well. Michael Bronski and Drewey Wayne Gunn have mapped out the terrain,[3] and the many gay pulp titles that started appearing with greater and greater frequency seem to attest to the fact that not only were there more working gay authors on the scene than ever before, but also many more gay readers. David Leavitt and Mark Mitchell's anthologies have testified that early gay texts were oftentimes "passed hand to hand," from one gay reader to another.[4] Prime-Stevenson's writings, under the pseudonym of Xavier Mayne, were personally distributed to friends and acquaintances or sold only at "particular" bookstores in large European cities and even in New York. How remarkable, then, is the leap within decades of finding gay books mixed in with heterosexual racy titles at practically any newsstand, and all this before the great demarcation of Stonewall. While gay historians continue their focus on authors such as Fuller and Carl Van Vechten and Hart Crane as they hopscotch their way along the great irregular arc of American gay writing, where each title seems a distinctive and isolated breakthrough in gay publishing, it now seems clear that there were many more titles available after World War II, and widely so. Had I been sleeping not to realize that these pulps were a major and under-appreciated part of this trend? Throughout the second half of the twentieth century gay fiction transmuted itself, and production snowballed. While the irregular appearance of gay characters and titles during the 1920s and 1930s tentatively showed their faces without any seeming reference to one another, the arrival of gay pulp fiction was explosive.

Yes, the authors of pulps were as anonymous as the writers of *Imre* and *A Marriage below Zero* and Claude Hartland's *The Story of a Life* (1901); and yes, paperbacks were surprisingly as guarded a format in some ways as earlier books being published abroad or privately or via a medical press. Once purchased, covers of paperbacks could easily be ripped off and titles stowed anonymously in coat pockets and under book piles. But more than the format, something else was going on in the type of fiction that was being written. Very gradually there was a shift in the style of gay writing as well. Certainly many of these pulps bear lurid titles (*Man into Boy* and *Faggots to Burn!*) and include melodramatic plots, but others, such as the *Idylls* I was holding in my hand, are full of everyday people and everyday situations—only, the heroes are gay. Instead of the odd, idiosyncratic, even pathological gay people that characterized such widely heralded novels as *The Fall of Valor* (1946) and *The City and the Pillar* (1948), pulps tended to show gay people more like people you would be apt to run into on the street, anywhere.

And they were being sold for the most part in the open air! For even if they were relegated to kiosks in the adult section, such newsstands existed practically everywhere.

I continued *Idylls* with a new appreciation. Different thoughts kept occurring to me as I read. There is more than a little self-conscious hokeyness in the men's Western patois (one story is called "Pancakes and Pulkrytood"), and sometimes the language is curiously quaint ("Chick Sale" meaning "outhouse," for example). But there are many literary references as well. Isn't that Alfred Lord Tennyson being lampooned in the book's title, after all? One story called "Disinherited" begins with a sonnet that the hero has written, no less, and later on the muscly military policeman quotes poet A.E. Housman. The stories are peppered with references to *Sturm und Drang* and Praxiteles, but author Carl Branch apparently saw no anomaly even where characters often speak with an uneducated twang. Such references would seem to be accessible only to college-educated readers, which suggests he was writing for a broad audience.

Remarkably, these stories have a strong morality attached to them. Branch misses no chance to allow his characters a chance to lecture on not losing hope, the dangers of sexual repression, and the difference between love and lust (love "is a grim dedication, a demanding hunger which is seldom fed": "When you love someone you want to do something for *him*. When you're *in* love with them, you want them to do things for *you* too"⁵). His lovers don't bed each other until there's a promise of fidelity. (And this in a pulp!) Branch shows us an interracial gay relationship in "Fallen Sparrow," where a black nurse is berated by a white patient for his constant self-belittling racial comments. "Us minorities. We must stick together!" he says.⁶ I occasionally winced at the obviousness of Branch's frequent use of symbolism. Several stories take place near foothills called the Superstitions. The hero in "The Quest" has a large red itching spot on his chest that keeps growing, and it won't go away until he declares the truth about his love for another man (the one place in the collection where Branch avoids strict realism). The eponymous hero in "Kissing Bug," in the simplicity of his country background, grows up kissing every boy and man he meets, and his straight neighbors accept it as part of his personality. As I read story after story, another prejudice fell by the wayside: that the heroes (and readers!) of pulps must've been uneducated and sleazy themselves.

The collection reveals that Branch felt under some compunction to stay true to a formula as Harlequin romances do, even if each tale has a plot quite distinct from its brothers. The author's writing often is witty, and if the tales follow an obvious formula, Branch never hesitates to create characters that are psychologically consistent and credible. The final pair of stories in *Queens* is a *coup de maître* in that they tell the same story but from the opposing sides of the two lovers. Always, the emphasis is on *romance*, not sex—something else that surprised me. Also astonishing in the pairing of these same-sex couples is the heavy suggestion of Fate, for in this book, men do not meet each other when they are on the hunt in gay bars or haunts. The idea is rather that partners find each other by Fate, willy-nilly. In this, Branch hearkens way back to *Joseph and His Friend*, where the two heroes meet each other accidentally and form an almost-immediate bond. Love at first sight is hardly remarkable, but the emphasis is decidedly on believable events to track the chance meeting of the two people, though there is occasionally just enough of fantasy in them to be titillating. A doctor's car runs into trouble on a lonely road in the middle of the night, where he is rescued by a handsome wrangler on a horse in "Line Shack." In "The Need" two men share a foxhole and fall in love. A man newly out of jail spends the night at a Catholic monastery

("Jail Bird"). A drug user finds sympathy from the orderly who helps him through a night of detoxing in a hospital ("Fallen Sparrow"). The message infallibly is: hang in there—you will meet someone yet. And out of nowhere the Right Person steps in. Although several of these couples are forthright in declaring their attraction, there are a few pining over undeclared love. But true to the formula he writes by, Branch concludes each story with the heroes leaping into bed together. Interestingly enough, however, they don't get there until they plight their troth. For example:

"Say what you mean, Ard," said Tom softly.
"I mean, I love you! I have from that first day when you took me in and said, 'You are very welcome here!'"
"And I loved you from that moment. I left my vocation for you, and I've waited so long...so long...for you to tell me!"
"Then come here, Red Wolf, and let us devour each other!"[7]

Also surprising is that none of the gay men evinces any stereotypes. They are for the most part straightforward about who they are, seeing themselves as part of the spectrum of human nature, the way God created them. Most often the straight people around them accept them that way too. There are supportive parents, friends, a friendly postman, even Granny in "The Quest"! Further, there are no derogatory terms to describe being gay. No flouncing or bouncing or mincing in this book, though the cover art may reveal effeminate eyes or poses.[8] Instead, the author uses masculine prototypes—the cowboy and the military man and the farmer as his gay heroes. (It reminds me of Prime-Stevenson's insistence that his hero Imre be an outstanding soldier.) These bastions of virility are war heroes, marines, cattle farmers, salt-of-the-earth types. Many long to start a spread and create a home for themselves, to settle down ideally with a partner. The World War II vet appears so many times in these stories that clearly the author had an especial empathy for them, for their sense of isolation and their longing to connect. In 1968 veterans were the perfect image of men who had been badly used and shown the worst that humanity can inflict on each other. They become the ideal types who long to love men, not fight them. It is interesting that in the midst of the Vietnamese War, Branch could create sympathetic and manly heroes out of military men.

And though there are some unsavory situations in the collection (a military lighthouse keeper who sexually traps the men assigned to him, a sailor who tries to kill himself), the most remarkable attribute of the majority of the gay men we meet is a sense of their kindness. The story "Disinherited" traces the nightly rounds of a tough but compassionate MP as he searches through a single night for down-and-out and victimized sailors, only to wind up falling in love with the would-be suicide he's saved. Instead of bringing the book down on men often victimized by their own naïveté, the macho MP is kind and helping, non-condemnatory, anxious to salvage bad situations and restore to the luckless their dignity and sense of self-worth. "South Forty" features a gay couple who nurse a cattle rustler back to health, and find him a partner and a new life in the process. It's actually rather touching. A sense of brotherhood pervades *Idylls*. Men kid each other, watch out for each other, keep their eyes open for possible partners for their friends. One cowboy readily suggests that the hero meet a pal of his, a good friend with whom he'll likely get along. When a Marine stumbles on two soldiers arm-in-arm out on duty, he shrugs, "Well God Bless! Glad someone has found something in this screwy war!"[9] Another story features a father who unwittingly (or not) becomes the means to his son and another man getting together.

Am I making too much of this one book, chosen pretty much at random? How could *Idylls of the Queens* be representative among so many gay pulps? Is it just the English teacher in me typically over-analyzing?

I think not.

From what I know of the literary past, gay authors have had a history of co-opting what genres they can, in hopes of getting their voices on record. Homosexuals grabbed at the case-history format early on, for instance, to tell their stories (*The Story of a Life*, *Imre*), because the age of dynamic psychology gave them access to a new literary structure. Westerns too with their all-male cast of characters were easy venues to express male-male feelings (Theodore Winthrop's *John Brent*, 1861; Owen Wister's *The Virginian*, 1902). Belles-lettres, always written with specific and limited audiences in mind, could be co-opted too, Fuller's *Bertram Cope's Year* (1919) being an example. With the mass marketing of paperbacks, how quickly gay writers assimilated *that* medium. If mainstream publishers were only gradually beginning to accept homosexuality in novels (and then grudgingly and often with restrictions), why not use the freer medium of the paperback original? Were some pulp novels pornographic? Of course. But *Idylls of the Queens* shows that at least some authors used the platform as a way to romanticize, even normalize, gay feelings. The positive portrayal of same-sex relationships was stunning to me in this 1968 collection. Idylls exhibits all the happy endings that Forster and Prime-Stevenson had only dreamed about. And I had picked this book at random.

If I were to pick a gay literary production from the past that is closest in tone and spirit to *Idylls of the Queens*, it would be Charles Warren Stoddard's *South Sea Idyls* (1874), and not just because of the title. In that collection of homoerotic tales, most of the stories feature the loving relationships of Stoddard himself with a number of native boys he encountered on his travels through Pacific islands. Their time together is always brief and edenic. But they all end unhappily, with the ever-fickle author taking his leave of the heart-broken boys. Although Stoddard had to be circumspect about specifics, readers in the know clearly understood what kind of love he was really talking about. The joyous freedom of the island culture and the laissez-faire attitude toward sex they represented fit Stoddard perfectly. Years later, Charles Branch writes in a similarly joyful fashion, with an open and liberated attitude toward sex—except that his lovers bond for life. The jump from *Idyls* to *Idylls* is ninety-four years: it's an eon when you're talking about American gay literature.

I always thought that the number of gay-themed books before Stonewall was provocatively and annoyingly small, each one like a rare jewel set in a crown. Now I realize that some pulps of post mid-century America shone like glitter around such "canonical" titles. Indeed, many of these pulps may be jewels themselves. Am I saying that *Idylls of the Queens* is great literature? I am not sure. But are it and its brothers worth investigating? The answer is definitely yes.

Because pulps are often sexually explicit, and since that is the impression that enters one's head even at hearing the word "pulp," I thought I would be remiss (having lost my pulp virginity, so to speak) if I didn't take a look at an example as part of my self-introduction to gay pulp fiction. Obviously such pulps were written with both provocative as well as money-making aims in mind. But were such pulps, as gay authors handled them, merely pornographic or were they genuine erotica? I am not sure the line of demarcation is clear, or even if there is one. But I assume erotica has a more literary bent, handling sexual formulas cleverly, and maybe even including ideas, themes, and purposes as any literature might. Could there be any redeeming features if an author tells a salacious tale?

I picked up *The Fag End* by Dick Dale, 1969, also a Greenleaf production.[10] The author's name is too good not to be a pseudonym, and the title is an obvious pun. If, as I have heard, some authors had to submit to publishers' adding sex to their already-formulated tales, Mr. Dale's writing did not seem to have been submitted to such editorial intrusion. The book was pretty nonstop when it came to sexual action: explicit scenes did not look like mere decoration layered onto a pre-determined story. In fact, the more I read, the more I, surprisingly, felt that sex was integral to the plot.

Briefly, the story revolves around two mid-teen boys, Jim and Tommy, who meet each other "by Fate" and gradually develop strong feelings for each other. They attend a Sunday School camping trip overseen by Reverend Leonard Smith, who is an amalgamation of all one's worst fears about the ministry. Sex-obsessed and a pederast to boot, Smith resembles Robert Mitchum's Reverend Powell in *The Night of the Hunter* (1955) with his evil focus on two children, but he more anticipates the clichéd and sex-riddled Reverend Peter Shayne played by Tony Perkins in *Crimes of Passion* (1984). Dale shows us (in detail) just about every character's sexual initiation; but Jim's, at the hands of a muscle-bound stevedore, is the only one with a saving grace. The older man is careful not to abuse the boy, though Jim clearly wants more. Smith's initiation, in a flashback to years before, is not so happy, however, as his partner turns on him when it's over. Thereafter, we are to understand, Smith longs for reciprocal and loving feelings with a partner, something he is unable to find, though he looks hard enough and even fathers children. This rejection turns him into an evil man who eventually turns to boys as sexual objects as a way to find an experience that will make up for his first loss. Young Frankie, his son, complicates matters, as both he and his father focus on Jim as their object of desire. But Jim faces the reverend down in the book's strongest scene, and the story closes with Jim and Tommy finding romance with each other, and the reverend somehow at peace with his demons.

I have probably dignified this story a bit more than it deserves. The book is full of typos and misprints, as though it were a rush job, whether by author or printer. The story's heavy insistence on sex, however, does not disguise some deeper ideas. As a cautionary tale, *Fag End* certainly delivers. For all its insistence on portraying teenage sex, the reverend is a loathsome figure, obsessively caught up with his own devils, subverting religion into an unholy dominance over any boys he can. Pederasty is certainly not shown as admirable in this book, and in fact Smith suffers greatly for his predilection, which, it is suggested, was a conscious choice on his part. Dale's rationale for Smith's behavior is weak at best, but there is no denying that the book's examination of his psychopathology is eerily fascinating. Although the purple prose might repel some readers, the progress of events keeps one turning pages. (Or at least I did.) In that sense the book sidesteps a charge of pornography, wherein to my mind plots are merely decorative devices. Still, *The Fag End* is certainly no *Tom Jones*.

Though explicit, the description of burgeoning sexual feelings seems truthfully portrayed, and in its way Dale's book captures the sexual struggles and desires and feelings of some aspects of growing up gay. If Mark Twain had been truthful enough, some of this material might have easily been put into *Huckleberry Finn*. Though we may all have such sexual thoughts, it is easy enough to contemn an author who dares to set them down. I sidestepped the sex to try to find similarities between this book and *Idylls of the Queens*, for there are echoes. For one thing, there is a strong element of Fate in the meeting of the two friends. They find each other and are immediately and inexplicably drawn to one another. They overcome obstacles and stand up for each other. And by the story's end they are in each other's arms. Oddly, there is a strong emphasis on kindness and thinking about the other person in both books. But the mere thought of sexual feelings in those not of legal age, not to mention the pederast's, could be a sufficient turn-off for many readers. It is almost as though the author has incongruously chosen some of the diciest material he could in order to tell a moral tale. For the predator villain is punished (perhaps cured), and the two boys learn that their love and respect for each other trump every other temptation, that *sex and love go together*. That is perhaps the most surprising thing I take away from *The Fag End*.

Bizarrely, minus the overt sexuality, the tale reminds me of Edward Prime-Stevenson's early boy's book *Left to Themselves* (1891). In that work, which the author himself later admitted (in *The Intersexes*, 1909) couched homoerotic undertones, we see two boys of the same age as Jim and Tommy as they meet, become friends, go through a series of adventures, and wind up in each other's company for life. Indeed, when a tramp attacks the younger boy, the older bravely steps in to save him just as Jim confronts the reverend. Both stories have as their focus the relationship between two boys and how they learn to care for and assume responsibility for one another. That also seems to be the backbone of *The Fag End*.

So I leave Dale's book with a confusion of feelings. The sexual explicitness is strong, but weirdly enough the moral message is equally strong. The material is not always attractive, but by book's end there seems to be a *point* (besides titillation) to it. Pederasty is distasteful to most people, especially in an age where the Catholic clergy seem to be daily fighting such charges in the news, but we have to admit that pederasts exist. Whether they deserve pity or prosecution, the condition is part of the human spectrum. If, as I believe, the author of *The Fag End* has scruples embedded in his tale, only the individual reader can decide whether they redeem the scurrilous prose that conveys the story.

It is impossible for me to contextualize gay pulp erotica within the tradition of erotica in general, although that would be an interesting undertaking. Steven Marcus years ago remarked that he had discovered very little gay pornography in his look at the Victorian era. Whatever was there was folded into generally heterosexual stories. When did American gay literary porn make its first appearance? What was the first pulp to provide gay sex-specific scenes? If *The Fag End* is typical of that tradition, is it fair to say that gay erotica has a moral backbone to it that erotica in general does not have? Does such intended lewdness represent another step in the history of American gay writing? Or are such productions better studied by a psychologist rather than a literary critic?

The sheer number of volumes from Greenleaf Classics and like presses says something. Clearly there was an audience, and the public availability of such works seems startling in retrospect to one who thinks of the 1950s and 1960s in terms of the television sitcom *Happy Days*. *Idylls*, *The Fag End*, and other pulp titles were right out in plain sight at newsstands. I can remember seeing them! Suddenly, it occurs to me how much easier it was for gay men of that time to find out about homosexuality than it was for earlier generations, who had to hunt for subterranean and medical texts, for brief mentions in novels like *David Copperfield* or books of poetry.

To think of such novels for sale in Dubuque and Oklahoma City! For such pulps were available pretty much everywhere apparently. Such new connectivity among gay readers is astounding to consider.

At least some of the pulp books that I had despised (or worse, thought nothing of) were in reality the fodder for Stonewall, nothing less. These books added to a consciousness that homosexuality was as wide-spread a phenomenon as the 1948 Kinsey Report had suggested. Further, gay men could see themselves represented happily and (yes) lustily and not alone and still basically moral; and how could that not add up to a sense of strength in numbers and self-esteem? The queens who fought back at the Stonewall Inn in 1969 were brave, to be sure, but in many ways they were standing on the shoulders of the pulp writers who had preceded them. These pioneers were laying the groundwork that helped gay men realize a positive self-image. Their books were loudly proclaiming to their readers that they had the right to love and settle down, an equal entitlement to live and not be ashamed.

And now, having read my first pulp fiction (*and lived!* as a pulp cover might exclaim), maybe I can give a bit of advice to readers who are wondering whether they too should try one. Here are a few tips:

1. *Come at them with an open mind.* Give the book a break. Do not assume that every pulp is a piece of sleaze or an undiscovered masterpiece. Let those presumptions go. Give the book the chance to be a good read. Keep a sense of humor and listen to what the story has to say.

2. *Be conscious that each book is a product of its time.* All books have publication dates. Try to recall what stage of gay life generated the story you're reading. In the present day, where homosexuality is proud to stand up and be counted, remember that your forebears had to be more circuitous about themselves. Keeping gay lives hidden was commonplace, and still is with some people. Try to see how this book reflects that sense or, more likely, struggles against it. Be grateful you do not live then, if nothing else, but do not be patronizing. See where this book is coming from.

3. *That said, do not be surprised if it still has a few things to say to*

the present day. Romance, as the song goes, "is never out of date." The dynamics of finding someone and making him your own never fails to be fascinating. The author of the pulp you're considering may well have a new or clever way of telling an age-old story. Or even something new about yourself. (And unfortunately sexual predators are not likely to go away either.)

4. *A pragmatic note: you may have to spend some money.* Pulps have become collector's items, and some can command quite a hefty price. Or you can sample Michael Bronski's anthology of highlights in his *Pulp Friction* (2003). And I must warn you that this may become a compulsive hobby. (Now that I think of it, why am I urging you to buy the very copies of the works that I will soon be hunting for?)

5. *Above all, enjoy the freedom that this pulp represents and sends down the decades to you.*

And what about me, you may ask. Will I go on and read other pulps?

Let me just say this: Charles Branch, I discovered, also wrote two other Greenleaf titles that I found on the Internet: *A Few of the Boys* and *All Shades of Gay*. They just arrived in the mail today.

Notes

1 David D. Irwin, Executive Director of the Quatrefoil Library has suggested that "Carl Branch" may be a pseudonym for the writer James H. Ramp. See *Gay Bookworm*, 4.6 (Nov. 1989): 4-5: http://www.qlibrary.org/quatrefolios/Quatrefoli01989November.pdf.

2 For examples of multi-author recuperation efforts for pre-World War II American writers, see James Gifford, *Dayneford's Library: American Homosexual Writing, 1900-1913* (Amherst: University of Massachusetts Press, 1995); Devon W. Carbado, Dwight A. McBride, and Donald Weise, eds., *Black Like Us: A Century of Lesbian, Gay and Bisexual African American Fiction* (San Francisco: Cleis, 2002), 1-105; A.B. Christa Schwarz, *Gay Voices of the Harlem Renaissance* (Bloomington: Indiana University Press, 2003); Axel Nissen, ed., *The Romantic Friendship Reader: Love Stories between Men in Victorian America* (Boston: Northeastern University Press, 2003); Gifford, ed., *Glances Backward: An Anthology of American Homosexual Writing, 1830-1920* (Toronto: Broadview Press, 2007); Nissen, *Manly Love: Romantic Friendship in American Fiction* (Chicago: University of Chicago Press, 2009); Christopher Looby, "The Gay Novel in the United States, 1900-1950," *A Companion to the Modern American Novel, 1900-1950*, ed. John T. Matthews (West Sussex: Wiley-Blackwell, 2009), 414-36.

3   See Michael Bronski, ed., *Pulp Friction: Uncovering the Golden Age of Gay Male Pulps* (New York: St. Martin's Griffin, 2003); Drewey Wayne Gunn, *The Gay Male Sleuth in Print and Film: A History and Annotated Bibliography* (Lanham, MD: Scarecrow Press, 2005), and Gunn, ed., *The Golden Age of Gay Fiction* (Albion, NY: MLR Press, 2009).

4 See Mark Mitchell and David Leavitt, eds., *Pages Passed from Hand to Hand: The Hidden Tradition of Homosexual Literature in English from 1748 to 1914* (Boston: Houghton Mifflin, 1997). They also co-edited *The New Penguin Book of Gay Short Stories* (London: Viking, 2003). Mitchell edited *The Penguin Book of International Gay Writing* (New York: Penguin, 1995) with an introduction by Leavitt.

5 Carl Branch, *Idylls of the Queens* (San Diego, CA: Greenleaf Classics, 1968), 46, 89.

6 Ibid., 91.

7 Ibid., 33

8 The cover is reproduced in Gunn, *The Golden Age of Gay Fiction*, 228, and the web site *Gay on the Range*.

9 Branch, *Idylls of the Queens*, 120.

10 Dick Dale, *The Fag End* (San Diego: Greenleaf Classics, 1968). The cover (which has little relationship to the actual novel) is likewise reproduced on the web site Gay on the Range. (In fact, it is another novel by Dale that lends the web site its name.)

jimmy
stefan styrsky

I THOUGHT JIMMY WAS STILL IN JAIL WHEN I MET HIM AGAIN IN THE METRO. For a while it had been my habit to travel at the center of crowds. There's more safety there than along the edges, exposed. I wanted to avoid chance meetings.

Bottlenecks like stairwells and subway platforms were dangerous since none offered easy escape. Too late to duck away when he appeared on the mezzanine at Dupont Circle, I could do nothing but stop and let Jimmy take the last few steps between us.

"Seth, how are you?" Jimmy said, arms wide.

Wind howled through the station ahead of an incoming train, buffeting his sleeveless t-shirt and blowing into my face.

Yelling over the screech of iron wheels, I said, "Fine," afraid to ask "When did you get out?"

Then he hugged me. The eyebrow piercing was gone. His hair was darker too, no longer hay-colored but brown. He had even put on some meat around the chest and shoulders. Jimmy was always good looking. Now older, the boy I once knew had become a handsome man.

"I'm out on parole," Jimmy said. "Time off for good behavior."

He winked. A joke? Word was he had turned in his supplier and gotten a light sentence.

"I'm late for an appointment. I've got to run," I said.

"Wait." He flipped open a wallet and handed me a business card. "Call me."

"I will," I said, waving the paper at him but not reading it.

Jamming the thing into my notebook, I hurried onto the metal escalator steps rolling downward. I darted ahead of a woman carrying a bouquet of lilies so there was something between me and Jimmy. Even so, he could still watch the back of my head and I feared he might read my thoughts.

When they'd arrested Jimmy my cell rang for days. Friends, guys I'd met once, strangers, called and called.

"Jimmy's been busted."

Everyone wanted to know if he had started naming names; if he had worn a wire while dealing. I hadn't seen him for more than a year, how would I know?

"You were his best friend," was always the answer.

But that was later. I first met Jimmy when I tended bar at the 17th Street Lounge. I had graduated from college three years earlier. To support my career as a freelance writer, well, mostly to earn the money I didn't earn as a freelance writer, and save for graduate school, I worked the Thursday through Saturday shift . Our manager encouraged the bartenders to stoke the crowd—pat each other's asses, dance, even kiss—like we were all fuck buddies. He thought watching young guys fool around made people stay longer and drink more. Tips definitely increased when we did this. Mark, my roommate and my best friend, was a fellow bartender. The night he and I made out behind the taps someone dropped a twenty into each of our jars.

Jimmy showed up all limbs and angles. He was hired as a barback. The way the faces followed his progress you would've thought people had never seen a guy collect empty glasses. Jimmy was oblivious. The staring men might as well have been invisible.

When I tried dancing with him, he laughed and scurried off into the cigarette smoke brandishing a loaded rack for the dishwasher.

Jimmy lost nothing after the lights came up at the end of the shift. I asked him where he lived and he pointed at a Nintendo video-game console balanced on a duffel bag in a corner of the kitchen. "I'm kind of in between places," he said.

Mark and I agreed Jimmy could sleep on our couch until he found something better.

"Come on," I said to Jimmy. "We're close. We walk."

We were young, and therefore assholes. Confident in our looks, or at least confident the hordes of guys on the other side of the bar thought us attractive, we believed we were entitled to certain behavior. That meant making fun of people we deemed ugly or stupid or clueless. It also meant we took what we wanted, even if what we wanted was not ours to take.

Mark joked about the fat guy who hit on him all night. "He made sure I knew he was single." He imitated a drunk's slur: "I broke up with my boyfriend last week." Mark laughed. His silver incisor glinted in the streetlight. "He said his boyfriend had gotten too fat."

"He must have been a water buffalo," I said. I puffed out my cheeks, made a squishy noise like a frog being stepped on.

"Does everyone grab your ass all the time?" Jimmy said.

Mark lit a cigarette. "Drunk guys think it's funny. You get used to it."

"How come nobody cute copped one?" Jimmy said.

"It's all rank," I said. "Because then that means he's not the prize." I looked Jimmy full in the face. Few in our circle wouldn't have put him near the top of that order.

Mark clipped the cigarette from his mouth. "What Seth is saying in his typically complicated way is that if you act like a stuck-up asshole people will think you're hot because stuck-up assholes are supposed to be hot. And vice versa."

"I think I get it," Jimmy said. Bag slung over one shoulder, he was the traveling prince, ignorant of the new place he had arrived.

As on most weekend nights, we ordered pizza. Nearly gobbling the phone, Mark told the restaurant, "An extra five if it's here in ten."

I leaned forward on the couch where Jimmy and I watched television, cupped my hands around my nose, and made snorting sounds. "He wants his crack," I said.

"Like you aren't desperate for a bump," Mark said.

We had a rule: no drugs after work until we ate. Otherwise we might end up falling out the way Mark did at the bar in January, bruising a cheekbone on the way down. He had barely eaten the whole weekend and then danced at Nation until sunup.

I was desperate, but I held on. I fingered the bullet in my pocket every few minutes, making sure I hadn't lost it.

"Jimmy wants to know, but he ain't asking," Mark said. "He's pretending he's worldly."

Jimmy put on a smile and looked from me to Mark and back.

"You guys smoke crack?"

"Tina," I said. "Crystal meth. Speed."

The door buzzer rang and Mark went for the pizza. I showed Jimmy my bullet. "You turn it over, twist the knob, and suck out the powder caught in the scoop." A shot to the brain.

"But our rule is eat first," I said.

That meant we greedily chomped through a pizza slice, had a bump, and then forced down a second or third. What a bit of tina could do! After a long night on your feet you were starving. The smell of pepperoni made your stomach flutter. Some crystal and the pizza might as well have been part of the table.

Jimmy's eager face screamed for a hit. With his looks he would have no trouble getting all the drugs could ever want. A free bump or pill—party favors, they were called—the joke being the real party favor was not the drugs, but the boy you hoped to fuck. The other half of the hierarchy Jimmy would soon learn about.

I said, "If you're going to do this—"

"The mother-hen routine," Mark said.

"—understand that you won't fall asleep until tomorrow. You must drink juice. Also, you might act weird."

"Weird like what?" Jimmy said.

"Some guys it makes chatty, some it makes crabby, and some horny."

"I'm always horny," Jimmy said. "I won't notice a difference."

I demonstrated how the bullet worked by putting it to use.

Like most fist-timers Jimmy snorted too hard, and only knew something was up there when an eye started watering.

"Shit, that burns," he said, then deftly reloaded and hit the other nostril.

"Slow down there," I said.

Mark took a snort. Jimmy reached for the bullet, but I put it back in my pocket. "Wait until you need it," I said.

Fortified, we headed out. First stop: our dealer Victor's apartment.

"He hosts parties," I told Jimmy.

To which Mark added, "All the better to eat you, my sweetie."

We hustled towards 13th Street. A dozen guys were in Victor's living room, splayed across a couch and two love seats, watching porn on the television, the sound off, techno music vibrating from some unseen stereo.

Everyone was interested in Jimmy. Victor came around with a plate of lines—something he rarely did—and made it a point to offer Jimmy the first one.

"Party favor?" Victor said. His hands always smelled slightly of bleach, the result, we surmised, of handling crystal without gloves.

Jimmy zipped up a line. "Have another," Victor said. Jimmy shook his head.

Victor shrugged and sent the plate and straw around. "Where are you from?"

"He works with us," I said.

For the time we were there Jimmy stayed at my shoulder, even a little behind it. Now he seemed conscious of the men watching his every move. He whispered to me, "Is this the party?"

"It will get better once Nation closes," I said.

"I could use something to eat," he said. "Something with sugar."

"Donuts at 7-Eleven," I said.

"Let's go." He hauled me by the hand towards the door.

"Victor, we're going out for donuts," I said. "You want anything?"

He shook his head, staring hard at Jimmy, along with every other guy in that room.

In the elevator I said, "Sorry, it's usually better."

"I was feeling jumpy in that small space. Like the walls were closing in." Jimmy tapped his foot and drummed his fingers against the paneling.

"You're tweaked," I said. "You need a downer."

He grabbed my belt and pulled our hips together. He kissed me hard and I felt his dick pressing through his jeans.

"You were right," he said. "I'm fixing to explode."

We were young and drugs made us feel boundless, without consequence. It didn't matter if I had planned this all along, that when I saw Jimmy's duffel bag I played through an imagined evening that ended here. Or that Jimmy always (but only) wanted sex when he was high. Sober, I soon learned, he was moody and quiet, spending hours playing video games or chatting with strangers online. I just waited, gave him drugs, and fucked him. I thought it was owed me. I told myself it wasn't wrong, it was just the life.

That afternoon I had interviews with veterans lobbying Congress to overturn the ban on gay soldiers. I was the gay guy at the newspaper, sort of pigeonholed with these stories. Things weren't unfriendly and you could make a career reporting gay political issues, especially in Washington. I called it a niche and felt comfortable. A niche story got me the job in the first place. It was only when rooting through my pockets for change for the subway that I read Jimmy's card:

JIMMY
A FREE MAN

Underneath was his telephone number. Everything came back in a rush—dancing shirtless with the boys at Nation, watching the sun rise, the power of a generous bump. I could have done it forever. I could do it forever. Jimmy certainly still knew people. He was in much deeper than I ever was.

I wanted it all again. Just once more.

At the office I typed my interview notes and transcribed the quotes I would use. Still thinking of Jimmy, I wandered to a window.

Desks of junior reporters looked over the alley behind the building. Like all city buildings, the rear presented a different world than the front with its security desk and marble-and-brass lobby.

We had put on a good show. We would have laughed at anyone who said we might have a problem. We were kids in a movie joyriding in a stolen Ferrari, free and careless and away from homes we thought we hated. Only the audience ever sees the truck approaching the crossroads.

One morning after the clubs we had crammed into Victor's car and rumbled up to the twenty-four-hour diner in Adams Morgan. In a booth, bouncing on the leather seats, the music still in our ears, we ordered eggs and hash browns and cup after cup of orange juice.

"You guys are up early," the waiter said.

"We're just getting back," I said. The guy looked at us, impressed, and Mark laughed and I did too, and Jimmy spooned a drum beat on the Formica table top because we were wide awake, not missing a second, taking in every moment of life.

And what a life it was. There was the Sunday afternoon Mark and I walked back to the apartment from a party on W Street, still buzzing, hoping the trudge would finally exhaust us so we could sleep. A car stopped—a convertible BMW, the song "Runaway" playing on the stereo, two men in the front. "Get in," the passenger said, and only then did I recognize Jimmy behind sunglasses.

We leapt into the back seat.

"Where you headed?" I asked. I didn't know the driver, a handsome older guy, a silver ring on the hand that worked the gear shift.

"Dave's place," Jimmy said. "We'll take you home."

We ended up on Dave's yacht. He motored us down the Potomac and laid anchor behind a jut of land in the Chesapeake. In the breezy shade Mark and I cut our crystal high with juice and swirl while Jimmy and Dave used the cabin. Later Dave handed out pills and took us back upriver. We were in the car before sunset.

Dave dropped us at our building. After he and Jimmy had spun off, Mark said, "From wallflower to crack whore in one easy step."

Jokes were one way we convinced ourselves we didn't have a problem. We marshaled other excuses in defense. I had a job. I used only on the weekend. Every other week I stayed home and slept and watched television to prove I didn't need drugs. Plus it did wonders for my waistline. When Mark started injecting tina we said it was to save money since less went farther that way. It also hooked you harder. He stopped showing up at work because he was strung out so often. Eventually he couldn't even afford fresh needles. He used the same ones over and over until his arms were bruised ropes. I watched him do it, fronted him the rent, and never suggested rehab because that might mean I also had a problem.

I dialed the number on Jimmy's card. I hung up. What happened after Jimmy I mostly believed scared me off drugs for good. But there were nights working against deadline I needed a bump so much it hurt. Then there were times I was just bored, flipping channels on the television, and remembered how tina got rid of all that. Everything was right. You knew what you wanted to do, felt capable of doing it and immune to everything.

Miles, the last guy I dated, had said I needed help. He said I got irritable. He said I complained about being bored but never did anything about it. I was afraid of what I might do. What I might do is trade Jimmy for drugs. I let the phone ring until he answered.

"Jimmy," I said.

"Seth, I'm surprised you called."

He told me about his life. He was living at Whitman Walker's group home on T Street. He had a year to get himself together and then he had to move out. He sold clothes at Universal Gear.

"I wouldn't think they hired—" I stumbled over the right words, "people in your position."

"My program has an arrangement with them."

I suggested we have lunch the next day at the Java House around the corner from the store. This time Jimmy wore a tank top, revealing arms and shoulders with a heft not present in my memories. It was not just age, it was beef. And it wasn't bulk. He was lean and corded like an athlete.

We sat on the patio. I ordered coffee and sandwiches. Jimmy changed his coffee to orange juice.

"Certain stimulants rub me the wrong way these days," he said. "But I will take one of your cigarettes."

I handed over a cigarette and lit us both, glad he wanted a smoke. A cigarette would keep the tremor that bounced through my legs from crawling up into my arms and hands.

We watched each other across the empty table. I wondered if Jimmy's body was a product of the prison weight room, but I couldn't imagine him pumping iron amid a sea of thugs. Whatever did it, I only felt more self-conscious. Staring in the mirror recently, I had finally admitted I was fat. Too many cigarettes and late-night sandwiches dripping with mayonnaise while working on deadline.

I had no desire for exercise.

"My sponsor would not approve this," Jimmy said.

"I won't bite," I said.

"You're not in recovery. He'd call you a dry addict."

"It's been a long time," I said. "That must count."

"Time means nothing."

It did seem like it was all only yesterday. "I went to a meeting once."

"It means nothing because you're the same," Jimmy said. "After rehab you're supposed to be new." Here he threw his arms up and out, wings of a bird taking flight, with one tip smoldering, trailing a white spiral where the cigarette burned.

"Is that where the muscles come from?" I kept my envy in check. "Did you work out a lot in jail?"

"Never went," Jimmy said. "I wasn't carrying enough for a distribution charge. The PD got me six months in residential rehab and then a year with an ankle monitor."

He propped his foot on the arm of my chair and pulled back his jeans cuff . A white stripe ran around his ankle. "I still think it's there sometimes."

"I'm sorry," I said.

"Sometimes I wake up after a bad dream and panic because it's gone."

I looked away. That was something I wasn't ready to confront. Some days I consoled myself with the thought he would have found it all anyway. It didn't change I gave him his first bump. Or that I wanted it all over again.

"Anyway, you wouldn't believe it," he said.

"I don't believe most things."

"Karate," he said.

"When did you start that?"

"My counselor encourages regular exercise. We do tons of pushups."

"And break a lot of boards," I said.

"It's not like that. It's hard and there's something totally satisfying about it."

He described how he practiced one move over and over just to get a single step right. It was all self-motivated, he said. It forced you beyond boredom and fatigue to a place where you had the will to do anything.

I offered him another smoke. He shook his head.

"Think about it," he said. "You do a hundred kicks and punches, pushups, squats, and then you demonstrate a really hard technique. Your legs shake. Sweat's in your eyes. You want to sit down, but you won't. That feeling is better than anything."

Behind Jimmy, out on the sidewalk, men and women in business clothes sauntered past. A few talked on cell phones, but all were dressed in that dull Washington style that marked success. The view hadn't changed in ten years.

"How can you not hate me?" I said.

"Now you're worried?" He was angry. Just hit me, I silently urged him, let out all the hate and all the fear. Give it to the person who really deserved it.

He talked instead. The anger was gone. "I worry when I walk by Victor's place. Or an old buddy comes into the store, some guy who still's very much into it. He tells me to call him. I know if I do, I'll be tweaked out of my gourd in a matter of hours."

"I'm sorry," I said, and not for what he was going through, but for what I had almost made him go through.

"I worry that I have to move out of the house in a year and I'll be alone again and I don't know what's supposed to happen next."

"I shouldn't have called you," I said. "I hoped you still had connections."

He stood. For a moment it seemed he would walk away, but he settled back in the chair, hands in his lap. There was something resigned, as if he knew this was part of it.

"Don't ask me that," he said.

"I won't. But so much makes you want it again."

"That's why running away doesn't work. If it's in you, you'll find it no matter where you go."

In my best faux-Chinese accent I said, "So now the grasshopper is the master."

"Okay, first, I hate that," Jimmy said. "Second, that's kung-fu, not karate."

The difference escaped me.

Jimmy moved off our couch for his own place. Soon after, he quit his job at the bar and started working for Victor. As Victor's delivery boy, he cut down on the traffic in and out of Victor's condo, always a giveaway someone was dealing. Delivery also increased Victor's business twice over. Who would want to trudge out for drugs when they would come to you?

I didn't see Jimmy much after he left the bar. He was usually working when I was off so one afternoon I dropped by his place when I knew he'd be sleeping in.

His apartment door was wide open. The door handle was gone and the deadbolt had been drilled out. Inside, a *Donnie Darko* movie poster was tacked on the wall over the radiator. A sock lay in front of the dresser, drawers dangling and empty.

I found him sleeping on Victor's couch. His clothes were stuffed into a garbage bag near his feet. The cord of his videogame trailed sullenly from the bag's crooked mouth.

"What the hell happened?" I said.

"Landlord kicked me out when I tried to pay the rent in cash. Said he knew a dealer when he saw one."

Jimmy did look haggard. With his job came all the free crystal he wanted. Puffy, dark circles—real scoops of exhaustion—hung below his eyes. Somehow it made him look younger, not an exhausted dealer, but a kid with black eyes from a schoolyard fistfight.

"This is not what you need to be doing," I said.

"I'm tired. Tell Victor I said you can have something wholesale."

He plunged back into the couch and covered his head with a pillow.

When I shook him he wormed deeper into the cushions, groaned and swatted at me.

The next weekend I was back, but not for Jimmy. I had the idea I could do a couple of expose articles on crystal meth in DC's gay scene. I pitched the series to an editor I had worked with before and he was eager for something edgy and provocative.

I interviewed Jimmy as the dealer willing to talk. We sat in Victor's living room. Jimmy powdered a quarter bag and cut lines with a dead credit card.

"Write I have six hundred clients," Jimmy said. "I sell to guys on Capitol Hill, guys who work in the Senate and a real-estate developer. I once made a drop at the World Bank."

"As long as I'm quoting you it doesn't matter," I said.

"It's all true except I have no idea how many clients I have."

Jimmy offered me a bump which I gladly accepted.

"Helps the ideas flow," I said.

"I've got one. Tell them all crystal dealers are addicts except for the lesbians. Lesbians are too practical to use and deal at the same time."

"There are lesbian dealers?"

"Who the fuck knows," he said.

"Let's do some background." I flipped the page of my notepad.

"Tell us where you're from and all that."

"I was born in Scranton, PA. I never met my dad and I had three sisters by the time I was five."

"Great stuff," I said, scribbling. "How do you make this up?"

"I'm not," Jimmy said. He licked the powder from the end of the straw and leaned back in the cushions. "One day my mom said, 'Time to be a man,' and left me at a shopping mall. I didn't know where I lived so I ended up in foster care."

"I had no idea," I said.

"Shit happens." Jimmy piled a tiny scoop of white power onto the plane of skin between his forefinger and thumb. "Bump?" he said.

Gently I steadied his hand and placed it against my face. I sucked it all in. Over Jimmy's shoulder in the doorway stood Victor, watching us.

Miles couldn't stand my pacing. Before he was around, it was the way I fell asleep nights. I'd find myself in front of the window, walking up and down its length. Sometimes I would stare into the beacon of the streetlight hanging at eye level. I knew there were parties happening right then somewhere in the city, guys and powder. I refused to leave the apartment.

You have to go back and forth a lot in an apartment if you want your pacing to wear you out. Floorboards creak.

At first Miles was worried. "What's wrong?" he'd ask. He knew some of my story, how the last time I used I was almost fired, and he knew I had promised myself I wasn't doing drugs again.

"I had an idea," I would say and sit down at my computer until he was back in bed.

It wasn't so much Jimmy I thought about—what might have been if I was stronger—it was my own survival. I was bored. I was convinced only a bump could relieve my boredom. I knew where that led.

Eventually, annoyance replaced concern. We'd lie down, hold each other, and when he breathed in the deep rhythm of a sleeper I'd untangle myself and start the ritual.

"You're keeping me up." Miles would say.

"I'm bored," I'd say. "Everything is the same all the time."

We tried watching television. I flipped channels, never satisfied.

"You're making me crazy." Miles would snatch the remote out of my hand. The oozy television light always gave him a moon face, round and pale, and a dull gaze that rarely showed surprise or disdain. And we didn't like the same programs. I had a weakness for cartoons. He followed cooking shows.

Instead of pacing I tried rearranging the kitchen cabinets. One night I cleaned the oven, but the fumes woke Miles.

"Are you embalming somebody?" he said.

I went back to stalking the apartment. The place couldn't hold both of us and Miles eventually moved out.

The articles were good enough to get me hired full-time at the paper where I work now. Jimmy was really excited. He planned on never having an honest job, but that didn't stop him from being happy I had finally gotten a job I wanted.

I asked him to celebrate with me by having dinner at Tortilla Coast. I was a bit put off when I met Victor in the waiting area, but no Jimmy.

"Congratulations." Victor shook my hand. "The intrepid reporter at last."

"Where's Jimmy?"

"He'll be here. He's in a mood," Victor said. "I told him he needed a break. A bit too much." Victor closed one nostril with a thumb and sucked air in the other.

"It's been a while since I've seen him when he wasn't tweaked," I said.

"He was getting strung out. Not a good scene." Victor collected a margarita from the bar. "The sex is great," he continued. "He's just crazy for it when he's high, but he wasn't sleeping, he wasn't eating."

There was the clang of forks and knives on dinner plates. The place was noisy with conversation the way a restaurant gets on the weekend.

"I hadn't guessed," I said.

Victor smiled as if he couldn't believe it either. "I guess you could say we're boyfriends."

Jimmy arrived wearing sunglasses. He mumbled congratulations and I opened my arms for a hug. His hand shot forward, offering a shake instead. Sober Jimmy. While we waited for a table he sucked at the salty rim of a margarita. He ordered a second drink when we sat down and finished it before the waiter brought around the basket of chips and salsa.

"I was just telling Seth how you won't shut up about him," Victor said.

Jimmy suddenly brightened. "He's my best friend." He patted my knee under the table then rested his hand there.

"We hardly see each other," I said. But I thought, "How could he be fucking Victor?"

Victor was nice and all, not a thing wrong with him, but he wasn't a catch either. His hair was thinning. He was older. Sitting in front of the computer all day had not benefited his physique. The guy was a drug dealer.

I left them at Victor's place despite Jimmy's pleas I come up. I got the hurt look I wanted and went home.

Of course, I partied that weekend, and Jimmy was the delivery boy. His face glowed from healthy bumps of tina.

I handed him my bills and he offered his bullet.

"What are you doing tonight?" I said.

"You," he said, and grabbed my crotch. I readily accepted him as much as I did his free drugs. He stripped me naked. He pushed me back onto the couch and speared himself, his nipples hard copper disks dancing in my vision.

I never came so fast in my life. He shot right after. We kissed once long and hard, and then he was up to the bathroom. When he came out I was still naked, lazily reminiscing in the image of his chest, his thighs against my waist.

"Stay," I said.

"Got business."

"Come over after."

"Everyone is going to Nation. Meet me there," he said.

Even in the press of shirtless men on the dance floor, Jimmy wasn't hard to find. He was the one everybody stared at and none dared approach. He had that wall, the "I'm too good for you so don't even try" look. But he wrapped his arms around me and we danced, our chests and tummies sweating against each other, our hips swirling together, him sometimes behind me, me behind him.

I clamped my mouth to his neck, tasted cologne and salt, felt his breathy moans close to my ear.

Victor arrived later, an apparition materializing under the strobes. I leaned off Jimmy, afraid of what Victor might have seen.

When Jimmy saw Victor, he waved him over and turned on his charms. "I never thought you'd come out," Jimmy said, hugging Victor.

Nothing in Victor's face showed if he was angry or jealous. He smiled, gave me a hug, and danced with us, although now we stood in a ring, the three of us facing each other.

Jimmy tried lifting Victor's shirt, but Victor pushed his hands away. Victor didn't have the body for it. Next to us his pudgy stomach would be all the more obvious. But there was little that dissuaded Jimmy when he was high and wanted something. He wanted Victor's shirt off. He danced around Victor and tried it from behind.

Victor scowled. He shoved Jimmy and walked off the floor.

Jimmy looked at me, worry in his mouth, then shrugged and plunged right in, taking up the beat with hips and shoulders.

We went back to my place. We showered together, rinsing the night's sweat from each other's bodies, washing the smoke out of our hair, making out under the stream. Jimmy left me in bed, too tired to dress or get up, too wired to fall asleep, a feeling entirely pleasant, a mellow high that made everything seem worth it.

We were young and we didn't talk about love. We talked about fucking and the cute boys we met at clubs. We thought that's what we wanted. Sure, there were boyfriends, but that hardly ever lasted a season. Crystal made us not care. About anything. We thought we were in control. We thought, high and spinning, there were no missed chances.

Jimmy called from the street. His voice on the phone was nearly lost beneath car horns and truck engines.

"Victor says he needs to see you," he said. "Come over."

"He can call me," I said.

"Seth, I'm in trouble. Just do it."

Victor gave me the rundown. "No more fooling around with Jimmy. He's with me."

Jimmy stood in the doorway between kitchen and living room, head drooping and hands behind his back, a scolded child. I wanted him to say something.

"That's Jimmy's choice," I said.

"I'll make it easy," Victor said. "Don't come around anymore. Mark too."

"That's not necessary," I said.

"You're not the king here," Victor said. "If I cut you off I'll make it real hard for you to find another connection."

What terrified me most was not having my stash when I need it. Weekends were these abysses of time that left me depressed if I wasn't tweaking. I was afraid the only thing that kept me on deadline, able to crank out two thousand words in two days, was a bump. I feared never having that feeling again.

"Fine," I said. "I agree."

And then a week later Mark said Victor kicked Jimmy out after a fight. He was now in Northeast staying with some other dealer. He didn't answer his phone and then the number eventually stopped working.

I saw him later at Nation, how long after I'm not sure, a few months, dancing in a crowd of muscle boys. They passed him from one to another like the party favor he had become.

I joined the group. When Jimmy came my way, I shouted into his ear, "Let's get out of here."

He smiled and turned around.

"Not that way," I said, spinning him back. I flipped up his sunglasses.

His face, loosened through a haze of crystal, ecstasy, special K, who knew what else, had the blank openness of a child. He looked exposed, impossibly vulnerable.

"You didn't choose me." Jimmy nodded his head. The sunglasses fell back into place. He slid out of my arms and over to a man twice his size. The guy fed Jimmy a pill. From behind another man licked at Jimmy's neck and stroked his arms. I left so I wouldn't see the rest.

After Jimmy, after Mark left for rehab, I tried living the clean life.

My calendar filled with X's, a double slash each day sober. For almost a year my job satisfied me. I craved the buzz of deadlines.

I loved how each day was different. You never knew what story would come up, who you might interview, where you might land in the city. It satisfied that part of me that hated routine, which needed the unexpected.

Then one evening I knew I wouldn't make it through the weekend without a bump. But drop out of the scene for a while and everything changes. Victor's number didn't work so I ended up scamming a guy on one of the hookup sites. He had a flabby body and eager hands. A year before I would have sneered—way below my league (even where he lived, a basement apartment)—but I was desperate. Squelching disgust over his aging, lonely hips, I fooled around enough he seemed satisfied, then gave him thirty dollars for the final, sandy dregs at the bottom of a plastic baggy.

I danced at Nation. I caught a ride to a party in Virginia. Not just a party where guys sat around passing the glass pipe: some birthday shindig held in a faux-Georgian mansion for the owner's much younger boyfriend. There was a hot tub, a DJ, food (untouched, of course) and a fire breather. He came out every now and then and wowed us with orange bursts from his mouth or juggled torches and flaming rings.

Even Victor was there, dealing from the bathroom. He sold me a quarter bag and we never mentioned Jimmy. I'm not sure he recognized me. We commented on the DJ's music and concluded business.

When I asked about the host, I was pointed towards a daddy type in a muscle T-shirt and a fading bleach job. Nestled against his bench-press pectorals was a slip of a kid, his hair at least a true shade of yellow. I laughed.

On the ride back to the city I giggled every time I remembered the pair. No one else in the car thought it was funny. The bullet went around and I shut up.

Those last few bumps must have sent me somewhere else because I thought it was a good idea to keep my Monday appointments. At the first one the secretary of the Congressman I was scheduled to interview told me to go away.

My editor called a few minutes later. "You apparently smell like a bum," he said.

A shower before putting on my slacks and blazer had never occurred to me. Reflected in the plate glass of an office window I saw a guy who hadn't slept in three days. He was unshaven, his hair a bristled tangle on one side. I reached up to smooth it down and felt crusted sweat and styling gel.

"I'm not well," I said.

"You get one more shot," he said. "Pull yourself together if you want a future."

As the weeks went on, I dropped by Jimmy's work whenever I had the chance. Circumstances seemed to line up quite a bit. He wasn't always there, but the times he was he talked and I listened. The subjects moved back in time the more we met. He talked about the group home, then when he worked for Victor, our time at the bar.

He even said he was having trouble remembering what his mother looked like.

Jimmy had sobered. Not in the obvious way, but on a personal level. He could be serious without being sullen. He could laugh without being out of control. He could admit things. "I just feel like a jerk," he said. "I wasn't a nice person back then."

Mostly I was silent, afraid of what I might say.

During one of these semi-mute visits Jimmy invited me to his belt test.

"I'm testing for green belt on Saturday. I want you to be there," he said.

"Is that like a black belt?"

"Half way. It means you're serious about going farther. It's an important step."

"Why ask me?" I said.

"My sensei said we should share important tests with people. I think you'd find it interesting."

The studio was a walk-up on U Street. Sunlight from tall windows reflected on a lacquered wood floor as dark as a calm, deep lake. Sticks, pads, and boxing gloves were ordered along the walls. In the corner a punching bag hung, heavy and still.

About a dozen other people were there. All of them were dressed in white uniforms. Jimmy looked astounding in his white suit. A cinched yellow belt emphasized his athletic shoulders.

He introduced his teacher, Sensei Ian. He was a black man my height. I had imagined someone taller, and brutally muscled, though his handshake was like an iron vise.

"Pleased to meet you," he said. He had a friendly, inviting southern accent. "Jimmy's a very dedicated student."

A few feet away, a woman practiced maneuvers that made her uniform snap. "He's the best student here," she said.

Sensei Ian chuckled. He laughed with his body, his whole being in the movement. "Mary should know everyone has their strengths and weaknesses," he said.

"Jimmy has told me he really enjoys the class," I said.

"His enthusiasm makes me excited about teaching," Sensei Ian said.

The process was more mundane than I had imagined. They bowed to each other and uttered Japanese phrases I assumed were some sort of ritual courtesy. There was no kneeling or meditating or chanting. They did jumping jacks, waist twists, leg raises. Ian then made them do pushups at his count.

Mary wrapped Jimmy's hands in boxing tape. Another student braced his shoulder against the punching bag. At a word from his teacher Jimmy flew at the bag. He sent out a staccato of punches and kicks that rattled the suspending chain and made the man steadying the bag grunt. Jimmy pounded away, over and over—fists, elbows, feet. He gasped. Sweat colored a dark stripe down his back.

Again Sensei Ian growled a command. Jimmy stopped and went to stand alone in the middle of the floor. He began a series of moves that took him up and down the length of the room. The steps were not random, more like a ritual dance composed of punches, kicks and blocks.

We were young then. We wouldn't have understood this Jimmy. He had cast himself into a new way. Each step was known, each turn predictable. There was at least that here in the wide room overlooking the city streets.

a summer solstice
lou dellaguzzo

"THIS AIN'T THE GOLDBUG NO MORE." The curly-haired bouncer hands Frank back his cover charge.

"When did it change?"

"Back in May. We took down the old sign, but ain't got around to a new one yet."

"Think it might be a good idea if I stayed anyway?"

"Probably not." The bouncer smiles. "You didn't even have to ask me if the place'd changed. Knew right off you were expecting the Goldbug."

Frank takes a closer look around. Suddenly he feels conspicuous in his tight jeans and T-shirt that cover his thin, supple body like a glove. And his well-groomed black hair. It's so unlike the greasy, haphazard locks on the guys who lounge nearby in baggy pants. He shrugs and makes his way out of the nameless club. But what about that short kid with the mischievous face? The one Frank passed outside? Sure was friendly. Went out of his way to walk past and nod. And his eyes were talking. Be damned if he didn't look interested, in a good way.

He walks to his old Mercury Monterey—a.k.a. the Tank—parked at the edge of an expansive lot. Traffic is light on the highway. What he'd expect, considering it's officially morning. He remembers today's the summer solstice.

Big deal. Nothing much seems to have changed in his life. Here he is again, back in suburban Jersey. Back where he belongs?

When he moved to New York six months ago—after dropping out of Montclair State his sophomore year—he never expected to miss his old stomping grounds. Or make a weekend visit so soon. But his roommate's been a prick all week. And his dumb sales job at a clothing store's boring him to death. He'd like to go back to school come fall. If he can get his old man to help with the scratch.

"How's it goin'?" someone asks from behind. A car idles. Could use a tune-up from the sound of it. He turns to the questioning voice. It's the guy. The little one he encountered on his way in. The kid's driving a sweet '90s Lincoln. A red, four-door job.

"Thought you'd be coming out soon." The guy's big, round head bounces in time with the car's clunky engine. "Guess we made the same mistake, huh? About the bar."

"Thought it was some other place," Frank says.

"Like, maybe, the Goldbug?"

"Yeah."

"Me, too. By the way, me is George."

"And me is Frank."

The two shake hands. They only let go when a small group leaves the club.

"Those people are smart to cut out now," George says. "It's getting late."

"Real late." Frank takes the hint and runs with it. "So where do you live?"

George massages the injured leg, naked like the rest of his guest. Before the two guys could even get started Frank slammed his knee against a nightstand while he undressed in the dark.

"Feeling better now?"

"It'll be okay, I guess." Frank's annoyed about more than his knee. The drive to George's rural home took much longer than he was told. And the kid didn't want to turn on even one lamp or speak above a whisper.

He manages to get back in the mood as the pain subsides. Sure helps that George's small, well-proportioned body, molded in creamy skin, looks irresistible in spare moonlight. His big head has a pleasing roundness. Perfect to hold against your chest. The wide blue eyes, and one slightly lazy lid, evoke intense need. Frank likes needy. Attending to it excites him more than anything. Soon he's all over George, grabbing a handful of red hair.

"Georgie, you okay in there?" The deep voice comes from the other side of the bedroom door. Heavy knuckles rap on wood. "Heard you swear a couple times. You sounded different."

"Everything's fine," George nearly shouts.

"You came in awful late tonight. That ain't what we agreed."

"Sorry. Guess I lost track."

George whispers to his bedmate to hide under the covers and lie flat. "Don't worry," he says.

Don't worry! Frank thinks. He burrows into the mattress, waits for George to turn away so he can peer outside the blanket and see what he might be in for. The door opens. A tall man appears. He's well-built, his age indistinguishable in silhouette. A streak of moonlight casts a stark band across his deep-set eyes. Not at all like George's. These unfamiliar eyes are dark. They meet Frank's dead-on. No question about it.

"Thought we had an agreement," the man says to George.

"Told you a second ago I was sorry."

"Just wanted to make sure everything's okay with you." The man looks again at the young face pressed against the mattress. "Guess I'll say goodnight."

"See you at breakfast. We'll talk about it then."

"Who was that?" Frank whispers. He asks a second time when there's no answer.

"It's okay." George says, eventually. "Don't worry. We won't be bothered again. Everything's fine now."

"Think I'm feeling otherwise." If his host won't talk, Frank won't stay. It might not be safe. Things could turn nasty. And him in the middle of Nowhere, New Jersey. He hops over the other boy and dresses in the dimness. The kid's dejected face makes him soften. "Look man, it's really late and I'm dead tired. It's better I leave now. Doing you a favor, really. I'm not good company when I'm beat." Or scared about what'll happen next. Why didn't George lock his door after that creepy visit? Are locks forbidden in this place? And by that big, nameless guy?

His right side hurts from taking a tumble after looking backwards while he walked. He keeps his guard way up. Woodsy back roads spook him. He'll take buildings. Concrete sidewalks. Bright street lights that make discernible shadows. The car door creaks when he opens it.

"You okay?" someone says from the leafy darkness.

Despite his panic Frank recognizes the voice. He also remembers the man's form, as the stranger, intrusive yet again, makes his way toward the graveled road and into moonlight. He doesn't buy the friendly tone. "Don't worry, mister, I'm going now. No more drama tonight, okay?"

Tall and sturdy, the man's smooth pate reflects the lunar glow. His small features are sharp, his jaw and mouth edged with brownish bristles. And get a load of those arms! "We need to talk." His tone implies an order. "Name's Mark." He extends his hand. "Georgie's father. His *dad*."

Frank gives his name, meets the large hand with his own, half-expecting to get it crushed.

"Thought you was a girl," Mark says.

"What?"

"Back at the house. You under the blanket staring at me through your long bangs. Thought Georgie was with a girl. Wanted to make sure what was going on. When I heard you leave from the kitchen, I went out the front. Took the long way back of the bushes. I knew where to find your car." He regards the four-door, ocher behemoth. "My son's a real creature of habit."

The man's weary monotone assures Frank a little. It's way different from the shouting he would've heard if his dad were standing here instead.

"Let's get down to it," Mark says. "You two do any drugs tonight?"

"I don't do drugs." Frank studies the handsomely lined face, the small nose that resonates like a bassoon when Mark speaks. Damn it. Why does the guy look angrier?

"You want me to say I'm a junkie or something? You want to hear a bad answer?"

"Young people lie so easy."

Again the weary, sonorous tone that pulls at Frank, who's surprised by the word "young." The guy doesn't look much past his thirties.

"I don't even drink fruit juice," he says.

"Juice?" Mark pulls a sour face. "You trying to be funny?"

"Not at all. It's the simple carbohydrates. Fruit juice is loaded with them. They put me in a major stupor, like I'm going to fall asleep. Well, it's true," Frank says, annoyed by the skeptical look. He smiles hard, striving for sincerity.

And a safe exit.

"Simple carbohydrates," Mark says. "That's a good one. I'd laugh if I wasn't so damn tired." He gazes at the sky then down a dark, tree-filled slope. "Let's take a walk around. I'm feeling on edge."

"Thanks, but I got to get home."

"You can't leave. Not yet. There's things I need to know about Georgie. Things I can't ask him direct." He places a hand on the boy's shoulder.

Frank looks at the man's worried, haunted eyes. He hates the way Mark makes him feel—like he wants to run and stay at the same time.

"Do I have a choice here?" he says.

The strong, heavy hand resting on his shoulder grows tense, presses against his collar bone, not hurting. But not comfortable.

"What would your dad do in this situation?" Mark asks.

"He'd probably deck me."

"That's a real shame. No way to treat a kid."

"Glad you think so." Though his hip no longer hurts him, Frank's muscles are getting stiff from all the tension. "I got to sit down."

"You're old Merc looks comfortable."

"That's not a good idea." He doesn't want to invite the man into his potential getaway car. If his getting away is an option.

"Let's look for a spot to sit along the creek," Mark says. "It's no darker than this road. "Even brighter. The moonlight reflects off the water. Makes everything magical, especially when the creek's in a talkative mood. Like now.

Frank nods his okay. Anything to get this over with.

To his relief the creek really is beautiful—and shallow. He walks along its generous bank; the soil grows fragrant under his feet. The scene's like an old black-and-white movie. A film noir, he imagines with bleak humor, since they always end badly.

"So what do you want to know?"

"What were you boys doing when I barged in on you?" Mark says. "Under different circumstances, it wouldn't be my business. Maybe. But we got a situation in our house. Georgie's been sick. Got in over his head with drugs at college. Freshman year, too." He leans his bristly chin into his plaid shirt collar. "Had to put him away a while for his own good. No other choice. A single dad can't play nursemaid and make a living. That clinic Georgie went to. It was top of the line."

Frank takes a few more steps before turning to face Mark. George's dad. It's odd that he's spending more time with the father than with the son who picked him up. He smiles, not knowing why.

"You got to level with me," Mark says. "I'm treating you like an adult here, even if you're still a kid. I'll ask this one more time. Did you guys take any drugs? I won't blame you." He pats the boy's arm and holds on. "I promise. Just tell me yes or no, so I'll know how to handle my boy. Get him more help if he needs it."

Frank's not sure where to go with the question, how much to tell. He's too tired to make up a story on the spot. "I met your son tonight for the first time," he says. "Outside a club. We both went to this club by mistake. It used to be a different kind of place. A disco." He takes a deep breath. "A gay disco called the Goldbug. It stayed open until dawn nearly. Anyway, the Goldbug got changed to a straight place while Georgie—I mean George—was away. After I'd moved to Manhattan. That's where I live now."

He turns to the creek, watches the flickering water flow past him.

"Your son picked me up to have sex. Not to do drugs." Still a little scared, he looks back at the man. "That's what happened. Or would've happened if you hadn't interrupted us."

Mark leans forward about to speak, then seems to think better of it. He rubs his hand along a willow tree, stares at it as if examining the rough bark in the darkness. "When you guys are.... What do you do about protection?"

"I'm safe," Frank says. "Very safe. Think George is too. We talked about it before I agreed to come up here. We both had our stuff with us, you know? We were both prepared in case the other guy wasn't. That's about as safe as it gets with strangers."

"You like my boy?"

"What I heard I like. You've told me more about George than he ever did. I don't mean any disrespect here, but look. A guy's dad doesn't always know everything about his son." Frank thinks of his own father, the huge disconnect between them. "You seem to care for him a lot. His welfare and all. That's really nice." He takes a seat on a long, flat rock, holds his legs tight against his chest like an anxious child, waiting.

George's dad sits down as well. Inches apart, they share the same mossy stone and let time pass in silence.

Their arms graze as Mark keeps shifting about. "Got a tricky back," he explains. He offers Frank his cigarette pack. The boy shakes his head no, grinning thanks.

"Think I forgot my matches." Mark pats his shirt pocket, extends his long legs to reach into worn jeans. "Just as well, I guess. Georgie keeps telling me I should stop. Imagine that." His sigh triggers a long yawn. He stretches like a cat. His work boots dig into moist earth. "I'm about shot for sleep. You hungry? Want to stay for some breakfast? Bet my son'd like it." He points to the surrounding tree tops. They display more definition in the barely lightening sky. "Today's the summer solstice, you know. Longest day of the year."

Frank rests his head on his knees. "Yeah, Mark, I know."

The yellow Formica table dazzles his bleary eyes. Metal tube chairs, thickly upholstered and candy green, remind him of cough drops. All the kitchen appliances—finished in yellow or avocado—look retro. Clearly not by design.

Mark eases bacon into a black iron skillet.

He's probably like my dad, Frank thinks. Never throws anything out.

The smell of sizzling fat makes his mouth water, his stomach growl. He hopes Mark has whole-wheat bread, maybe some fresh fruit, but doesn't ask. Tired, hungry, and a little cranky, he admits he's enjoying himself. He likes the early morning light that streams through the window. It's a different light from Manhattan's. Not better, only different.

"Wakes you up, don't it?" Mark says loudly. He bends over the browning fat, inhales deeply. "Can't beat a smell like this."

Before Frank can answer, George shouts from the hallway: "Okay, okay, I got the hint. Hope you made a lot."

He rounds the kitchen doorway and freezes at the sight of the other boy.

Frank offers a sheepish grin and shrugs his shoulders.

George blushes crimson and looks at his father, who turns away, makes a show of moving the bacon slices with a fork.

"Hi," Frank says to the boy he left quickly and never expected to see again.

"What's going on, Dad?" George doesn't get an answer so he asks Frank. "What're you still doing here?"

"He never left," Mark says. "I met him on one of my walks along the creek. We got to talking. Before we knew it, the sky was beginning to turn, so I asked Frank to join me for breakfast. That all right with you?" With huge tongs, he removes the bacon from the pan. He cracks eggs over a white porcelain bowl, dumps the shells into the empty box and checks on the old coffee maker's progress.

"Since when do you go for a walk so early?" George says.

"Since this morning."

"Oh yeah? So what'd you talk about?" He takes a seat across from the other boy. "You okay?" he asks. "You look way tired."

"I'm fine," Frank tells him.

"What?" Mark says.

"Said I'm fine. Your son asked me if I was okay."

"Of course you're okay." Mark grabs four crisp bread slices from an old toaster and refills it.

"So what'd you guys talk about?" George says.

Neither of them speaks.

"Will someone please answer me?"

"Relax, Georgie."

"Dad, it's George. Not Georgie."

Mark begins to scramble the eggs with a metal whisk. "We talked about the place you and Frank went to last night. The one that changed hands. I think Frank called it the Golden Bug."

"Goldbug," Frank says.

"Right. Anyway, we had a long talk." Mark stops whisking and turns his level gaze at George. "Your old man learned a lot last night." He turns back to the stove and pours beaten eggs into the reheated pan. The golden puddle he encourages with a spatula.

"Hope you don't mind," Frank says.

There's a long pause.

"I don't mind," Mark says quietly.

"No, sorry. I was talking to your son. I hope he doesn't mind we were talking about him."

George's blue eyes squint and seem to darken. His tongue squeezes past dry, full lips. He licks them nervously, twirls a patch of rebellious red hair around one finger.

Frank slouches in his chair, wanting to help, knowing he'd like a second chance more than anything. He extends his calf, brushes it against the other boy's leg.

No response.

He drops his hand below the table, resting it on George's thigh. Soon he feels a warm hand cover his own, squeezing it tight.

"I guess it's okay you guys were talking about me," George says.

"Well good then," his father tells him. "Sounds like we're all okay."

pelion
mario alberto zambrano

I DON'T REMEMBER WHERE IT WAS, OR WHEN, BUT I SUPPOSE I WAS TOURING WITH
the company. A few of us had taken a trip to someone's house—a house of
a friend—outside of the city where there was wilderness in the backyard.
Now that I think of it, it could've been somewhere in northern Italy. I
remember we were in a town known for their pumpkin mousse ravioli,
near Bologna.

From the kitchen door a field sloped down to a creek with lots of
trees, orange and fig, I think. Everyone gathered around a table covered in
dirt and dust from when it had last rained and took with them plates of
cheese and fresh loaves of bread. A few meters away there was a hammock
in the shade. It's where I kept myself that afternoon, afar from everyone,
but where I could hear conversation. I was reading *Orlando* for the second
time, aloud to myself under my breath, under the shade of two lemon
trees. I still do that, you know, read aloud when I'm alone. Nothing in that
sort of thing has changed about me.

At some point, you walked to the kitchen to get some wine, and on
your way back you must've heard me.

"You reading to yourself?" you asked.

"I am," I said. "I see the story differently if I read out loud."

You nodded and asked, "You all right here by yourself?"

"I am," I said, and smiled to prove it.

"We're about to have some wine if you want some," you said. I shook
my head and lifted my book. Then you understood.

Now I'm at your house, the one you helped build a few years ago in
Pelion where they say Greek gods used to come holiday. As I sit here on

the terrace taking in the sun, it's as though I am on that hammock again and I hear your voice even though you aren't here.

After I wrote to you and told you I wanted to be alone for a while and to wake up to the sea, you offered your home to me.

It's beautiful here, really.

This house is built out of stone and wood, and is filled with all the parts of you I have never gotten to know: your tens and tens of pillows covered in Moroccan textiles strewn along the couch on the bottom floor that I'm sure come from that Middle Eastern shop close to the soup stand in Lyon, where you live; your piles of magazines that range from *National Geographic* to a German edition of *Architectural Digest*; candles of all different sizes and colors you have on the coffee table, and on shelves, and on windowsills, still dripping from that night you must've been here with a group of friends, or with a lover, chatting through the night with nothing but the sounds of cicadas outside the glass door; and your serpentine branch as thick as my arm hanging from the ceiling, yellow holiday lights strung through it, set to a blinking sequence that keeps the light in the room changing as I read by your fireplace in one of those low seats that has a wooden footstool at its end; your postcards from Alaska and Mt. Fuji and Iceland snug behind wooden beams where they hold, and behind pantries, half-shown—a few of them are photographs of you standing atop a mountain surrounded by clouds with a hiking stick in one hand; in the open kitchen there are your old-fashioned tea cups, glass-blue shot glasses, old plates you've collected over the years; your Japanese tea kettles and wooden spoons, your pink whisk that is surely part of a kid's collection from some kitchen play box; a small radio with a long antennae by the window set to a station that plays classical music all day and all night. I've been listening to it ever since I arrived. There's a jingle that comes on every few minutes between pieces like "Bacchus' Cup" and "Nessun dorma." "*Acontento de la programa!*" Or something like that. It might not even be Greek. It could be Italian for all I know. But I love it.

I know you're not here, but you are.

I wanted to wake up to the sound of waves crashing in the distance and the view of an island across the bluest horizon—lapis lazuli and sapphire and whatever flower is the bluest. But then, in my head I hear your voice: "Are you all right here by yourself?"

Instead of lifting a book, I'm writing this.

I heard a lot about you before I met you. We danced for the same company but at different times. I got your roles after you left . It was you I watched on the videos whenever we had to learn the choreography of a ballet being brought back to the repertoire. The director and dancers who knew you spoke highly of you—you had moved to France to join another company the year before I arrived.

Just a year and we missed each other.

It wasn't until four years later when I was performing in Kalamata at an amphitheater near Athens when I saw you for the first time. In the middle of a piece we were performing, we had to go out into the audience and take someone onstage. We had only two minutes to find someone. We had to be selective—choose someone with bright clothing; an elderly woman who might seem willing to participate; someone eccentric; someone bashful. I can't remember why, but I had trouble finding someone. All the other dancers—there were sixteen of us—had already chosen their partners and were escorting them onstage. Pressured for time with the music cue only seconds away, I reached out to someone four seats in from the aisle on one of the top rows. He wore a summer fedora, and I suppose that's what caught my eye, the Robert Redford fedora. He stepped out into the aisle and left his hat with a friend. That's when I recognized you.

It dawned on me that you were part Greek and you must've been home visiting family. It was the middle of July. But what were the chances?

I pulled you down the aisle, practically running down the steps and to the stage so that we'd make it in time.

Then we danced.

You were strong and playful and lifted me in classical positions as though I were a girl. When you put me down I ran around you the way a squirrel runs around the trunk of a tree. Part of my costume was a black hat similar to the one you'd been wearing. You grabbed it and put it on. A crowd in the audience cheered. But without my hat, I felt exposed. I wondered if you knew me, if you'd heard about me the way I'd heard about you.

At the end of the section, after the music changed to a number by Dean Martin, we had to do a three-step with our partners. Then slowly, one by one, we'd ask the audience members who'd joined us to return to their seats. You and I were upstage, in the corner, and the lights were beginning to dim as they were supposed to. I couldn't look up at you. I stared at your chest where your buttons had come undone. We were dancing so close our foreheads were only an inch apart.

Someone in the company knew you. When she was off-stage I heard her whispering your name in the wings, but neither you nor I turned our heads. It felt as though you were staring at the tops of my eyes, waiting for me to look up.

After the show, backstage, we laughed about the coincidence. Someone asked if I'd done it on purpose. We weren't supposed to grab someone we knew. But I didn't know you, I said. I'd never met you until then.

The night sky was dark and all of the stars could be seen. I was standing by the backstage door with my bag ready to leave. I can't remember why, or how, but you appeared suddenly and grabbed my hand and led me down to where some of your friends had gathered near the theater's entrance. They were having a glass of wine at the outside bar, greeting some of the other dancers who'd already gotten dressed. You introduced me to them and spoke of plans for the following day since we didn't have class until late afternoon. Everyone seemed excited about it. We'd go to a vineyard of a friend in a small village up the mountain, have fish and Greek salad for lunch by the shore.

The entire time, you never let go of my hand.

In the morning we met downstairs in the hotel lobby, the few of us who wanted to go, and by noon we were all in a great mood from the wine we'd drunk. Then, at a long table under a canopy overlooking the sea, we were served small red fish—it was the first time I'd ever bitten off the head off a creature and swallowed it entire. It was delicious, and I asked for more.

We never sat together, at that table or in the car, or stood next to one another as we all walked through the vineyard. We never had a chance to speak to one another. We were a group of ten, at least, and everyone wanted to be next to you. At the end of our excursion, we said good-bye.

I didn't see you again after that. Perhaps you'd left to the north, to your house here off Mt. Pelion, or had traveled to Athens to meet some friends. I didn't know it then, but the next time I'd see you I'd have to keep my distance from you.

I was in the middle of a five-year relationship—but that wasn't the reason.

I woke up this morning and found a white cat with a gold tail waiting for me on the terrace. It's so bright out that she has to shut her eyes when she walks around me. I guess she can sense where things are because she doesn't bump into anything. She purrs and bends her head to my ankles, rubs her face there and begs for attention. She wants food, I know. I found the cans of cat food you left under the countertop. But I don't want to spoil her so I give her one feeding a day, three generous spoonfuls at the hour I have breakfast. We eat together. As she eats, I peel a banana and read over what I've written.

In the company you were in, you were single. A close friend of mine—my closest, in fact—joined the company. (I don't want to say his name because by saying his name the story will be his instead of mine—but you know who I'm talking about.) He left a boyfriend behind, a pianist, from where he moved, and they had decided to try to make it work, the long-distance.

Three months after he started working with the company, he called me, and it wasn't until he told me your name that I knew I'd lost my chance in getting to know you any better. First, he said he'd been having an affair, then, that he was having an affair. But apart from the tone of guilt in his voice there was enchantment. It was all in the way he spoke about you.

There was no reason for my stomach to have dropped when he said your name—I was still with my boyfriend—but it did. He thought I'd never heard of you before. He went on describing you, how generous you were with him, how talented a dancer you are. When he said your name, I said it with him because I knew it had to be you.

But having an affair with my closest friend wasn't the reason I couldn't speak to you when I saw you again. It's what happened after, with the pianist. When I found out about it a compass of loyalty was thrown in front of me and I had to make a choice as to which direction to move in.

You were not the direction I moved in.

In the weeks after you slept with my friend he confessed to his boyfriend what had happened and it caused a rift between them, as expected—long arguments into the night, bottles thrown across a room, silent treatments. Up to there, I understood. I could understand how difficult it must've been for two beautiful boys to resist one another, you, and my friend. But what happened next was what I had a hard time wrapping my head around.

The pianist wanted to meet you, he said. He was furious and couldn't control his rage or his jealousy. He thought that if he met you his fury would subside, that the demonic vision of you would calm into something human and ordinary. When you heard he wanted to meet you, you agreed. And so, you met. Then you slept with him.

In fact, you didn't just sleep with him, you fell in love with him, and he, somehow, fell in love with you.

My friend was devastated, which is obvious. It was last thing he ever expected and it ensnared him into a deep depression. He loved you both, and now, he had neither of you. Worse, he had to go to work and see you, loving you and hating you in every instant as he circled the room around you. He had fallen for you, but now, you'd taken the pianist from him. Not just the pianist. But his lover. It was so unbearable he asked the director for a leave of absence, which he was granted. Three months passed and when he returned to work, he found the pain just as unbearable as if it had just happened.

He came to visit me in Spain where I was living. I remember him sitting by the window, stunned silent as he sat on my couch for most of the day. When I asked him if he wanted to talk about it, all he could say was that he had trouble breathing, and that the room felt tight.

"No matter how much I try to get over it," he said, "there are times my chest starts to contract and I can't breathe. No matter what I tell myself, it doesn't stop."

I held his hand and sat beside him, but when it was time to run errands or prepare dinner, I had to leave him in the corner. I knew he was hurting because he never spoke badly about either of you. He understood how both of you had fallen for each other; after all, he'd fallen for both of you. But still, he'd been hurt.

Soon after his visit, he returned to work and asked me to visit him. The director of the company, having seen me dance before, asked me to join the company. By then, I had already wanted to dedicate myself to something besides dancing. I'd started taking online classes for a degree in literature. As a means to be close to my friend, I agreed. But only as a guest artist, which meant no obligation greater than working with the company for only weeks at a time.

Besides, I needed money.

It was a big company, at least thirty or more people than I was used to. We worked in the opera house, on the top floor, where on one side of the room there was a wall of windows that overlooked the river running through the city. Everyone was coy at the start, but they warmed up to me quickly when they learned that my motivation didn't stem from any ambition. I was there simply to dance with them. As innocent as that.

I saw you at the end of the barre on that first day I arrived. I don't think we said hello to one another. Maybe we did. If so, it was brief and I don't remember. What's certain is that we never found a moment to talk or have dinner. And in the roles I was cast in there was never a moment when I had to interact with you. When we passed each other in the hall or downstairs in the canteen, we greeted each other, but in the way strangers greet each other at a supermarket. You knew how dear my friend was to me, and without words, it was as though we had sealed an agreement: I wouldn't get close to you for fear of hurting him.

As time passed, you turned into someone else.

That's how it was for the years I worked in the company. I grew used to forgetting about the way we had first met. During rehearsals I heard other dancers speak of you in a negative light, how you would sleep with anyone who joined the company, how you'd break their hearts and then move on to the next person, how, it always seemed, that you had a man in every city we performed in.

You were with the pianist for two years, I think, then that too ended.

After I arrived in Pelion I wrote to you and told you this house had turned me into an arachnid slayer. I suppose it comes with the beauty of the wilderness and having a stone house. A stone house comes with spiders in it. Above the sink, where you keep the silverware in that small wooden tray, there are cobwebs around it, and a web around the faucet and its handle, and around the shower head upstairs, and in the boxed window of the bathroom where the biggest spider I've seen lives. Her body is as big as my thumb and she's striped gold and orange with pinpricks of emerald. The first time I took a shower, I set the water on her. She'd made at least three webs, like a layered mansion, and I demolished it with the force of the water. When I duck my head under the shower, I close my eyes. One day, when I opened them, she was standing at the edge of the windowsill starting at me. I'd destroyed her home and she was at her edge, ready to kill me if she could.

I didn't kill her, but I've killed lots of others. Until you told me to stop.

But still, it's not just the spiders, but the snakes and lizards that make noise in the dark after the sun has left , and the wasps and bees and mosquitoes and ants that never give me peace when I read or try to write, and those unidentified rodents that run through the woods in the middle of the night. They are everywhere. Even when I'm inside, after the sun's gone down, after I've locked the door and closed the windows, they're around. I know there's nothing to be afraid of, but it's just me here and I am in a country I'm not familiar with.

You mentioned that the spiders help take care of the flies so I've stopped killing them. When I clean the dishes, I let them watch me. When I read at night by the fireplace, I try to think that they're peeking at what's on the page. One night, I found new webs I hadn't seen before around the books you have stacked on the mantle. I find them casting webs between the candles in the center of the coffee table. Sometimes in the morning when I am still nude and going down to make some coffee, I feel a thin spider's thread breaking around my hip. Even when I can't see them, they're there.

I've gotten used to them, but I do not love them.

When I stopped dancing for the company, I moved to New York to finish my studies. It was five years before I graduated with an MFA, and when I finished, I wanted to visit Europe again.

A few months ago, I wrote to you. I'd heard about your house from my friend whose heart you'd broken. Time had healed him and he was dating someone, had even come to Greece to visit you. He couldn't stop telling me how beautiful it was here. "And the tomatoes!" he kept insisting. "There's this local herb called *kritama* that only grows there. You should go. It's paradise."

Now that the both of you had become friends, I felt it was all right to reach out to you—for the second time. When I saw a photograph of you both, down from your house on the beach, with his arm over your shoulders, I knew the tides of what had happened between you had subsided.

A day before I arrived we spoke on the phone so you could explain to me how the alarm worked. You didn't have much time, so we kept it brief. You said, "But I want to catch up and hear about what's going on with your life."

What's going on with my life?

I'm writing stories, I wanted to tell you.

But I didn't.

Perhaps I'll leave this letter on your table with a stone over it. But then, with the shutters shut and everything closed there will be no breeze, no risk that it will be caught and swept under a piece of furniture—so perhaps there's no need for stone. Perhaps this story will exist in some invisible web that neither of us can actually see, but feel.

The house further up the mountain still has its windows boarded, and the one below me with the white hydrangeas doesn't have anyone living in it either. The rest is nothing but trees and wilderness, until you hit the winding road that leads down to the sea. But with the string of lights you've woven around the hanging branch above the coffee table, the way it flickers, the way every light illuminates at different times, then, all at once, it's a marvel. You've made it quite magical. At night when I'm feeling lonely, I stop reading whatever I'm reading and look up at it. It's as though the sequence is set to some dated rhythm of Morse code and it's trying to tell me something. When they fade to nothing all at once, there is that pitch-black darkness again and I make sure the door is properly locked. I look out, hoping to see a sliver of a silver moon but not even that can be seen. All I can sense are the sounds beyond the trees. And I know that in some way you're here, but really, I'm in the middle of darkness with you.

In a few days, I'll clean this house and pack my things. After I'm gone, you'll come; and still, no matter how close we came, it'd be as though we never got to know each other.

the hat prize
jason schneiderman

I WAS SO EXCITED FOR OUR SECOND DATE THAT I BOUGHT A NEW SWEATER. It was a really cute sweater. I was late to meet Michael because I was buying that sweater. But unlike our first date, the chemistry seemed wrong from the moment I arrived. The restaurant was a Greek restaurant. I always forget that I don't really like Greek food. When we sat down, my Prince Charming announced that he was about to take a Valium. I thought: Couldn't you just tell me you're taking an Advil? Valium? I watched a filmstrip in fifth grade about the dangers of Valium. You can't even kill yourself with Valium. Addictive, retro, lame.

The night I met Michael, we talked all night. On our first date, we talked so long the maitre d' had to let us know that the restaurant was closing. But now I was searching a menu for the least offensive option while the man across from me took a drug popular among 1950s housewives. Our conversation couldn't find a groove. I'd told my friends about him, which I figured was the jinx. I'd ruined it.

I'd been playing hard to get. My friend had just read The Rules (Remember that book?), and I was no longer falling into bed on first dates. On our first date, he'd walked me to my door, but I didn't invite him up. I walked him to the subway instead. I thought it had been a good move, but now I was doubting myself. I should have gotten laid and been done with it.

Things were going so badly that I was on the verge of excusing myself and just walking out of the restaurant. I was trying to formulate the words in my head. Sorry, this just isn't working? Too vague. Too formulaic. Look, I'm just not feeling the connection I did last Friday? Also unworkable.

And what would I do if I left? I didn't want to leave. I just wanted him to be the guy I remembered.

He ordered an appetizer, and then he broke the awkward silence. "I should probably tell you I have a boyfriend."

A boyfriend?

Seriously?

What's the line from Party Girl? Ah yes. You lower my real estate.

I'd just gone through this—though technically, I had been the boyfriend. I had spent my study-abroad year dating a man named Alexei. He had cheated on me with roughly half the men in St. Petersburg. I had been completely duped, and it had been humiliating.

Well, at least I no longer had to excuse myself. "A boyfriend?" I said. He sheepishly nodded. "Have I been unclear?" I asked him. "Have I somehow sent you mixed messages? Were you not under the impression that this was a date?" I could feel the Joan Crawford in me rising. I was sitting up straighter, speaking with a level of disdain that I usually reserve for the what-I-should-have-said-but-would-never-be-so-bold-as-to-actually-say after game. I unleashed all the vitriol I had. When I finished, I sat back, self righteous and wounded.

"You're being so nice about this," he said.

Nice? I was doing my best to be a total bitch about this.

"What's his name?" I asked.

"Fernan." He said.

"Is Fernan a name? Shouldn't it be Fernando?"

He laughed. "It's actually Fernan Fernandez."

I laughed too. How could I not? I figured that the evening shouldn't be a total waste. "Can I still have sex with you?" I asked. To be honest, I wanted to see his apartment as much I wanted to have sex. I really liked seeing people's apartments.

"I was hoping you would ask that," he replied.

He had the best apartment I'd ever seen. It was a two-bedroom off Columbus Circle in the building where Bela Bartok had died. The sex was fantastic. His taste in bedding was exquisite. His bedroom was cozy and perfect. I wanted to stay in his bed forever. My apartment had a bathtub that filled up with raw sewage and had to be bailed into the toilet. I had been showering at the gym for weeks. His bathroom, with its white porcelain tub and sliding glass doors, was heaven.

As I came out of the shower the next morning, he was on the phone with Fernan Fernandez. Michael was telling him about me. Or rather, he mentioned my existence, and listed my qualities. It was as odd as it sounds.

As I listened to them talk, I realized that they weren't talking. They were just recounting events. I thought to myself, why don't you two just exchange calendars and get it over with? But now that Michael was taken, and there was no risk of actually having to fall in love with him, we went back to the easiness of our first date. For the first time in my life, I wasn't auditioning a man for life partnership. For the first time in my life, I fell in love.

It happened gradually. Michael and I would often spend two or three nights a week together. Sometimes I'd spend the evening at his place, and sometimes he'd come to my place. He would leave my apartment at six a.m. to get back to his place to shower and change and be at work by nine a.m., which I found consistently impressive. Michael seemed to find all of my faults endearing. I am an incredible klutz, and Michael never minded when I spilled coffee—which I did every single morning we were together. I had a habit of basically living in my bed, and even after Michael was poked by the sharp end of a compass (I'd been drawing circles) while trying to sleep, he never objected.

We never seemed to stop talking. Once when we were walking around Central Park with our Sunday morning coffees, I made some sententious statement or other and Michael asked me who had said that. "I did," I said, slightly annoyed. "If I'm giving you someone else's idea, I'll tell you. If it's not footnoted, it's mine." I was in my first year of grad school; I was belligerent and insecure. Michael responded, "You're the first guy that's ever been smart enough for me." I was a little insulted. "Have you been dating morons?" I asked. (Twelve years later, I've met many of Michael's exes. There is one whom I'm quite fond of, but for the most part I can confirm: Yes, he'd been dating morons.)

Michael also seemed to enjoy my mean streak. Once when we were discussing writing, he explained that for him writing poetry was a personal project. He told me that it was about self-expression and personal growth. I looked at him incredulously. "That's," I said, "what bad writers say when they can't get published."

Inexplicably, he found this endearing.

I kept the subject of Fernan off limits. Michael's roommate had developed a strong dislike of Fernan, and Michael often wanted to defend Fernan to me against the accusations of his roommate. Channeling Jeanne Tripplehorn in Sliding Doors, I had to point out that I was trying to be his boyfriend. "I'm not impartial here," I would say, "You talk about him to someone else."

Still, despite our growing affection, and increasing time together, there were times when Fernan would visit and I would have to disappear. I would meekly retreat to my post-apocalyptic apartment with its bad plumbing, aggressive rodents, and eviction threats. I would spend the time waiting for my life to restart when Michael would put his real boyfriend on a plane back to San Juan.

If I'd been following my own plan, those weekends without Michael would have been my most active husband-hunting time. I'd explained my plan to Michael: Until Fernan was living in New York full-time, Michael was my pretend boyfriend. Since it's a proven fact that people in a relationship are always more appealing to single people, I would be using the extra attraction boost from having a pretend boyfriend to attract a real boyfriend. But of course, I spent most of our time apart wondering when I could see him again.

During one of the blackout weekends, I was having lunch with a friend when my jaw locked up. I was explaining my plan and suddenly I experienced intense pain in my jaw and I could barely move it. Clearly, my body knew how ridiculous the plan was, even if I didn't. Thank god for chiropractors.

Over time, Michael and Fernan's relationship went into an irrevocable downward spiral, and it suddenly seemed like he wanted to complain to me about Fernan all the time. Again, I had to insist that I was not an impartial observer—I had a vested interest. I wanted Michael, but only if I could get him free and clear.

I began to insist on two points: 1) If you break up with Fernan, you do it because you don't want to be with him, not because you want to be with me. 2) I'm not plan B. Don't think that breaking up makes us instant boyfriends.

Michael wrestled with his feelings. It was almost impossible not to talk his relationship through. We discussed almost everything, and this one piece of our lives—perhaps the most consequential piece of our lives—was under conversational quarantine.

The night that Michael called me to tell me that he had broken it off with his boyfriend, he said all the right things. It was as though I had coached him. And of course, I had.

"It's over," he said, "and I know that doesn't mean that you're my boyfriend. I didn't break up with him to be with you—I did it because he wasn't right for me."

I cut him off . "We have to go to a Kentucky Derby party tonight. What do you have that we can put on your head? There are prizes for hats."

"I have a double-headed dildo," he replied.

"Awesome," I said. "Bring it. We'll run them through a pair of my briefs, and you can wear that for a hat."

We met up, and as we waited for the subway to Brooklyn, I wondered how long I would have to keep up this back-to-square-one charade. I'd been so focused on being certain that I had him free and clear, I wasn't sure how to actually have him. He looked down the track, waiting for the light, and holding a brown paper bag containing the illicit makings of his hat.

"You're my boyfriend," I said. I just blurted it out.

"What?" he said.

"You're my boyfriend," I repeated. "I know I said we'd have to wait and all, but you are. You just are."

"Okay," he said.

He won the hat prize by a landslide.

king
max steele

IT'S LIKE I HAD AN ACCIDENT. Or I've been hit by a car, or broken my legs while skiing. Maybe I had some kind of childhood disease, like polio or scoliosis. Something happened and it means I can't really walk right. Locomoting like the rest of you, like anybody else does without thinking about it, is a lifelong source of pain and embarrassment for me. Maybe you can't tell. I hide it well. I've had titanium screws drilled into my legs. Or, my spine still remembers the cold metallic feel of the back brace I learned to masturbate while wearing. You can't see my limp, it's imperceptible, but I know it's there. Sometimes I think this way. Pretend I'm disabled. Like Snow White. Do you remember her? She had a chunk of poison apple lodged in her throat, and the prince came and took it out.

We filed into this room, an art gallery, and sat against the walls while you lay on your stomach on the floor in the middle of the room. It was a performance but it wasn't anything special, the moving. Just warming up. You were stretching onstage and your movements became exaggerated; it looked like you were humping the floor. You flipped onto your back and let out a loud groan and that's how we knew the show had started.

You leapt up and twisted through the space in an arc, your face an expression of exquisite agony. Taut and convulsing, you paused, turned around, did it again, moving back. You did this kind of thing a few times; on the way there your movement looked random, impulsive, and madeup. But then replicating it, doing it backwards proved a kind of mastery. The movements back and forth got smaller and smaller, as you slowly led yourself back to the floor. You were showing off how in control you were, it was almost embarrassing. And we could tell you almost felt bad about it, the showing off, but not bad enough not to do it. Like there was some underlying rightness to it. The tension was seductive; we all held our breath. I felt increasingly tense watching you, but I liked it. I think it took me much too long to identify it, that anxiety of pleasure. I was definitely behind the rest of the audience in realizing that it was sex, was about sex. You were acting out if not fucking then your feelings about fucking. The experience, internally of getting fucked. Best expressed as a dance. The inside part of the inside part. Lying on your back, now on your knees, then again on your back but now with your legs spread out. An imaginary boyfriend. Watching you get fucked by a ghost. I wanted to be that ghost (to get to haunt you). Maybe you were thinking of a boyfriend you used to have. It made a space for me to imagine myself in, to see you like that. Like I was privy to something visceral and precious and I know I wasn't the only person in the room who felt like that.

I wonder what you were like as a kid. Did you have sex as a teenager? Is that an unfair question? I bet you're great in bed, the way only someone with lots of practice can be. You're a dancer so you know about pacing. Your body is your instrument. You can never take it off; you're always ready, fingering the keys. I like to imagine that you were a slut in college. That you fucked men, women, students, professors, janitors, cab drivers. And in the fantasy we're in college together and you're getting rimmed by the cafeteria chef while upstairs I'm in my room doing my physical therapy just waiting for our paths to cross.

You threw yourself on the floor. I bet you've been there a hundred times. It seemed like a habitual position. I bet this is what you do with your free time. Throw yourself at the floor. It looked familiar. Demonstrating how spontaneous you are, how good you are at sex, how comfortable you are even face down on linoleum. How uninhibited! Wriggling your pert little ass in the air, your white cotton shorts so practical for dancing, so clean, with no dance belt underneath. There was a challenge there as well, a gloat. A kind of hinting at some kind of violence, getting the shit beaten out of you and bouncing back. We all know about pain: mine makes me a cripple and you wear yours like a crown. It made me feel differently about abjection. Can you get off with a black eye? Can you come without making any sound? To survive and locate pleasure there, on the floor. I saw you do it.

Rolling across the floor and then suddenly stopping, standing on your feet with legs spread wide. Bending over so achingly slow, kind of hovering. Those seated behind you could probably see you engaging those muscles that run between your asshole and your balls. The one that cuts off the flow of piss. Seeing you, I thought of church, the thing of the mortification of the flesh. That spectacle. It's like worship, right? Your body is magic, mine is broken. You're performing, I paid to be here. You're showing what's inside and I'm on the outside watching. You're like a king, I'm a subject. You can fly, I'm buried up to my neck.

I kept thinking about how compared to you my body was so feeble, overwhelmed by my appetite. And your body seems to live in service of your imagination, to take the form of your will. I went on to fantasize about you all summer. You as horny hospital nurse, sneaking into my room at night to let me suck your cock from my hospital bed. Or you as star quarterback, muscular insatiable bottom who secretly loves to ride the cock of the horse-hung autistic band geek.

Your breathing got heavier. I saw sweat glisten on the sides of your face. You struggled to breathe into your muscles. Standing on your left leg only, taking tremendous balance and exertion. You held your right leg up and out until the muscles began to shake and give out. You collapsed to the floor and I saw your veins swollen, pumping hard in your neck. You gasped for air. You caught your breath, stood up and walked out of the room and the show was over.

Walking down Tenth Avenue, it was summer and sweltering and sunset. The sun had finally just gone down, and we stumbled through the soft wet pink light. Dusty like a rosebud, an anus. A little bit drunk on free white wine, and sweating in the heat. Sick with humidity. And we're all tops (all my friends are) and we were all thinking about fucking you. We didn't talk about it or anything but I know that's what we were all thinking about. I'm kind of psychic. I wish you had come with us. We went to a gay bar with dingy seats. We sat under a light bulb in the back and took turns talking about how successful we were gonna get, what we would spend our fortunes on, what it was gonna be like when each of us in turn were king.

about the
contributors

michael alenyikov is the pen name for the author of *Ivan and Misha*, which won the Northern California Book Award for Fiction and was nominated for the Edmund White Award for Debut Fiction. In 2013, he received the Gina Berriault Award. His work has appeared in *14 Hills*, the *Georgia Review, The James White Review, Descant, Black Heart, New York Stories, Modern Words*, and the *Gay & Lesbian Review*; and has been anthologized in *Best Gay Stories*. He has been a MacDowell Fellow and was nominated for a Pushcart Prize. He was raised in the outer reaches of NY's three large outer boroughs (with a few years in Phoenix and LA wedged in between the Bronx and Brooklyn). He currently lives in San Francisco.

alexei bayer was born in Moscow. In 1974 he immigrated to the United States, where he works as an economist and economic writer. His fiction works have been published in various American literary journals, including *Kenyon Review* and *New England Review*. Bayer and Andrei Gelasimov have cooperated in translating each other's works. A collection of Bayer's short stories, *Eurotrash*, was translated by Gelasimov and published in Moscow in 2004.

richard bowes has published several novels—including the Lambda Literary Award winning *Minions of the Moon*—four collections of short fiction and numerous short stories and articles. He has also won a World Fantasy Award and an International Horror Guild Award.

michael carroll's first collection of short fiction, *Little Reef and Other Stories*, debuts in summer of 2014 from University of Wisconsin Press. He has been published in *Boulevard, Ontario Review, Southwest Review*, and *The Yale Review*. He resides in New York City.

lou dellaguzzo has published numerous short stories in various anthologies and literary journals. These include *Chroma, Best Gay Love Stories, Best Gay Romance* and *Jonathan*. Lou lives in Washington, DC, with his partner.

l.a. fields is the author of the *Disorder Series* and *My Dear Watson*, a queer Sherlock Holmes pastiche that was a Lambda Literary

Award finalist for Best Gay Romance. Her short fiction has appeared in anthologies of horror, erotica, and academia. Find her online at la-fields. livejournal.com.

michael thomas ford is the author of numerous books, including the novels *Full Circle, Changing Tides, What We Remember, The Road Home, Suicide Notes,* and a blackly-comic trilogy featuring Jane Austen living as a modern-day vampire. The winner of five Lambda Literary Awards, he was also a finalist for the Bram Stoker Award. Visit him at michaelthomasford.com.

An Associate Professor of English at Bowdoin College, **guy mark foster** has written numerous stories. His first collection, *The Rest of Us,* was published by the Tincture imprint of Lethe Press in 2013 and was a finalist for the Lambda Literary Award for Best Debut Fiction.

james gifford is Professor Emeritus at Mohawk Valley Community College. He is the author of the acclaimed *Dayneford's Library: American Homosexual Writing, 1900-1913* and edited *Glances Backward: An Anthology of American Homosexual Writing, 1830-1920.* He resides in Utica, NY.

trebor healey was awarded a Lambda Literary Award in 2013 and has received two Publishing Triangle Ferro-Grumley fiction awards and a Violet Quill award. He is the author of the novels *A Horse Named Sorrow, Faun* and *Through It Came Bright Colors,* as well as a collection of poems, *Sweet Son of Pan,* and a story collection, *A Perfect Scar & Other Stories.* He co-edited (with Marci Blackman) *Beyond Definition: New Writing from Gay and Lesbian San Francisco* and co-edited (with Amie M. Evans) *Queer & Catholic.*

andrew holleran is one of the most prominent novelists, essayists, and short story writers of post-Stonewall gay literature. He was a member of the Violet Quill. His first novel, *Dancer from the Dance* should be required reading in all university English classes. He received the Bill Whitehead Award for Lifetime Achievement from the Publishing Triangle in 2007.

ed kurtz is the author of *A Wind of Knives, Dead Trash, Control,* and the forthcoming crime novel *Angel of the Abyss*. His short fiction has appeared in *Thuglit, Needle, Shotgun Honey, Beat to a Pulp,* and numerous anthologies. Ed lives in Texas, where he is at work on his next novel. Visit him online at edkurtz.net.

dmitri kuzmin has taught literature in colleges and worked as assistant professor of foreign literatures and literary translation. In 1989 Kuzmin founded the Vavilon Union of Young Poets, which was the organizational hub for Moscow's experimental poetry scene. Since 1993 he has been the head of ARGO-RISK Publishers (which publishes about twenty titles of current Russian poetry yearly). Since 1996 he has edited the Vavilon Internet project, which includes an anthology of contemporary Russian writing. Since 2006 he has also been editor in chief of *Vozdukh,* a quarterly poetry magazine. Kuzmin's poems have been published in translation in the USA (*A Public Space, St. Petersburg Review, Habitus, Aufgabe, Fulcrum*), England, France, Poland, China, Italy, Estonia, and Slovenia. Kuzmin's selected poems and translations were published in a hardcover edition, *Horosho byt' zhivym,* and won the Moskovsky Schet award for the best debut poetry collection.

tommi avicolli mecca is editor of *Smash the Church, Smash the State: the early years of gay liberation*. His writings have appeared in about fifty anthologies since the '70s. He lives in San Francisco where he often performs his original songs at cafes and rallies. His website is avicollimecca.com.

sam j. miller is a writer and a community organizer. His fiction has appeared or is forthcoming in *Strange Horizons, Electric Velocipede, Shimmer, Daily Science Fiction, Nightmare Magazine, Beneath Ceaseless Skies, The Minnesota Review,* and *The Rumpus,* among others. He is a graduate of the 2012 Clarion Writer's Workshop and the co-editor of *Horror after 9/11,* an anthology published by the University of Texas Press. Visit him at samjmiller.com.

About the Contributors

james powers-black's work has been published in
Jonathan, Theodate, Anon, and the anthology The New Queer Aesthetic
on Television. He is working on his first novel, a re-imagining of
Penelope's story from The Odyssey that focuses on the partner left behind
by a closeted, gay soldier stationed in Iraq. Originally from Kansas City,
Missouri, he now lives in central Pennsylvania with his husband and dogs.

jason schneiderman, essayist and poet, is the author
of Sublimation Point and Striking Surface. His poetry and essays have
appeared in numerous journals and anthologies, including American Poetry
Review, The Best American Poetry, Poetry London, Story Quarterly, and
Tin House. Jason directs the Writing Center at the Borough of Manhattan
Community College.

max steele is a performer and writer living in Brooklyn. He
has presented work at the New Museum, Rapture Cafe, Deitch Projects,
PPOW Gallery, Envoy Enterprises, Dixon Place, La MaMa, Participant,
Inc., Munch Gallery, RADAR Reading Series at the San Francisco Public
Library, Kelly Writers House, and the Queens Museum of Art. He writes
the psychedelic porno poetry zine Scorcher, and his writing has been
featured in Dossier Journal, Spank, Spunk, East Village Boys, Birdsong,
and Noisey.

stefen styrsky's fiction has appeared in The James White
Review, Harrington Gay Men's Fiction Quarterly, and Fresh Men 2: New
Voices in Gay Fiction. He has also written for the Lambda Book Report
and Gay City News. He lives and works in Washington, DC.

adrian west has published original fiction in McSweeney's and
3:AM, and translations from Spanish, German, and Catalan in Aldus, The
Brooklyn Rail, Fwriction, and Asymptote, where he is also a contributing
editor. He lives in Philadelphia with the cinema critic Beatriz Leal Riesco.

josef winkler is the author of fourteen books, among them the
award-winning trilogy Das wilde Kärnten. His major themes are suicide,
homosexuality, and the corrosive influence of Catholicism and Nazism in
Austrian country life. Winner of the 2008 Buchner prize, subject of the

235

award-winning film *Josef Winkler, der Kinoleinwandgeher,* and current president of the Austrian Art Senate, Winkler lives in Klagenfurt.

mario alberto zambrano was a contemporary

ballet dancer before dedicating his time to writing fiction. He has lived in Israel, the Netherlands, Germany, Spain, and Japan, and has danced for Hubbard Street Dance Chicago, Nederlands Dans Theater, Ballett Frankfurt, and Batsheva Dance Company. He graduated from The New School as a Riggio Honors Fellow and the Iowa Writers' Workshop as an Iowa Arts Fellow, where he also received a John C. Schupes Fellowship for Excellence in Fiction. He has been selected as a Barnes and Noble Discover Great New Writer for Fall 2013, and Booklist chose his first book, *Lotería,* as one of ten top debuts for 2013.

the editor

As an editor, steve berman has been a finalist for the Lambda Literary Award three times as well as the Shirley Jackson Award and the Golden Crown Literary Award. As an author, he is an excellent fabulist. As a gay man, he is an excellent liar. It has been confirmed he resides in southern New Jersey.

best gay stories

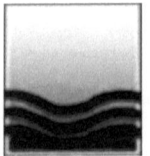